CW01501907

Book Cover by Pixel Perfect

CONTENTS

DREAM ESCAPE TO ROSE COTTAGE

Michelle J Nagy

CHAPTER ONE

Laura pulled up in the taxi outside of the large semi-detached house in Vale Street, where her best friend Becky lived. After quickly settling the fare, the driver quickly left for his next job, the tyres screeching on the road in his haste. Feeling the brush of cold air against her face, with a small shiver running down her spine, came a stark reminder that winter was just around the corner.

Gingerly, she made her way up the short pathway of the semi-detached property, clutching the card and present, so carefully chosen for her best friend's special day. In her voicemail, Becky mentioned that she'd invited a few other people along to celebrate her birthday; nothing major she promised, knowing her friend was no party animal. Just a small get-together to celebrate becoming another year older!

Laura grimaced, wondering if she'd made the right decision in coming along this evening. Having just recovered from yet another migraine from hell, felt both tired and drained, and really wasn't in the frame of mind for mingling with people she'd never met before.

As much as she hated admitting this to herself, her reluctance was largely down to feeling more than a little apprehensive about meeting Becky after such a long time; which was crazy when she'd known her for the best part of her life. For reasons she preferred to keep to herself, Laura no longer celebrated her own birthdays, but to miss the big day of the friend who was more like a sister, would have been completely unforgivable.

Much to her own curiosity from her last message, Becky mysteriously mentioned there would be someone there she knew she would be pleased to see; but despite her best efforts at coaxing her to elaborate, her friend refused to give away any further details.

Just as she was about to press the bell, the door swiftly opened with the sound of music and laughter escaping from the house. Becky stood there expectantly, the short length of the tunic dress she wore emphasising her long shapely legs, with the electric blue colour complementing her long blonde hair perfectly. For a few brief moments, they gazed at each other, almost transfixed before finally hugging tightly.

As she embraced her friend, a tear ran down her cheek. 'Oh, just look at me!' she smiled apologetically, feeling more than a little foolish about her emotional outburst. 'Here I am on what's supposed to be one of your happiest days of the year and I turn up on your doorstep a blubbering wreck!' Trying to compose herself, she smiled brightly. 'Oh, Becks, Happy Birthday! It's *so* good to see you!' She stepped back slightly to admire her. 'Wow! You look absolutely stunning - blue's definitely your colour!'

Becky smiled softly with affection, her own eyes welled up with unshed tears. 'Oh, never mind me and what I'm wearing! Gosh, it's *so* lovely to see you Laura - it's been much too long! Come on in, you look frozen!'

Excitedly, she quickly led her into the hallway, taking the present from the silver gift bag that Laura handed to her. 'Oh, my favourite *Angel* Perfume! You must be psychic - I've just about finished off my last bottle. Thank you *so much!*' Her attention focused back to her friend, regarding her with unmasked concern. 'I hope you don't mind me saying, but you're looking a bit pale.'

Letting out a small sigh, gave a shrug. 'Oh, don't mind me, I had another one of those migraines. You know how it is - my head was pounding for ages despite taking a couple of tablets.'

Becky gently placed a hand to her friend's forehead, brushing back the fringe of her dark long brown hair. 'You've been getting a lot of these lately, haven't you? It might be worth popping along to the doctor to get things checked out.'

Laura shook her head defiantly. 'Well, I know this is *definitely* a migraine - Mum and Lou also suffer from them so I know all the signs - besides, there's not much a doctor can do. The best thing is just to rest in a darkened room and let it takes its course.'

Knowing just how stubborn her friend could be at times, gave a shrug. She gazed in admiration at her emerald laced dress before quickly hanging up her jacket in the nearby cloakroom.

'Well, I think it's about time I introduced you to everybody - come this way!' she beckoned, taking her through to the lounge.

As she entered the dimly lit room, the loud chatter heard only moments earlier from the four people standing around, came to an abrupt silence, with just the sound of a James Blunt song playing along in the background. She glanced at the other guests looking over her way, the only familiar face was of Becky's husband, Chris. He immediately rushed over with a welcoming smile and placed a friendly peck on her cheek.

'Wow Laura, it's *so great* to see you - it's been a while! I hope life's been treating you well in Minsden.'

'Oh, I mustn't grumble,' she replied with a wry smile. 'I

have a roof over my head and a job that pays the bills.'

'Aren't you forgetting your manners?' Becky chided, rolling her eyes to the ceiling before shaking her head in despair as she looked up to her tall athletically built husband. '*Honestly* – you just can't get the staff these days!'

Laura gratefully accepted Chris's offer of a drink, opting for a glass of Rose wine.

'Let me introduce you to the rest of the guys,' Becky gushed excitedly, quickly placing Laura's gift and card onto the nearby coffee table. She peered over to her friends, all waiting in eager anticipation. '*Finally*, I get to introduce you to my dearest friend Laura, who I'm forever banging on about – as I keep mentioning, we go way back and have been practically joined at the hip since secondary school!'

'This is Marsha who works at the salon and Frank her lovely fiancée who's dead clever with all things IT and works as a programmer.' Shaking hands in greeting with the strikingly exotic couple both of West Indian origin, noticed the slightly puzzled expression registering on Marsha's face. Realising she'd been staring towards the woman, clearly making her feel slightly uncomfortable, Laura quickly explained. 'Oh, sorry if I seem to be giving you bit of a strange look - it's just that I'm *sure* I've seen you somewhere before.' Never one to forget a face, was certain sometime in the past their paths had crossed.

Marsha who she would have guessed to be in her early thirties, looking slightly taken aback for a moment, gave a blink before laughing warmly, her dark almond-shaped eyes shining brightly. 'Oh, I don't *think* so, but it's funny really because people often make that remark - I guess I just must have one of those kinds of faces!' She took a sip of her wine. 'Mind you, I *almost* feel as if I know you as Becky never stops speaking about you and how lovely you are - now I can see why!'

'Marsha's our senior stylist at *Cuts & Curls*,' explained Becky, referring to the hair salon owned jointly with Chris. 'Without this lady, I just don't know how I would ever manage!

Becky's attention then focused to the man she suddenly became aware of, standing quietly alone in the corner of the room. For some inexplicable reason, Laura's heartbeat almost seemed to come to a stop as he studied her with his smiling inquisitive brown eyes. The room seemed to fall into silence or maybe she just simply became oblivious to the noise around them as they gazed at each other intently.

His smile was so warm and tender, appearing to share her surprise in the way you would feel when becoming reacquainted with a friend or perhaps a former lover that you hadn't seen in a long time. Just *why* was there something so incredibly familiar about him, she wondered, certain they couldn't have possibly met before. Had that been the case, Laura knew without a doubt his image would have been permanently etched on her mind!

Much to her embarrassment, his expression quickly turned to one of concern as she suddenly became aware of an overwhelming feel of an emotion that she couldn't quite define, so intense was literally trembling, as tears came to her eyes.

'This is Oscar,' Becky smiled sweetly, seemingly oblivious to the chemistry that was developing between them. 'Well, what can I say about this guy? Without wanting to over-inflate his ego, our world wouldn't be the same without his amazing sense of humour and endless puns! In fact, I would go as far as saying without him we would've been completely lost, because he really helped get us on the map!'

Desperately trying to compose herself, Laura smiled as she shook his hand, hoping he didn't feel her shaking like a leaf. With their eyes firmly fixed on one another, it was almost as if nobody else in the room existed.

'Lovely to finally meet you Laura,' Oscar smiled, his hand lingering on hers, feeling warm and somehow familiar to the touch. Not a great deal taller than herself, he looked deeply into her green eyes, still sparkling with unshed tears, the colour almost matching the emerald shade of her dress. 'Well what can I say? with an introduction like that, I've certainly got a lot to live up to!'

Judging by his appearance, with his thick, wavy dark brown hair perhaps a shade or two darker than her own, but peppered with grey, would have guessed him to be in his mid-forties, possibly around three years older than herself. Perhaps he couldn't be described as handsome in the classic sense, she mused; but his warm smile mixed with an air of confidence, made him appear as one of the most striking individuals she had ever encountered.

Aware she must be appearing to look completely dumbstruck standing there with her mouth wide open, tried to spark up a conversation.

'Nice to meet you too,' she replied, hoping she didn't sound as nervous as she felt. 'I take it you must work at the salon with Becky and Chris?'

For a moment Oscar looked a little taken aback before suddenly bursting out laughing, with all the others joining in much to her bemusement as if she'd made the funniest joke in the world.

Oscar turned to her, his face softening. 'I'm really sorry, but the last thing I can imagine is spending the entire day snipping hair and chatting about holidays and boyfriend troubles.'

Becky gave him a stern look. '*Oscar Devereux*, I'll have you know, that there's a whole lot more to hairdressing than *snipping hair* and discussing matters about all the problems you guys give us!'

'Ouch! grinned Oscar feigning a pained look on his face. 'You know I'm only teasing.' His attention turned back to Laura looking more than a little apologetic for embarrassing her. 'Well, for my sins, I'm a photographer – actually me and Chris go way back to our schooldays, pretty much like you and Becky.'

Placing her arm affectionately across Oscar's shoulder Becky informed her, 'This man's far too modest to say, but he really is the most amazing photographer. Not only is he much sought after for weddings and businesses, he's done so much for our publicity, taking pics of our clients showing off their fantastic hairstyles. And would you know, just like you Oscar's huge passion in life when he's relaxing is to draw and paint. You should see some of the stuff he's done - absolutely breath-taking!'

Laura felt her heart skip a beat. Never had she felt this excited about a man that she had literally only just met; not only was he drop-dead gorgeous, it seemed they shared one special thing in common with a love of art.

Inviting Oscar and Laura to make themselves

comfortable on the brown leather settee, Chris offered to refill her glass with more wine. Becky peered at her through narrowed eyes with a questioning look.

'Honestly, I'm fine,' insisted Laura as if reading her mind, while Chris topped up her glass. 'That headache's shifted and it's not likely to be coming back anytime soon!'

Oscar raised an eyebrow in question.

'As usual, my dear friend's making a big fuss over nothing!' she explained. 'I just happen to suffer the occasional migraine from time to time - but she makes such a fuss over them, that anyone would think she was my mother!'

He laughed warmly, emphasising the creases around his eyes, only succeeding in making him appear even more devastatingly attractive. Within a few brief seconds, Laura relaxed, her intuition sensing Oscar to be an animable person who was easy to get along with.

The six friends sat together, quickly getting into the party spirit, making small talk, with Marsha eager to learn as much as possible about Laura.

'So exactly how long have you and Becky known each other for?' Marsha enquired, handing her over a plate of vol-au-vents to take her pick.

Taking one of the small pastries, she chewed thoughtfully. 'Well, as Becky mentioned earlier, our friendship goes way back to when be both started at the all-girls secondary school in our home town.' She giggled as she thought back to that very first day of the new term. 'I remember being so terribly nervous and shy and it didn't help matters very much when my only other friend, Jackie Finch went on to the local comprehensive instead. Well, Becks who's always been very confident, even at that young age, soon took me under her wing and from that day onwards we've been practically inseparable.'

'From that day on this one was nothing but *trouble*!' added Becky with a grin as she sat perched on her husband's knee on one of the surrounding armchairs. 'We were *so* bad that we'd got thrown out of the school library more times than I could care to mention!'

Her eyes narrowed as she glanced towards Laura. 'So, don't be fooled by that sweet butter-wouldn't-melt in the mouth look - madam here would open up this large human biology book and show me some very graphic pictures. Of course, that would set us both off into hysterics and without fail our miserable physics teacher who got roped onto the lunchtime duty rota would get us thrown out!'

Feeling herself blush, Laura suddenly remembered something that would embarrass her friend like crazy. 'Well, I haven't forgotten about Mr Elliott the dashing geography teacher!'

'Oh no, *please*!' exclaimed Becky in mock despair, much to the amusement of Chris.

'Hmm, now what's all this?' he probed teasingly, gently kissing her on top of the head. 'So, you had a crush on the geography teacher? That's a new one to me!'

'Only *big* time!' Laura revealed with a mischievous grin. 'She would do just about anything to get his attention. Being such a teacher's pet, she would always spend ages studying the capitals of all the cities of the world so Mr. Elliot would lavish all his praise on her - when I came to her house after school, she would drag me to her bedroom. On her dressing table, she had this large atlas globe which she would make me spin and get me to ask her random questions about what the capital of Bulgaria or China was, or any other country that came to mind.'

Chris studied his wife with amusement as her face turned a dark shade of red.

On a roll, Laura continued to enlighten the others in the room. 'Her crush got so bad, that she would drop her hanky *accidentally* so Mr Elliott being the perfect gentleman that he was would pick it up and hand it to her!'

Putting her hand over her face that had turned an even deeper shade of crimson, Becky peeped at her friend through a gap in her fingers. 'Laura Winters you are *so* going to pay for embarrassing me like this on my birthday!'

'Have you *anymore* amusing stories, Laura?' asked Marsha, dabbing a tear from her eye.

'Oh, I haven't finished with this one yet,' she informed her audience, much to their delight, glancing briefly towards Oscar who was clearly enjoying the walk down memory lane. 'The *Big Crush* ended abruptly when one day, we sneaked off to the stock room when we saw the door was left open and decided to nick some pencils and some other goodies - but as we turned on the light, we noticed we were not alone! Who should we see, but Mr Elliott snogging the young chemistry teacher, Miss Armstrong, with his hand up her skirt!'

With that everybody in the room burst out into peals of laughter.

'Wow! Looks like there was some *chemistry* going on there!' exclaimed Chris. 'Did you report them?'

Laura shook her head. 'Becks was completely heartbroken and ran off in floods of tears - completely inconsolable for ages. Of course, the two teachers tried to make us believe there had been a big misunderstanding - they had gone to look for pens, according to Mr. Elliott but couldn't get the light to work! Looking back now, it all sounds so pathetic.'

Frank nodded his head in agreement as he chuckled. 'I

don't think these days those two would have gotten away with it - I'm sure they would've received instant dismissal and been named and shamed in the newspapers!'

Marsha peered down the front of her dress in horror as she realised she'd spilt some white wine soaking her gold coloured dress with a large wet patch. Quickly, Laura grabbed a few serviettes from the coffee table, which Marsha gratefully accepted.

She quickly set to work at mopping up the liquid. 'Phew, thank goodness it wasn't Shiraz - that red stain would have really made me look like an extra in a horror film!'

Getting up slowly from her husband's knee, Becky gave a small yawn. 'I'd better see to that Chicken Enchilada. Marsha, perhaps you could give me a hand - you're the expert on Mexican cuisine. Maybe you could tell me if it needs a little longer in the oven.'

Seeing Laura about to get up to offer her assistance, waved her hand for her to stay put. 'It's ok hon, I don't need any more help - chill out and give your head a chance to recover.' She gave her husband a wink. 'Why don't you take Frank to the garage and show him all the work you've been doing on the T-Bird? It's really come a long way in the past few months.'

When he wasn't working hard at the salon, Chris's one

big passion in life was vintage cars and his latest project was restoring an American T-Bird from the 60's. Obediently, Frank followed his friend to the large double garage that adjoined the house, leaving both Laura and Oscar alone in the lounge.

The pair sitting closely together on the leather settee, looked to one another smiling, both correctly suspecting this had been a setup to give them some time alone together. She soon came to realise that Oscar was the person Becky hinted she would be pleased to see; all through the banter during the evening Laura had been very much aware of him, certain the feeling was mutual, noticing he could barely take his eyes off her.

In the background, as the song changed to *Wonderful Tonight* by Eric Clapton, Oscar dutifully refilled her wine glass and then his own, studying her faraway expression.

'Oh, I'm sorry,' she apologised, realising she must have looked as if she was in some trance. 'It's just that I find that song *so* beautiful.' The truth was that the song transported her back to a much happier time in her life, to the very first time she connected to that special person. Somebody she could never have envisaged in a thousand years would leave her the way in which he had.

'Yep, it's a great song,' he agreed, his voice softly, bringing her back from the fringes of those dark times she would prefer to forget. 'Becky tells me it's been a while since you last spent some time together.'

She nodded, nervously biting her bottom lip in shame. 'Actually, it's been a few years - much longer than I would have liked, but it wasn't from choice. Before you know it, four years have slipped by in a blink of an eye.'

'Tell me about it,' he said with a wry smile, taking a sip of his wine and leaning his head back on the settee, closing his eyes momentarily, before opening them again. Studying her, his eyes appeared as dark as coals of fire seeming to search into the depths of her soul. Just *why* couldn't she get out of her head this feeling that there was something so familiar and just so *comforting* about him?

'Well, now you know that I'm a professional photographer and not a renowned hairstylist, what exactly is it *you* do for a living?'

Laura looked thoughtfully into her wineglass. 'Well, for the past three years I've been working for a large finance company specialising in retirement products.' She gazed at him with a twinkle in her eyes. 'Yes, *very* exciting, I know.'

'Would you say it's a job that you enjoy?'

She shrugged her shoulders. 'Well, I guess I'm reasonably happy - the work is ok and I get on well with my colleagues. I suppose I must be fairly good at what I do as I've worked my way up in the department to a team manager.' She helped herself to a sweet from a dish on the coffee table. 'How about you - would you say your career gives you great job satisfaction?'

He looked momentarily at his own wine glass. 'Well, I've considered it a great privilege to get paid reasonably well for something that I've loved doing and gives pleasure to others - but I've got to say painting is my *real* passion.'

He sat up, giving her a long, lingering smile that made her heart melt. 'So, what does Laura Winters do in her spare time? Is there a special someone to share your time with when you're not working at Global Life?'

She grimaced, as she let out a deep sigh. 'There hasn't been anybody special since...since...' Her mind regressed back to those times that she would prefer to forget.

Seeing the troubled frown creasing her forehead, he waved his hands dismissively. 'Hey, it's ok, you don't have to tell me anything that makes you feel uncomfortable - I'm sorry.'

He looked clearly relieved as she reassured him with a smile. 'There's nothing to be sorry for. It's just something I find it hard to think about... a part of my life I don't like to dwell on, that's all.' Not wanting to scare him away, she quickly moved onto a safer subject, something she had so much passion for.

'Well, when I'm not working I hang out with my good friend Karen who also works at Global. In my spare time as Becks mentioned, like you, I love to draw and paint.' She gave a mischievous smile. 'Can I ask if there is a special person in your life?'

For a moment, he looked slightly taken aback by the question. 'Actually, there is - her name is Jessica.'

Seeing the look of surprise and perhaps a tinge of disappointment registering on Laura's face, went quickly on to explain, 'Jessica's my ten-year old daughter. Sadly, her mother is no longer on the scene - it's a long story, but we had to part company, so my little girl is with me.'

'Oh, I see.' Really, she didn't see and couldn't understand why the mother no longer featured in their daughter's life. But she didn't want to press any further knowing this wasn't the moment to be asking those kinds of deeply personal questions.

He swiftly changed the subject. 'So, in your spare time you love to draw and paint? Well, that's definitely something we share in common! I absolutely love my photography with a passion, but most of all I do love to paint - they are both forms of art, after all. Do you have any favourite subjects you prefer to paint? My particular love is for landscapes, though I do like to turn my hand to other things.'

Laura's face flushed excitedly. 'Actually, I *also* love

painting landscapes - sometimes in water colours and other times I work with oils. But what I love to do *most* of all are portraits - I just find the human face so interesting, the expressions, the bone structures, most of all the eyes. It's so true what they say about them being windows to the soul!'

Oscar studied her, clearly finding her enthusiasm infectious. 'Yes, we certainly are a diverse and interesting species. I guess I'm fairly adequate at drawing and painting people, but find woodlands or seascapes tend to be more my forte.'

Nobody in any of her previous relationships had ever shared her love of art. At the time, she would never consider this to be an issue, even if that person could never fully understand her need to express herself on canvas nor her need to spend her time in art galleries appreciating the works of the great painters.

But here she was now, sitting next to this most intriguing man at the moment still shrouded with an air of mystery who shared her interest, and without a doubt completely understood that passion. For the very first time in her entire life, Laura now realised what it was like to experience instant attraction; never before had she felt such an immediate connection to another individual she had only just met. Yes, she had heard of others that professed to have experienced this, but didn't really believe this to be true. Surely that kind of thing only happened in stories or was it a thing that just grew with time? Although she couldn't be one hundred per cent sure, felt as certain as she could that Oscar also felt the chemistry developing between them.

As if reading her thoughts, his face lit up with excitement. 'Then you'll understand what it feels like to work on an oil or watercolour so hard and to see something come to life - there's nothing to quite compare with that, is there?'

She shook her head, smiling radiantly. He completely got it that to create a work of art was a labour of love.

Oscar peered towards the kitchen where both Becky and Marsha were seeing to the meal then glanced back to Laura as a thought came to him. 'I know we won't have much chance to really get to know each other this evening as we'll need to divide our time between the Birthday Girl and the others - would it be ok to make a note of your phone number so maybe we could arrange a day to catch up, perhaps over a drink or a meal?'

Laura asked him to pass his mobile, where she tapped in her number, which he immediately saved to his contacts. Just as she was about to add his details on her own phone, Becky and Marsha reappeared from the kitchen, the fragrant aroma of the food wafting through the open door.

'Well, it looks like you two have been getting on like a house on fire,' remarked Marsha with a knowing smile, the wet stain having faded slightly on her gold satin dress. 'I'm sure you'll both be pleased to know dinner should be ready within the next five minutes or so.'

Holding a tea towel in her hand, Becky rolled her eyes to the ceiling. 'I guess our better halves are still in the garage discussing their *toys*.'

Feeling she hadn't really contributed anything of real use throughout the evening, Laura offered to let their partners know dinner was about to be served.

She opened the side door located from the large kitchen she remembered from previous visits. A puzzled frown immediately marked her forehead, as she discovered the garage to be shrouded in a penetrating darkness, making this impossible to see anything ahead. Gingerly, she took a step forward, as a shiver run down her spine, unsure if that was down to the sudden coldness that enveloped her, or the ominous silence. Feeling more than a hint of apprehension mixed with fear, suddenly gave a yelp of surprise as her foot touched a step that she hadn't been aware of, causing her to stumble and trip forward, crying out helplessly as she fell into what seemed to be a cold, endless void.

Having lost all sense of time, she slowly opened her eyes,

aware she was lying on her side, with her left leg numbed with cramp as if she had been laying in one position for too long.

Much to her astonishment, instead of laying hurt on Becky's garage floor, was in her own bed with the sheet pulled back. Taking in the surroundings of her bedroom as if only aware of them for the very first time, glanced towards the glowing LED alarm clock on her bedside table the time showing three a.m. in the morning.

Holding her forehead, which was pounding from the migraine she'd previously believed had eased, realised that the whole evening at her friend's birthday had been an entire dream. Even more shocking came the realisation that Oscar, or come to that Becky, Chris, Marsha and Frank actually didn't exist outside of her imagination!

CHAPTER TWO

With a shiver, Laura sat up quickly lifting up the bedsheet before covering this over her shoulders. Despite this being the height of summer in her real life, was feeling distinctly cold. She looked vacantly across the room towards the open window, focusing on the amber of the streetlight shining through a gap in her curtains, flapping lazily by the gentle breeze coming from outside.

For a split second, her mind desperately grasped onto the idea that when she had tripped on the step in her friend's garage, had managed to knock herself out, and what she was experiencing *now* in the bedroom was in fact the dream.

Knowing deep down the idea was absurd, Laura switched on her bedside lamp, lighting up the room, the instant brightness dazzling her momentarily, before her eyes slowly became accustomed to the brightness. After a few minutes, she reluctantly stepped out from the comfort of her bed, wincing as she experienced a wave of dizziness with the room seeming to spin around her. Slowly, as the floor beneath her feet steadied, reality sunk in as her attention focused on the laptop placed upon her bedroom stool; a reminder of the work presentation she had been working on relentlessly the previous evening.

Slowly, she walked over to the large mirror covering the door of her fitted wardrobe and gazed at her reflection. The long dark brown hair almost down to her waist in the dream was now styled in the short sleek bob she'd since sported for the past few years; normally glossy and immaculate, was now ruffled after having tossed and turned in her sleep, with the strap of her nightdress slipping off her shoulder.

She studied her reflection, noticing as if for the first time how pale her complexion appeared, with the dark shadows under her eyes telling a story of many weeks of broken sleep. Maybe she did look younger than her 43 years as others had suggested, she mused, with barely a line on her face; but at the rate her insomnia was continuing, knew it was just a matter of time before she would begin to look like a zombie extra from some horror film!

Laura thought back to the dream and her encounter with Oscar. Never in her entire life had she felt such an instant attraction to anybody. Within a short space of time knew without a shadow of doubt he was the very person she'd spent her entire life searching for. Yes, it was true she did find him physically attractive, with those smouldering brown eyes and that heart-melting smile; but most importantly it was the way in which they immediately bonded, the way they seemed to connect with one another. She recalled so vividly the wave of excitement that rippled through her entire body when he finally asked for her number, along with the promise of meeting up and the chance for them to get to know each other better.

Slowly, with a weary sigh she sat down on the corner of the bed, with a feeling of both sadness and despair creeping over her, as came the realisation the entire evening had been nothing more than one big dream. With Oscar not existing anywhere outside her imagination, there was absolutely no chance of that ever happening.

A tear came to her eye as her mind regressed back to Becky the vibrant, warm-hearted woman, convinced had been her best friend since childhood and to that moment of pulling up in the taxi to her birthday party, remembering that feeling of excitement at reuniting after the best part of four years; that feeling you get with that special kind of friendship where you can easily pick up where you'd left off after a long absence.

How was it possible to feel such love for a person, and share cherished memories of their schooldays when in truth those events had never actually taken place? As for Marsha and Frank, to think the loving couple that seemed made for one other only lived inside of her head. She pulled up the strap of her nightdress back over her shoulder before a tear trickled slowly down her cheek. Had her life truly become so empty that she had now begun to make up imaginary friends? Feeling a sudden wave of nausea as her head pounded with the relentless migraine, rushed quickly to the bathroom where she vomited.

After realising her attempts at returning to sleep were proving to be unfruitful, Laura finally got up at 7.30 that morning. With her headache easing slightly after taking a shower, decided she would be well enough to go to work. However, with the aftereffects of the migraine lingering, her appetite was poor, and only managed a spoonful of the porridge she would normally have for breakfast, washed down with just a few sips of coffee.

Work proved to be equally challenging, as Edwina Charlton the customer service manager at Global Life called a last-minute meeting, announcing to her team managers that some big changes were to take place over the coming months. She explained due to an increase in work volumes, a large recruitment campaign was set to take place, informing her management team that advertising would begin with immediate effect and interviews planned to commence within the next three weeks.

Nobody in the meeting room was quite prepared for what came next as Edwina dropped a bombshell by announcing after the end of the next couple of months she would be stepping down and leaving the business. Gasps of shock came from around the room, followed by a stunned silence as the woman now aged 56 had worked for the company for many years having begun her career as an apprentice before working her way to the top.

Although known as a person who spoke her mind, Edwina was also considered to be a fair person and would always stand up for those she considered had been treated unfairly. Laura was particularly saddened at the news as her boss around thirteen years her senior, had personally taken her on as a customer service representative when she first moved to the town of Minsden three years ago. During that time, she found the older woman to be extremely supportive after sharing with her the some most difficult episodes of her life.

As everybody left the meeting in a sombre mood, some shaking their heads in disbelief, Karen glanced at Laura, her face set with a grim expression. 'Well, I don't know about you, but I didn't see that one coming. Do you think there might be a bit more to this than what we know? She was on sick leave for a few weeks, supposedly with a gastric virus which did seem a bit strange at the time - makes me wonder.'

Still feeling jaded from the night before, Laura gave a non-committed shrug. 'Who knows? I guess in time we're bound to hear something.'

'Hey, are you feeling ok?' Karen asked with concern, studying her face which looked distinctly pale. 'You're not looking too great if you don't mind me saying. Don't tell me you've had another of those migraines?'

Laura smiled apologetically at her deputy team manager and close friend. 'There's just no hiding the truth from you.'

It was just over three years ago on the very day she first arrived in Minsden, when she first become acquainted with Karen Bright; happening in the most unexpected way after having reached a major crossroads in her life. Had it not been for this kind-hearted soul who took her under her wing, heaven knows what route her destiny might have taken.

Having arrived at the small market town from the tranquil Dorset village where she had spent most of her life, checked into the Maple Leaf Hotel following a recommendation by a lady working at the local newsagents who she later came to know as Stella.

Sitting in the lounge bar, nursing a large spritzer, and

desperately contemplating what to do next with her life, began browsing through a local paper for places to rent. As she flicked over to the next page, a young woman joined her at the bar ordering a double vodka and coke. It was clear to see from her face looking distinctively flushed that she was both angry and upset; from the redness of her eyes was obvious she had shed more than a few tears. At a guess, Laura would have said she was about her age or possibly slightly younger. Feeling concerned, asked the woman if she was ok, knowing nothing could be further from the truth.

At first the woman with the shoulder length fair hair and a figure that might be described as curvy, but nevertheless quite attractive, looked at her sternly as if she was about to tell her to mind her own business. Instead, however, her face softened as she burst into a fresh flood tears, explaining although she didn't normally go to bars on her own, had just thrown her rotten boyfriend out of the house after catching him cheating with another woman.

Laura listened sympathetically as the woman who introduced herself as Karen, poured out her heart about Graham, the man she had spent the best part of five years of her life with and discovered after some suspicion had been having an affair with his work colleague. Over her second drink, Karen went into some detail about how glad she was her daughter Emma had been had been staying with a friend that evening and was spared having to witness the breakup.

Karen looked apologetically for burdening her with all her mess, but the truth was that Laura was glad to think of something other than her own troubles and was more than happy to listen. Her newly discovered acquaintance enquired about what brought her to Minsden, seeing that she was looking at the property section of the local paper. Laura admitted truthfully that she wanted to get away from her old life and happened to see Minsden after Googling for market towns, seeing this as the perfect place to make a brand-new start once she found somewhere to live and hopefully with time, a job.

She regarded Laura with both surprise and admiration, remarking how brave she was to make such a bold change in her life, and wasn't sure if she would have had the courage to have done the same. Sensing that the attractive, smartly dressed woman that had come to town wasn't forthcoming about her reasons for leaving her old life behind, Karen felt it wasn't appropriate to probe any further. Despite that, her instincts told her that Laura came across as pleasant and trustworthy, informing her about some customer service vacancies going at Global Life, the pensions company she had worked for the past four years.

After asking the hotel receptionist to provide her with a pen and some paper, Karen jotted down the details of the job role for Laura, including contact number and also her own mobile number. By the end of the evening with both feeling merry after a few alcoholic beverages, the beginnings of what would prove to be a special friendship had formed, before parting company and Laura also giving her own contact details.

Over the coming weeks, much to her delight, Laura was successful in her application for customer service representative. During the interview, Edwina Charlton listened carefully as Laura truthfully revealed the reasons why she decided to change her life so drastically, studying her sad face as she regressed over the previous twelve months. Once the young woman finally came to the end of her story, the manager was for a moment rendered speechless as the news of her very tragic past slowly sunk in, before finally getting up from her chair to give her a gentle hug, with tears glistening in her own eyes.

Although the job was a far cry from her previously high-profile role, with the work being far below her capabilities, Laura felt this was exactly what was needed to get herself back on track, enabling her to come to terms with all she had experienced. As discussed with her new boss, had readily agreed to go for some further counselling if the need should arise.

During her transitional period as Laura came to think of this, had taken up Karen's generous offer to move in with her and her teenage daughter Emma. Although both clearly enjoyed her company and was plain to see her new friend was more than happy to have her stay as long as she needed, as helped to take her mind away from her recently broken relationship, Laura preferred her own space, making the decision to sell the home she'd abandoned in the quaint Dorset village, and bought a two-bedroomed flat in what was known as a desirable area of Minsden.

Since settling into her new life in her adopted town, Laura was determined to focus on the present and the future, choosing to firmly place the past to the back of her mind. Whilst at Global Life her career had gone from strength to strength and within a year in the Investment Solutions team, quickly worked her way from customer service representative to Deputy before finally securing the role of team manager.

It was no secret that Karen also had her own aspirations for a more senior role, but was more than happy to be offered the Deputy position appreciating her friend, three years her senior, deserved the promotion after all the hard work she'd undertaken to quickly to learn about the pensions industry. Together they worked well to ensure the smooth running of their small team and were well-liked and respected by most of their colleagues.

After returning back to their desks where they sat side by side, Karen looked sternly at her friend over her reading glasses, reminding Laura of her history teacher Miss Rogers when she would forget to complete her homework. 'Now *what* is it?' she enquired knowing all too well what was to come next.

'*Oh Laura*, you should be going to the doctors!' I'm sure there's something that can be done for people like you that suffer from frequent migraines.'

Laura waved her hand dismissively as she logged back onto her PC. 'Maybe there *is* medication that can be prescribed, but to be honest I would rather avoid going down that route - you often hear about the side effects from drugs being worse than the original symptoms!'

Karen's face softened. 'Sorry for coming over like some busybody, but you know it's only because I care.'

Frowning, eager to change the subject, Laura glanced at her email. 'Looks like Edwina's made official her big announcement as promised - I guess we'd better bring forward the team huddle as there's bound to be some questions. Not that there's much more I can share at the moment!' She looked back to Karen apologetically. 'Look I know you care and it really does mean a lot to me, but I promise I'll be fine.' She had a thought, 'Actually, there's something I need to tell you. About something amazing that happened to me last night.'

'Hmm, now that sounds *interesting*,' Karen remarked with a knowing grin.'

Laura rolled her eyes in despair towards the ceiling. 'Yes, *interesting* but not in the way you're probably thinking! But it's something really strange that I want to share with you - I'll tell you about it at lunch, but let's get moving with that huddle!'

'Now I'm *intrigued*! Roll on one o'clock!'

At lunchtime, the two women went to one of the nearby coffee shops, their favourite retreat to catch up and unwind during their normally hectic day. Unlike the wintery feel of the weather in her dream, the small market town was basked in warm sunshine, making this a glorious June day for both the workforce and shoppers to enjoy the sunshine. Being fortunate to work in the heart of Minsden meant being able to take advantage of the many shops and eateries that the small market town had to offer.

Having both decided on a cappuccino along with a toasted cheese and ham sandwich, settled down at a table in a quiet corner of the cafe. Karen added a sachet of sugar to her own coffee while Laura told her friend in great detail about the vivid dream she had the night before.'

After carefully listening until Laura came to the end of her story, Karen paused for a moment before shaking her head in disbelief. 'Well, I've got to say that sounds a pretty *amazing* dream - I mean, to remember things in such detail. I've got to admit by morning, most of my dreams have usually been forgotten. That's unless I've woken up from some nightmare.' She looked at her friend with sympathy. 'You must have been well gutted thinking you'd met this gorgeous guy who felt the same about you, then you wake to find it was just all a dream.'

Laura nodded glumly as she took a bite of her sandwich. 'I've never experienced anything like this *ever* before. Oscar just seemed so real - so special. I mean, he wasn't *perfect* like some Hollywood film star, though he was quite good-looking. But really, it's his personality that was just the icing on the cake. There I was thinking I'd met this incredible guy who seemed to have so much in common with me - wouldn't *you* feel disappointed in my shoes if you discovered the whole thing was a dream?'

Karen stirred her coffee thoughtfully, nodding her head. 'I know I would've been devastated. Do you remember much about the others in the dream?'

'They're all still so vivid in my mind,' Laura admitted, blowing on her coffee before taking a sip of the hot liquid. 'Now I look back it was all so strange, pulling up in that taxi in Vale Street, a town I've no idea about, convinced I was reuniting with a close friend that I hadn't seen in ages. The feelings that I had about missing Becky and the feeling of excitement turning up at her doorstep for her birthday just felt so real - I was *so* convinced this Becky was my lifelong friend.' She placed her cup down on the saucer as she thought back. 'The memories about what we'd done together over the years seemed every bit as real as any moment I've shared with you. Then of course there was her husband Chris mad about all things to do with cars and the lovely Marsha and her computer geek husband, Frank.'

The troubled look shadowing Karen's face didn't go unmissed by Laura. 'Look, I *know* it was just a dream, but I just want you to realise that you've been a really great friend to me. My life was a real mess before I moved to Minsden and started work at Global Life. But you, Karen Bright soon made me feel welcome, and for the first time in ages I regained a sense of belonging and helped me get my life back on track. I really don't know what I would have done without you.'

Looking clearly moved, her friend's features softened with a smile that added radiance to her round and pretty face.

'Gosh Laura, in a moment you'll have me in tears!'

Although some may have described her unkindly as petite but on the plump side, Laura would have argued her warm personality and positive nature made her appear both young and attractive. Those that didn't know her well, would have been surprised to learn that she had recently just celebrated her fortieth birthday.

'Well, it works both ways because I can say hand on heart that you've been a great pal to me - always there for me no matter what, helping to pick up the pieces after my string of failed relationships. All I can say is *thank goodness* you were there for me that night at the Maple Leaf when I stormed out after that row with Graham - it's never easy when these things happen, especially when raising a kid on your own.'

Laura picked up her sandwich. 'Well, I've got to say things are looking promising with Andrew - surely it must be coming up to your first anniversary?'

'A year this Sunday,' her friend confirmed, looking blissfully happy. 'I know it's still early days, but I've got to say he makes me feel good. What's more important is that Emma likes him and is really cool about him moving in. So now she's off to Leeds University to study Healthcare Management, it's great knowing she can leave home feeling reassured!'

'Takes after her mum for brains!'

Karen smiled at the compliment. 'Now you're just going to make my head swell - don't mind me and my *Proud Mum* moment!' Her expression became more serious. 'Have you given any more thought to giving online dating a try? It worked for me and Andrew!'

Laura shook her head firmly. 'No way! As far as I'm concerned, online dating is a risky business.'

'But is it any riskier than meeting somebody at a pub or a nightclub?' questioned her friend. 'Just think about it - you meet some fit looking guy who could tell you absolutely anything about himself, but it could all be a pack of lies. For all you know, he could be married or be a psychopath!'

Laura remained cynical. 'But surely it's better to meet somebody face to face? I've heard so many stories about online dating - about players on there with one thing on their mind. Often married men out for just a bit of fun!'

'*Tell* me about it!' Karen winced as she thought back to her previous experiences. 'Remember Simon? Been dating him for three months and thought I'd met Mr Right. That is until I got a call from his wife!'

'Hmm, yes I remember Simon only too well and the poor wife who'd been getting suspicious that he was up to something - I can't *begin* to imagine how she must have felt when she checked out his phone and saw all his texts and photos of you…and the string of other ladies who believed in his lies!'

Karen shook her head with a pained expression. 'I *really* had no idea. Now I look back I can see he was so full of bull - making out he had this amazing business consulting job and had to go off at the last minute to meetings here and there as a cover for his busy love life. I *so* wish you'd told me he'd also been coming on to you behind my back.'

Laura deeply regretted not telling her that Simon had also started sending her texts. She first had the misfortune of meeting him when Karen invited her out for a birthday drink. Despite her protests at not wanting to play gooseberry, her friend insisted on introducing him to her *wonderful* new boyfriend.

Within about ten minutes she decided she didn't like him, finding him both patronising and smarmy as he seem to undress her with his eyes. Having found out during their conversation that she was looking for a new MacBook Pro, took her mobile number, offering to find her the best deal. True to his word he sought out the brand and specification she was looking for at a reasonable price. But her suspicions became aroused when he would regularly call her to ask how she was getting on with her new purchase; then the subject would change to questions of a personal nature, enquiring if she was seeing anybody.

She looked to her friend apologetically, before gazing into her coffee mug. 'I could see you were completely smitten with him - but I just didn't want to hurt you. At first, I thought I was imagining things and that he was just being friendly. But when he started asking what I was like in the bedroom, then I knew for sure that he was coming on to me. I told him to back off, but nothing would stop him until I blocked his number. I kept toying with the idea whether I should tell you and just as I'd made up my mind to break it to you, his wife jumped in first!'

Karen reflected with sadness. 'I felt such a fool for falling for all his lies, but I guess it's true that love makes us blind. But please don't blame yourself - you were just being a good friend who didn't want to see me getting hurt after all my other past mistakes.'

She thoughtfully took another sip of her coffee 'Going back to what we were originally talking about - yes it's true I met Simon online, but I could just as easily have met a similar liar if I'd been in a club or a pub. If anything in most cases, it's better to meet someone on a dating site because you can take all the time you need getting to know them - on that occasion, I just happened to be unlucky.'

The look of scepticism didn't go unnoticed on Karen.

'Look, I can see you had some bad experience before you moved to Minsden that you've never talked about, and that's entirely your own business. But I'm sure life for you would feel a little sweeter if you had somebody special to share it with - sometimes we just have to take a chance. I'm so glad I decided not to be put off as I would never have got to know Andrew!'

Both gave a start as Laura's mobile phone sprang to life, rudely breaking up their conversation with the loud ring tone. Picking it up from the table, she declined the call before placing it back into her handbag.

'Who was that?' enquired Karen with a frown.

'Oh, just another of those withheld calls - probably yet another of those PPI ones. I've had so many of those in the last few weeks, that I've lost count.' She decided to swiftly change the subject. 'Anyway, never mind me and my crazy dreams!'

'*Then give that dating site a go*!' interjected Karen. 'At least if you met some creep on there you can reject him from the safety of your home - it's *just* possible that you might meet somebody who is looking for somebody special like you.'

After returning to work, her mind was firmly fixed on the telephone call she received earlier at the cafe, and went to the Ladies to check her mobile.

In total, there had been three missed calls along with a

voicemail. She listened to the message from her mother.

'Hello sweetheart. Just your old mum here calling to say she's thinking of you and hoping everything's going well - Lou sends her love and just to say we both miss you *very much*. It's been a few weeks since we've heard from you and just want to make sure you're ok.' She could hear the emotion thickening in her mother's throat and was sure she was about to cry. 'Anyway, when you do get the time, *please* give us a call - it would be lovely to catch up on all the news. Hope everything's going well with your job! Take care darling and speak to you soon.'

As she hung up, she placed her mobile back inside her handbag, with an overwhelming feeling of loneliness and sadness sweeping over her.

CHAPTER THREE

L aura heated up a ready meal of cottage pie for one in the microwave, hastily bought on the way home from *Simply Food*. Normally not a huge fan of convenience foods, after her particularly demanding day, just wasn't in the mood to cook a meal from scratch. Sitting at her small table in the kitchen, toying with the food on her plate with her fork, discovered that although her migraine had finally disappeared, still didn't have much of an appetite. Despite all her best efforts to finish her meal, ended up throwing most of the contents into the food bin.

After washing the few dishes from her evening dinner, switched on her laptop perched on the coffee table in the living-room, thinking back to her earlier conversation with Karen. Maybe it was time to move on, she thought reluctantly; after all, as amazing as her connection had with been Oscar, this was one relationship guaranteed not to go places. With a sigh, she went on to the dating site her friend recommended and set about creating her profile. After searching through photo albums on her MacBook Pro, found a picture taken at the firm's latest Christmas party, wearing a flattering red dress that complimented her dark brown hair. Biting her lip nervously, finally took the plunge and uploaded the image onto the site, before composing a few brief details about herself: -

Single Female aged 43
Non-smoker
Profession: Team Manager for a finance company
Interests: Art, Painting, Reading, Eating Out, Walking
Seeking: Single Professional Male aged 40-50 with similar interests

At first, she added *happy and carefree* but after some deliberation deleted the words, fearing this might give the wrong impression that she was looking for something more casual; heaven knows, there were enough players on dating sites without attracting them like a magnet! Tapping away quickly on the keyboard, she included: *Has a good sense of humour, with a caring side.*

As she read through her newly created profile, Laura felt as satisfied as she could that she wasn't coming across as completely desperate before finally pressing the Submit button.

Oh, what have I just gone and done? she thought to herself with despair. *Why did I have to listen to Karen?* She took a sip of the now lukewarm tea from her mug before finally closing down her laptop. Well, at least she could deactivate her new account whenever she chose to.

Despite feeling shattered after her particularly manic day, Laura felt too unrelaxed for sleep.

In the spare bedroom that acted as her studio, she placed the large A3 drawing pad standing in the far corner, onto her easel. Whenever experiencing moments of stress when sleep eluded her, found that drawing or painting was a good way in which to unwind, as well as helping to express herself.

Feeling distinctly uncomfortable with the humidity, a sure sign a thunderstorm might well be on the horizon, opened the window to the small room, allowing some much-needed air to enter, enabling her the opportunity to gather her thoughts together.

She sat down for a moment on her stool, staring at the blank sheet of paper, not knowing what to draw. A gentle breeze came through from outside, sending a ripple of pleasure down her spine as the air, albeit muggy and fume-congested, gently caressed her skin.

Wouldn't it be just amazing to live somewhere in the heart of the countryside? she mused, not having to breath in all the traffic fumes of an urban environment; to live in her own small private retreat, a pleasant contrast to the two-bedroomed flat where she currently resided. Oh, she appreciated that she mustn't be ungrateful, as the property was entirely her own with no mortgage to pay. So really, there wasn't any reason to grumble and was conveniently located in a fairly central area of Minsden, making her journey to work a fairly stress-free experience.

As much as she was more than a little in love with the idea of a place not too far away, Laura had to admit, found the thought of living in a cottage set in a small quaint village very appealing. A home from where she could drive off to meet friends in town whenever there was a need for company.

Determined to apply her burst of inspiration to paper, began making a sketch of a large thatched cottage with three bay windows to the downstairs of the property. After a few seconds of studying her drawing beginning to take form, added a further window to the upstairs that would probably be to the master bedroom with the smaller one on the left for a spare room or nursery, and lastly a considerably smaller one immediately to the right providing a view from what could be the bathroom.

Licking her lips in concentration, applied further detail to the large brass knocker attached to the front door of the property. Taking a step back, she studied her work, seeing her creation beginning to slowly take shape. What could possibly be more inviting than the thought of sitting in front of a warm glowing fireplace on a cold winter's evening? she pondered, before adding a chimney to the roof of the dwelling.

Pausing for a moment, Laura studied the quaint country cottage knowing without a doubt this was exactly the kind of place she would love to live one day.

Although the minutes were quickly ticking by, felt compelled to continue, drawing a straight path leading up to the dwelling. Looking thoughtfully with a frown of concentration creasing her forehead, decided a nice winding path comprising of crazy paving instead would look much more in character, and used her eraser before adding the final touches.

Nodding in approval, provided some privacy to the dwelling by sketching picket fencing around the entrance with a white wooden gate displaying a small sign written in a gothic style to give any visitor a warm welcome when arriving to *Rose Cottage*.

Aware for the first time her eyes were beginning to feel heavy, gave a yawn in protest as tiredness washed over her; switching off the light before slowly making her way to the bedroom.

As Laura made her way slowly through the village, became

aware of the silence that surrounded her; a stark contrast to all the noise of the traffic during rush-hour in Minsden, a silence only broken by the sound of her shoes crunching against the gravelly path beneath her feet.

She gazed up at the night sky, becoming almost entranced with its dark, mysterious quality, the colour reminding her of a vast pool of deep bluey black ink.

Pausing for a moment she inhaled the sweet fragrance of the countryside, the clean, untainted air holding no trace of the traffic fumes she had long become accustomed to. Reassuming her walk, Laura came to what appeared to be the heart of the village with a small pub displaying the name, The Silver Lion with a picture of the animal of the same name and colour. Still open for business if the lighting coming from the windows was anything to go by, with peals of laughter coming from within, and the delicious aroma of cooked steak wafting her way soon reaffirmed this.

As she continued along the walkway overlooking the small village green, glimpsed a cluster of houses and bungalows with their curtains closed, indicating the evening was fairly late with most of the occupants having retired for the evening. A small grocery store that served the community, was set slightly back from its neighbouring buildings, also devoid of any lighting having long been closed for the day.

She turned around the corner on her unknown journey, to

be met with a penetrating darkness, with no artificial lighting to be seen, hampering her vision until her eyes adjusted to her surroundings; the only source of light came from the full moon above, casting an eerily silver glow over the road, still damp from an earlier rain shower. The gentle breeze caused the low clouds to race across the sky, momentarily covering the bright orb from which the light reflected, with the branches of nearby trees moving in gentle protest.

With a small shiver rippling down her spine, Laura frowned, feeling more than a little apprehensive as sudden realisation dawned on her that she had absolutely no idea of where she was; the silence became almost overwhelming without the sound of any vehicles in the distance to be heard. Her heart suddenly raced an as an owl perched on one of the larger trees along the opposite side of the narrow road, hooting loudly before taking flight into the sky and disappearing without a trace.

Once managing to compose herself after her brief moment of panic, Laura gingerly ventured further. Seeing no sign of any further houses, only woods, was about to turn back the way she came, before spotting something from the corner of her eye. Her attention immediately focused on some white picket fencing close to the far edge of the pavement, appearing to be a border to a nearby property. Looking further ahead she glimpsed the silhouette of a building not too far in the distance.

Squinting in concentration, and her fear momentarily forgotten, held onto the small wooden gate, looking curiously ahead. Laura studied the large thatched cottage set back from the road, just barely glimpsing through the darkness, plants and shrubs that bordered the long path leading up to the dwelling. Occasionally she would get a whiff of their pungent aroma through the air, made more intense by the earlier downpour of rain. The sound of something rustling through vegetation re-ignited her fear, only to discover the source of the noise came from either a cat or a fox, difficult to know for sure, scurrying through the garden.

Laura couldn't detect any lighting from the cottage, which somehow seemed familiar but certain she had never been here before. But her attention was drawn to one of the downstairs windows, believing she could just make out a slight orange glow, possibly from a fireplace. The thin, grey plume of smoke coming from the large chimney on the rooftop soon confirmed this.

Realising that somebody from within the home might well be watching her, quickly stepped back from the gate, not wanting to be seen as an intruder by whoever was living inside. As Laura listened carefully, was certain she could hear the sound of somebody crying. Or could it be the howling of a wild animal in the distance? Listening again, knew for sure this was the sobbing of a child, coming from inside the cottage.

Her attention was immediately diverted towards one of the

upstairs windows to what was probably to a bedroom, as a light was switched on, flooding the room in brightness. Quickly, she stooped down trying to hide behind the privet hedge adjoining the fencing, hoping that she hadn't been seen. As her eyes shifted back towards the source of light, could just about make out the silhouette of a person, possibly a man appearing to hold the child that was still crying, being gently rocked in the arms of the adult until the crying slowly came to an end. Within an instant, her heart seemed to jump into her mouth when in the distance but not too far way, heard the ear-splitting sound of a gun being fired.

Reluctantly opening her eyes, quickly looked around to make sure she wasn't in any immediate danger or at the very worst had been shot by whoever held the gun. But instead of finding herself in the great outdoors, was sitting up in her own bed.

For a split second, lost in confusion, gazed towards the bedroom window that had been left open, studying the curtain flapping with the now strong wind outside, the air remaining warm and humid despite the sound of rain pouring down relentlessly. Just as she was about to get up to take a look from the window, gave a start as a dazzling white flash lit up the room, followed immediately by an ear-splitting clap of thunder that sounded more like an explosion. Certain that something not too far away had been struck by lightning, came the realisation that all the events in the village and of the cottage...*Rose Cottage* her very own creation on paper had all happened inside her dream.

CHAPTER FOUR

After what proved to be a particularly demanding day at work, Laura gratefully accepted Karen's invitation to share takeaway pizza at her house. As Andrew was meeting up with a friend, meant they could enjoy some quality time together watching a Sandra Bullock movie on Netflix over a meal that required no cooking.

'Perhaps not the best of her films,' Laura remarked feeling a little disappointed as the movie came to an end, 'but definitely by no means her worst.'

'But always good when the girl gets her man and there's a *happy ever after*.' added Karen with a wry smile, offering her the remaining portion of the large Sloppy Giuseppe pizza that they had eaten before diving into the generous slices of strawberry cheesecake.

Laura declined, giving a large drawn out sigh as she patted her stomach, now feeling considerably bloated. 'Oh, not for me. Anymore and I think I'll be ready to explode!'

Karen leaned back on the sofa, discreetly undoing the top button to her trousers. 'Perhaps ordering the cheesecake was a little over-ambitious, but Luigi's desserts are just to die for - but I guess with that and the fizzy cola was maybe taking things a just bit too literally.'

Laura had to agree. 'But it was rather scrummy, if a bit fattening - but always a plus when it saves on a pile of washing-up,' she added glancing over to the empty pizza boxes stacked on the coffee table.'

A look of sadness shadowed her friend's face. 'True, but I *do* miss my Emma, even if she did leave a trail of mess and destruction in her path. Heaven knows how she's managing in her shared accommodation - she would never so much as wash a plate, unless it was under duress!'

'I'm sure uni and having a taste of independence will be the making of her!'

She nodded in agreement. 'I know you're absolutely right - once she realises Mum's not around to tidy up after her, she'll soon come down to earth with a bang.' Karen looked up to the ceiling, giving a sigh. 'I have these visions of her flat being overtaken by all kinds of takeaway boxes and cartons.'

Laura grinned. 'All part of student life!'

Unable to resist the last slice of pizza any longer, Karen finally succumbed, regarding the piece before taking a bite.

'Yes, I've got to accept my little girl has finally grown up and probably soon will have her first serious relationship.' Seeing her friend appeared distracted, gave a troubled frown. 'Hey, you're looking in a world of your own - what's up? I hope you're not getting another of those migraines.'

Laura shook her head apologetically as she wiped her mouth with a paper napkin before tossing it aside. 'No, with that storm kicking off, I didn't sleep too well last night. Definitely didn't help when going through those job applications practically the whole day - never thought we would get such a speedy response!' She thought for a moment, deciding honesty was the best policy. 'Well, I also had one of those weird dreams again last night.'

Karen sat up, her interest lost on the pizza slice which was dumped unceremoniously back into the box. 'You mean you dreamt again of your dream man? No wonder you seemed to be in a world of your own today!'

She shook her head. 'Not about the man…Oscar, but all the same it was rather strange.'

Seeing that she had gained her friend's undivided attention, explained, 'Because I was having difficulty unwinding, decided I'd do some drawing. Well, I began sketching this cottage - and after adding a few details including a path leading to the door and other details here and there, I finally managed to feel sleepy, and went to bed. Well, the next thing I knew, found myself walking through this mysterious village at night time and came to the very same cottage that I drew.'

For a moment, Karen sat there taken aback, not quite knowing what to say. 'Wow, that's pretty amazing - to draw a house, I mean a *cottage* and to see it in a dream! Did it look *exactly* the same as the one you sketched?'

Laura confirmed with a nod of her head.

'Gosh, how strange is that!' An idea suddenly came to Karen. 'Do you think it's possible you might've seen that cottage on TV or somewhere and you remembered subconsciously?'

Laura thought for a moment, giving a shrug. 'Not that I'm aware of.' She took a sip of her diet cola. 'The only thing that comes to mind is that I'm living in a town flat and I'm really in love with the idea of living in a nice house or cottage somewhere in the countryside.'

Karen gave a wry smile. 'Well, that's your answer - I'm always dreaming of winning the big one on the lottery and getting somewhere bigger and upgrade my car, but sadly that never happens!'

'And there's more,' she informed her friend. 'I was standing at the bottom of the garden just outside the gate and could hear this child crying. At first I thought it was some wild animal as there were these fields nearby - but I realised it was coming from the house, then saw a light being switched on to the room where the child must have been. The next thing I saw was an adult, from what I could see, a man picking up the youngster and rocking them until they stopped crying.'

'And?' Karen promoted.

Laura shrugged. 'And nothing – I heard what sounded like a gunshot and I woke up finding myself in bed.'

Karen refilled her glass with cola, looking completely taken aback. 'Well, you certainly have some interesting dreams! Do you think it might have something to do with those migraines? You've been getting a lot more of lately - there could well be a connection. It might be time to check it out with the doctor.'

Her friend shook her head defiantly. 'No. No, I'm sure it's nothing to do with the headaches. Ever since I was a young child, both mum and my art teacher said I had a vivid imagination - I guess with lack of sleep well, it just triggers those types of dreams when I do finally get to go off.'

'Maybe you should take up writing and make your fortune,' Karen suggested with a grin.

'I don't think so - although I'm good at reading other people's work, I know I would make a useless writer. I'll just stick to what I'm good at and that's just sketching and painting in my spare time.'

'So, how's it going with your online dating?' asked Karen, deciding to change the subject.

Her friend cringed, closing her eyes for moment. 'I hoped you weren't going to ask.'

'Haven't you set up your profile? Oh, come on Laura, how is anybody going to know you exist if you don't make yourself known?'

She pouted her lips teasingly. 'And who said I *haven't* set up my profile?'

'Oh, you're *such* a tease! Why didn't you say so? You know it would only stay between the two of us!'

Laura looked apologetic. 'Of course, I know you would keep it to yourself, but to be honest I only set the thing up just before going to bed last night.'

'So, you haven't even looked to see if any admirers have come your way?'

'Nope.'

Karen shook her head in disbelief. 'Oh, you're a *nightmare*! If that was me, I would be dying of curiosity – would've downloaded the phone app and be checking it out every five minutes! Shall we log on now and take a look?'

Laura looked hesitant. 'I'm not sure I really want to know

- I'd feel such a loser if I've not even had a flicker of interest.' She nervously bit her bottom lip for a few seconds before her curiosity getting the better of her. 'Oh, go on then, let's take a look! It might be a good idea for you to look through my profile to make sure I've not written anything too outrageous or come across as completely desperate.'

Within a few minutes the two friends huddled around the laptop, with Karen studying Laura's dating profile with her reading glasses perched on the end of her nose, as a look of pleasant surprise spread across her face.

'Well, it looks like you're more attractive than you realise, Miss Winters! In the space of less than 10 hours you've received twelve Winks and received five messages to your inbox - in total, you've had over 30 profile views. That's a pretty good start!'

Together they skimmed over the profile photos of men who'd expressed their interest, now and again having a giggle at the less than flattering ones.

'We're being much too unkind,' Karen remarked trying her best not to laugh. 'It's not the packaging that counts, but what's underneath.'

'Very true,' agreed Laura. 'But I feel it's important to find at least *some* physical attraction.' She pointed to a photo of Lawrence from St Albans. 'There are some things that can be overlooked as none of us are perfect, but just look at those teeth -from what I can see, there's at least three front ones missing and the rest look as if they've never seen the sight of a toothbrush!'

'Oh, yuck,' Karen winced. 'And he wonders *why* he's not able to pull.' She took a look at Mike from Reading. 'Hmm, not too bad looking, but has bit of a strange stare about him - perhaps he's just not photogenic.'

Laura burst out laughing as her attention turned to Gordon from Dunstable. 'If he's fifty, then I'm Victoria Beckham! It's not the fact he's probably older, but if somebody is lying about their age, then what else could they be hiding?'

Karen giggled. 'Maybe he's just had a hard life - and don't be so hard about the age thing, he wouldn't be the first. Look, you get this all the time on all these dating sites - it comes with the territory. There're loads on here who fib about their age or put on photos how they looked twenty years ago - others are married and serial cheats or just after for one thing.'

Laura grimaced. 'You're really *selling* this to me! I'm beginning to wish I hadn't bothered.'

Her friend's face softened. 'Stop being such a Negative Nelly - the secret is learning to look out for the liars and the way to do that is to spend as much time as possible getting to know them before even contemplate meeting up. There's no hurry - just take your time.' Her attention was diverted back to the laptop. 'Hey, let's take a look at the messages in your in box.'

Together they browsed, with Laura frowning in disgust as the first one contained an explicit photo. 'Well, he's going to get blocked for a start!' She went through the next three messages not particularly liking what she saw. Shallow she might be, but looks did have to play a part as far as she was concerned. Just as Laura was about to give up, came to the last one, noting the man in the picture appeared very pleasing to the eye.

'Now he looks rather tasty - got a nice smile too,' Karen agreed, encouraged by the flicker of interest registering on her friend's face as she studied the man with a head of dark wavy hair and the most sparkling green eyes.

'Well at first glance he *does* looks a lot more appealing than those others - but, as you keep telling me, it's not all about the looks! So, let's see what he's got to say about himself.' Laura clicked on the link which provided further details about her subject of her interest.

Putting on her spectacles again, Karen read slowly through his message. 'Well, his name's Julian and a sales director from Burrington. He says he's 46 and divorced with two grown-up children. Hmm, he states he read through your profile with great interest and believes you both have a lot in common with the drawing and also loves reading - he would love to learn a little more about you.'

Laura browsed through some of his other pictures. One in particular caught her attention, of him wearing a charcoal grey suit looking very striking. Judging by his athletic build was clear to see he took fitness seriously. She had to admit his warm friendly smile only added to his appeal.

'Why the cynical face?' questioned her friend.

'Well, he does seem very nice, and apart from the good looks he does come across as a genuinely nice person...'

'But...'

Laura gave a deep sigh 'But, there's got to be a catch - why does any guy who's particularly attractive with an interesting job and full of charisma need to look online to find somebody special?'

Karen rolled her eyes to the ceiling in despair. 'I'm sure it's all for the same reasons why an attractive woman with a great personality and an interesting job like *you* is doing the same thing. I guess like you Julian's got a full-time job and getting to that age where it's not quite so easy to go out and meet other people.'

Laura gazed back to the photos displayed on the laptop screen. 'Yes, I suppose it's not so easy for somebody our age as it would be for a young, fit twenty-something. Look, I'm not promising anything, but I just *might* reply to his message later and take it from there. He probably won't bother getting back as he's probably written the same message to half the women on that site.'

'Oh, don't be such a cynic!' Karen chided as she closed down her laptop. 'It's just possible that in you he saw a like-minded person and is simply interested in getting to know you a little better. There's one thing you can be sure about - the chances of you getting better acquainted with your dream guy, Oscar are zilch.'

The following day at work, with Karen taking a day's holiday Laura decided to have dinner in the canteen, feeling it would save her the trouble of cooking later. Having not long come out of a lengthy meeting with Edwina Charlton to discuss details about the recruitment campaign now having been put into place, and not having slept particularly well the previous night, found the whole ordeal emotionally draining.

With the canteen relatively quiet, had her pick of the tables and sat down wearily in the corner, glad to finally have some time to herself. Just as she started cutting in to her gammon slice, jumped with a start from her thoughts as a plate of salad was placed opposite to her meal of her mixed grill.

'Mind if I join you?'

She looked up to find Edwina looking down at her, smiling apologetically. 'Sorry if I startled you, I could see you were miles away!'

Laura beckoned her boss to take a seat, trying to appear more enthusiastic than she felt at having her peaceful lunchbreak interrupted. 'Of course, Edwina, I was just wrapped up in thought about all the interviewing coming up.'

Edwina grinned, feigning despair, wiping her brow as she sat down. 'Phew! Tell me about it! Well, if anything it's certainly going to prove to be a challenge.' The short, dark pixie-style haircut complemented her heart-shaped face, giving her a youthful appearance; the fashionable *M&S* burgundy trouser suit, emphasising a slender figure that was the envy of those half her age.

For a moment, she looked around to make sure nobody else was in their vicinity. 'To be perfectly honest with everything that's happened to me lately I won't be sorry when it's time to leave - especially with all the changes that are afoot!'

Laura raised her eyebrows quizzically, her suspicions raised that there had been other reasons to her boss's absence than some virus.

Edwina appeared momentarily flustered with a blush

colouring her cheeks a darker shade of pink. 'Oh, forget what I said - you know how things are here, nothing stays the same for long.' She peered at the younger woman with a smile, eager to change the subject. 'So, how's everything Laura? Things have been just so manic lately, that we just *never* seem to get the time to have a friendly chat.'

Laura shrugged. 'I'm fine - I guess there's really no room to complain. I have a nice flat to come home to after a busy day at the office.'

'So, no special man?' enquired Edwina before waving her hand dismissively, regretting her question. 'Oh, please forget I said that - I don't want you to think I'm prying!'

'Oh, don't worry about it, Edwina, I'm used to people asking me. And for the record, the answer is no.'

Edwina took a sip of her water. 'There's a lot to be said for being single - believe me, it has its advantages! Don't get me wrong, I love my Hugh to pieces and wouldn't swap him for the world.' She gave out a long, drawn sigh as she prodded her fork into a slice of tomato. 'But I must admit it's rather nice when I have an evening all to myself - he's taking the grandchildren out early this evening to see that new Disney film followed by a McDonald's. I say I'm going to make the most of the peace and quiet, but as usual I'll probably end up getting stuck into a pile of work.'

Laura toyed around with her mashed potato. 'Won't you miss this place after being a part of the furniture for so many years.'

Her boss gave a chuckle. 'Oh Laura, you're making me feel positively ancient! Yes, joking aside I'll miss being here despite all the highs and the lows. As you're already aware, I came here as a young apprentice when I was twenty - my first real job after university, opening the post, and not a computer to be seen in those days!' She smiled as she reminisced with fondness back to those days when life seemed so much simpler, if a little tough. 'For all my sins, I finally worked my way up to where I am now!'

She paused for a moment, looking at the pretty young woman sitting opposite, studying that haunted, faraway expression she had come to know so well. 'I'll be truthful with you Laura, and I know what I'm about to say you'll keep this to yourself, as I really don't want it known by everybody.'

Her curiosity getting the better of her, quickly assured her boss that anything she discussed would be treated with the strictest of confidence.

Feeling satisfied that Laura was definitely a person she could trust, continued. 'As you know I was absent for the best part of six weeks, and the official reason given was that I was on sick leave due to a viral infection.' She gently placed her knife and fork on to her plate, the contents only half-eaten. 'Well, that wasn't strictly true, because the real reason was I had a minor heart attack.'

Laura's face paled with shock. 'Oh Edwina, I had no...'

Her boss waved her hand dismissively, making it clear she wasn't looking for any sympathy. 'Don't worry, dear I'm absolutely fine and it was only a very small one, nothing to be too concerned about - more of a wakeup call, really.' Her expression grim as she reflected, 'But the whole incident made me realise I've made life too much about my work.' She took a sip from her glass of water, 'So that's my true reason for leaving Global Life and to dedicating more time to the family. We're moving down to Dorset to be with our eldest daughter Vanessa and her hubby. It'll be great to spend more time with the grandchildren - they're certainly growing up fast and I would like to see their best years. Before we know it, they'll soon turn into adults and be living their own lives!'

Laura completely agreed with her boss's way of thinking. 'Yes, life's much too short not to be doing the things we truly want to do.'

Edwina glanced around again to make sure nobody else was listening before she continued. 'Actually, I won't be completely put out to pasture - me and Hugh have been debating a possible internet business venture that might turn out to be quite lucrative. I won't go into any details at this point, but I feel this will give me something to get my teeth into, as well as spending more time with the family!'

Laura smiled brightly genuinely pleased for the older woman. 'That's fantastic! To be honest you don't strike me as the type to be sitting back doing nothing. I know only too well how busy you like to be - not that the grandchildren won't keep you occupied!'

Edwina laughed lightly before her expression turned to one of concern.

'Laura, how *is* everything? *Really?* I'm taking off my manager's hat now, so I'm not prying from an employer's perspective. You know I think highly of you and for everything that happened before…you know.'

The younger woman nodded her head, for a moment lost in thought. 'I know Edwina and it really means a lot - more than you could ever possibly realise. I could never thank you enough for all the opportunities you've given me after everything. I'm going to really miss you.'

Her boss shook her head. 'My dear, you got that job through your own merits and not because of what had happened! I knew when you came for that interview what a bright young woman you are and you have most definitely proven me right! Besides I'm hoping we can stay in touch when I move to Dorset and would be most put out if you didn't come down to visit - I'm only just a few miles from your mum!'

Laura smiled, though the fleeting moment of hesitation didn't go unmissed by Edwina. 'That goes without saying.' She put down her knife and fork, her meal barely eaten. 'Well, to be honest I don't think I have the appetite to eat this food - I'm more used to eating a main meal in the evening. So, it looks like I'll either be rustling up something quick tonight or having a takeaway.'

As Laura left the table, emptying the food from her almost full plate into one of the bins, was unaware of Edwina watching, with deep concern etched on her face. For some considerable time, she had noticed that the younger woman wasn't looking particularly well, having become thinner, almost gaunt with that sad expression and those dark shadows permanently under her eyes.

Her mind wandered back to that day several years ago when Laura came for that interview, when she learned with a combination of both shock and sadness the reasons that had brought her to Mindsen to begin a brand-new chapter of her very tragic life. Edwina would have happily been friends with her outside of work, but for some reason Laura seemed to detach herself from most people, but thankfully had become good friends with Karen Bright who apparently knew nothing about Laura's history.

After returning home, Laura prepared a tuna salad, unable to muster an appetite for anything heavier. As she rubbed her right temple, decided to give the glass of white wine a miss, detecting the tell-tale sign of the painful throbbing that precedes a migraine. Giving a weary sigh, noticed her sight distorting into double-vision and quickly swallowed a couple of headache tablets, hoping she had recognised the signs earlier enough to halt the migraine in its tracks.

She switched on her laptop, logging on to the dating site to see if there had been any further messages. Although in total saw that about ten men had viewed her profile, saw nothing further in her inbox. She looked back to the message that Julian had left the previous day and after some deliberation, decided to take the plunge and reply to his message.

Hi Julian, Great to hear from you. As you can see my name is Laura and I come from Minsden. As I mentioned before, I have worked for a finance company for several years and on the whole, I enjoy my job. I have been single since...

As her fingers moved swiftly over the keyboard, a troubled frown knotted her brow as she thought back to bygone days. Trying to gather her thoughts together despite her misgivings and the increasing pain in her head, felt determined to reply to Julian's message.

Well, I've been single for some time as have been busy with work commitments, but have come to appreciate there should be a happy balance between career and personal life. With this in mind, I am seeking a like-minded person who shares these views. I guess what I am looking for is that special someone for friendship and to see what goes on from there!

I hope your day has been a good one and look forward to hearing from you soon. Laura.

Before she had a chance to read over her words written from the heart, quickly sent her reply to Julian's message before there was a chance to change her mind.

Giving a shrug Laura closed down her laptop. The likelihood of him even bothering to reply was slim, she mused. All the best ones soon got snapped up by those that got there first.

CHAPTER FIVE

Laura woke during the night, holding her head in despair with the grim realisation that her migraine was now in full swing. Peering at the time through distorted vision to the bright display of the alarm clock, the large green luminescent digits showing two am. Switching on the bedside light, the brightness for a moment exacerbating the nauseous feeling welling up inside her stomach, reached inside the drawer to the bedside cabinet for the box of paracetamol tucked away. Taking out the last two tablets, quickly swallowed these with the glass of water always kept by her side at bedtimes, letting out a deep sigh as she became only too aware that she was medicating more frequently of late.

Perhaps Karen had a point, she pondered; maybe she should pop along to the doctors, before quickly dismissing the idea. No, before going down that road, she would buy those strips that you could stick on your forehead especially for migraines. Fiona Bradshaw in the drawdown team at work swore by them, so it was well worth giving them a try.

After tossing and turning in her bed, as sleep eluded her, finally picked up her Kindle and began reading a recently downloaded Martina Cole novel, in the hope this might relax her. But after getting through a couple of chapters, finally gave up on the idea and ventured into the kitchen to make a mug of tea.

Letting out a long yawn, she switched on the light to the spare room, her attention focusing on her latest sketch placed on the easel, as her mind regressed to the dream cottage in the mysterious village.

Although the dream had shown Rose Cottage at night, where colours appeared vague, shadowed by the darkness of night time, could clearly imagine the details of the small dwelling, surrounded by the natural beauty of the rural settings had she been there before on a bright summer's day. Feeling a sudden burst of inspiration, Laura set to work mixing paints in preparation to continue work on her latest project.

After spending what turned out to be a considerable length of time working on her painting, with her only interlude to eat some toast, finally glanced at the small round clock ticking loudly on the wall. To her astonishment the time was already just a few minutes after five pm. Giving a weary sigh, rubbed her throbbing right temple, all too aware that this migraine was likely to stay for at least the next day or so.

Taking a sip of the remainder of her now cold tea, carefully studied her painting, seeing it come slowly to life with the scene now bursting with vibrant colour, capturing so perfectly in minute detail, the pale almost orange hue of the Bath Stone exterior of the cottage with the dusky yellow thatch that topped the roof.

The garden displayed an abundance of the bold crimson petals of rosebushes, and the pale pinks and whites of carnations adorning the borders of the long green lawn, adding a bright contrast to the blue hydrangeas all in full bloom, ready to invite a bounty of wildlife into its fragrant sanctuary.

She smiled with satisfaction at the leafy effect she had managed to capture of the dark green fir trees around the privet fencing, affording privacy to the country retreat, the sunshine speckling the leaves with shimmers of gold.

Pursing her lips together in concentration, Laura could easily imagine sitting within this small oasis of tranquillity whilst having breakfast, gazing wistfully overhead at the large fluffy white clouds, appearing to drift along like floating cotton wool through the gentle breeze of a morning blue sky.

Finally, her attention wandered to the small white wooden gate to the entrance, with the name Rose Cottage painted on the sign in large black gothic style letters, enticing any visitor to walk along the long, narrow crazy paving path, mottled with clumps of moss, leading invitingly to the dark brown wooden door of the dwelling. Who knew what secrets might lie behind that closed door?

Her mood somewhat melancholy, placed her paintbrush on the small side table alongside her tubes of paints. What a beautiful thought to live in a place like this and to share her life with somebody special; somebody she could come home to after a busy day at work.

Despite her thumping headache was finally beginning to feel tired but regretfully didn't have enough time to go back to sleep. Giving a deep sigh, she slowly made her way to the bathroom to take her morning shower.

'I knew the day was set to go from bad to worse,' Laura grumbled, staring at her blank PC monitor in exasperation, causing Charlotte the team's young apprentice to turn her attention away from the incoming post that she was in the process of sorting.

'Oops, looks like the gremlins are in full force,' remarked Karen who'd just returned from a trip to the canteen placing on her desk a takeaway carton of bacon and egg with two Americano coffees, handing over one to her friend.

She held her head in despair. 'Tell me about it - knew it was going to be one of those days after a lousy sleep and another thumping migraine!'

Peering over her friend's shoulder to the display of numbers flashing up on the screen, her face pulled into a grimace. 'Hmm, I don't like the look of that. Might be best to give IT a call.' With that she sat back at her desk, opening up the polystyrene container, the smell of fried bacon making Laura feel slightly nauseous.

She rubbed her temples, letting out a large groan. 'And I know exactly what IT are like, especially this week when they're three people down with holidays. You're held for ages in a queue for at least twenty minutes before finally getting seen to. That's if you're lucky.' She gazed in frustration at the ominous error message on her screen. 'Of all the mornings when I've got to get those stats ready for that meeting with Edwina at eleven and arranging those job interviews - now I'm beginning I wish I'd stayed in bed!'

Karen busily cut into her fried egg with the plastic cutlery, the yoke running over the remainder of her breakfast. 'Just an idea, but Tracy Bishop in Claims is on holiday today. I guess you could always sit at her desk until it gets fixed. I know it's bit of a pain being at the other end of the office, but I suppose it'll work until you get that report done.' Then she had another idea. 'Or better still *I* could go there and you can log onto mine. It'll save you time moving all your stuff!'

Just as Laura was about to agree, Charlotte sprung up from her chair and came over, suggesting she could try rebooting the computer.

Although Laura whose own IT knowledge was very limited, knew that Charlotte was pretty good at all things technical, but still remained sceptical and worried any interference might cause the machine to crash and worst still wipe all her files away.

Nodding reluctantly, seeing her young apprentice didn't share her apprehension, looked on nervously as she restarted the computer, closing her eyes for a moment as the screen went blank. But Charlotte remained calm as the PC began to restart with a message appearing to press a key for Windows to reload. With confidence, she hit the keyboard as instructed, with the three of them watching, completely transfixed to the screen. Laura gave a huge sigh of relief as her desktop folders seemed to magically reappear on the monitor.

Charlotte blushed with pride as her manager lavished her with praise for saving the day, along with a Global Life £5.00 food token to treat herself to something in the canteen.

As she happily went off to choose something to buy, Laura sat down at her desk, feeling more than a little relieved. 'That girl's worth her weight in gold - what she doesn't know about computers definitely isn't worth knowing!'

Karen agreed. 'Tell me about it, she's wasted as an apprentice, that's for sure - she should be in IT.'

Her mood somewhat lighter, Laura giggled, putting a finger to her mouth. 'Hush, better not let Edwina hear you saying that - after all, she began her career at Global Life as an apprentice and sorting out the post. I for one reckon Charlotte's got massive potential and I don't see any reason why she shouldn't be able to climb all the way to the top if she wants to.'

'Yes, she's an absolute treasure.'

'Whatever you ask of her she never questions and gets straight on with it. I forgot to tell you the other day...' Taking the plastic lid from her large coffee, she gazed at the screen with a frown of concentration marking her forehead as something grabbed her attention, as her mouth slightly opened in astonishment.

'Oh no, has it crashed *again*?'

Laura waved her hand dismissively, shaking her head. 'No. No, I'm just going through my emails and you'll never guess what - I've received a nomination for the Global Life Employee Awards!'

Her interest aroused, Karen got up from her chair with

her coffee, peering over Laura's shoulder at the email. 'For *Most Loved Manager*, no less!' Taking a sip of her drink, read the message aloud.

'I would like to nominate Laura Winters for Most Loved Manager. As team manager for Investments Solutions, she's ace, as she really believes in us, and always encouraging us with all the things we're best at. She's very hard-working and always there when you need help, no matter how busy she might be. Not only is Laura one cool dude in a crisis, she's so funny and nice and makes coming to work such fun. As far as I'm concerned, Laura deserves to be voted for Most Loved Manager as she's the loveliest team manager ever!'

Karen looked over to her friend who was clearly moved at being nominated, giving her a hug as the others in the small team looked on with smiles on their faces, giving a burst of applause. 'Oh Laura, how lovely and so well deserved! It's just a reflection of how nice you are and how much everybody thinks so highly of you. Looks like you'll need to start thinking about getting a dress - the awards are only a month away!'

She gave a wry smile. 'To be honest if it wasn't for the fact I'm team manager and supporting our team, I wouldn't even bother going to these events. This is only the first stage and I might not even make it as a finalist anyway, but I suppose I should make the effort and buy an extra nice dress for the occasion just in case.' Shrugging her shoulders, she added, 'Well, I guess the day isn't turning out so badly after all.' Making sure her remark wasn't premature, she glanced back to her monitor to make sure everything was still working, before turning back her attention back to Karen through narrowed eyes. 'I wonder *who* was kind enough to have nominated me.'

Her friend sat back on her chair laughing. 'Hey, you know I think you're great and you really deserve to be nominated, but I can assure you it wasn't me - with words like *ace* and *cool dude*, I don't think so! Look, you're not likely to find out unless you start bribing suspects, so really the best thing is to just look at it a bit like receiving a valentine from a secret admirer - you'll probably never know for sure who was behind it, but just be happy that somebody took the time to consider you.'

Their eyes followed Charlotte as she returned to her desk with her blueberry muffin and a small bottle of Sprite, looking sheepishly their way. Seeing that she had their undivided attention, returned to her seat, quickly setting back to work on the incoming post, trying her best to conceal the smile appearing on her face.

After what turned out to be a particularly manic day at Global Life, Laura was glad to be home. Sitting on her black leather sofa, with her head rested back, slowly rubbed her temple in a vain attempt to ease her relentless headache. Her earlier plans had been to go out for after-works drinks with Karen and a few of the other team managers, but knew even sticking to soft drinks because of the drive home, the noise of the crowd in the pub would do nothing to ease that dull, throbbing sensation.

Remembering she had bought a box of migraine head strips, went into her handbag lying on the floor to retrieve one. After a struggle, she managed to tear open the foil sachet and applied it to her right temple, giving a deep sigh of satisfaction as she lied down, relaxing her head back on a plump red cushion. *Anything* was worth a try, she surmised; better than continuously swallowing endless tablets that did little or nothing at all to ease that dull ache and nausea. As she finally relaxed, her migraine began to ease with tiredness washing over her.

Laura opened her eyes finding herself standing outside of Rose Cottage. This time the place was in daylight, but only just, judging the by the large tangerine sun setting in the west. Her gaze drank in the sight of the quaint cottage and the surrounding area, realising that all the colours matched those on her painting, from the crimson petal rose bushes, to the pink and white carnations, and the purple-blue blossoms of the hydrangeas out in full bloom.

She listened out carefully for any signs of life, for people, or anything; but apart from the birds singing from the tall trees close by with their heavily leaved branches rustling gently in the wind, there wasn't another sound to be heard, not even from a passing car.

Again, she looked towards the cottage, this time with the hindsight that this was all a dream where nothing bad could possibly happen to her. Placing her hands on the small white gate to Rose Cottage, prompted it with gentle a push, as it let out just the smallest squeaks of protest from its weathered hinges, before opening with ease.

Gingerly, Laura strolled a short distance down the crazy paving path, peering over her shoulder, before diverting her attention back towards the cottage. From inside the large white paned window on the ground floor came the familiar orange glow from the fireplace as in her previous dream. A sudden gust of wind caused the gate to slam loudly behind her, rudely rousing Laura from her thoughts. A shiver ran down her spine as much from fear as the coolness of the breeze giving her cause to wonder how it was even *possible* to sense weather conditions inside of a dream.

Taking a deep intake of breath, she slowly ventured

further down the pathway, only too aware that somebody might well be home and was probably watching her from inside. The thought caused her to smile, realising that the idea was absurd when whoever was at home didn't actually exist. Even if it turned out to be something scary like a ghost, she took comfort from the thought she would wake up in the safety of her own home.

Composing herself, Laura summoned up the courage to walk over to the entrance of the cottage, oblivious in her concentration to the scent of the nearby rosebushes, infusing with the cool evening air. Nervously, she peered into the window, seeing the room shrouded in almost total darkness, the only source of light from the orange flickering flames she could now see more clearly coming from the fireplace. Carefully, she stepped onto the large lawn, much to her relief, appearing to be dry judging by the firmness of the ground beneath her feet. Mustering up some more courage she peered to the side of the building, noticing a large green privet hedge blocking the view to the rear of the property. As she returned to the front, decided to finally take the plunge and hit the brass knocker firmly on the large brown wooden door. From inside a dog barked furiously, alerting its owner to a possible intruder.

She waited a few seconds, with the dog inside continuing to make itself heard, beginning to wonder if anybody would answer. Just as she was about to walk away, gave a small yelp as the door suddenly opened. Her heart immediately began to race, not knowing quite who or what to expect and gave a gasp of complete surprise when standing at the entrance, watching her intently, was Oscar.

CHAPTER SIX

Appearing totally transfixed with unblinking eyes, Laura stood there staring at him with her mouth slightly agape. Once the shock had finally registered, her cheeks burned red with embarrassment, knowing in his eyes she probably looked about as delightful as a freshly boiled lobster. Which was crazy really, considering this was all just a dream. But to be standing right opposite the very man who'd managed to capture her heart in a single dream just days ago, and believed would never have the chance to see ever again, was something she could never have foreseen.

This time wearing a dark blue open-necked cotton shirt with faded jeans that fitted snugly over his long lean thighs, looked exactly as she remembered him; with that dark slightly ruffled hair, with a small peppering of grey, those same twinkling dark eyes that seemed to burn through to the core of her soul.

Oscar broke the almost hypnotic spell by treating her

to a teasing smile. 'Well, this is a most pleasant surprise.' He peered briefly towards the hedge from the direction she had only moments earlier been checking out. 'Um, if you've finished having a look around the place, perhaps would you'd like to come in, or shall I leave you to take a little longer?'

Not quite knowing what to say, and feeling more than a little foolish at being caught out, decided the best option was to follow him inside the cottage.

They entered a short hallway walking by the light wooden staircase leading to the bedrooms, as he took her straight through to a light, spacious sitting room. Her heart skipped a beat as she took in her surroundings. Unsure why, was struck by an immediate sense of déjà vu as if a bolt of lightning had coursed through her body as she studied the sofa opposite two comfy looking armchairs, all in a deep Bordeaux red, plumped with sumptuous light floral scatter cushions; the rug covering the wooden floor of polished pine in a complementary red and gold mixture. She raised her head, looking above to the low-ceiling, its wooden beading adding to the character of the country abode. Finally, her attention focused on the large open fireplace to the far side of the room, until now only just glimpsed from the outside; without a doubt the pinnacle of the room, she mused as she watched the flames, warm and inviting, licking gently around some recently added logs.

The quizzical frown marking her forehead didn't go unnoticed by Oscar as she listened to the sound of what could only be described as paws scratching behind a door at the other end of the room. Giving a wry smile, he strode across the floor, satisfying her curiosity by opening it. A small white West Highland terrier came unleashed like an uncoiled spring from where it had been shut away, bounding swiftly in her direction.

'This is Duke,' he informed her, with amusement as the dog immediately jumped up to her legs, his short tail wagging swiftly. Mistaking her wide-eyed expression for fear, was quick to reassure her, 'I promise he'd never hurt you - he'd make the most useless guard dog, he's much too soft!'

Laura quickly demonstrated she couldn't have been less afraid when she crouched down as Duke eagerly accepted her strokes of affection. Placing his two front paws on her knees, eagerly rewarded her to a lick or two to her face, as if reuniting with some long-lost friend.

She turned to Oscar who was studying her curiously, then realised much to her own surprise, she was shedding tears.

'I'm sorry, it's just that I once had a dog exactly like this one,' she explained apologetically. 'But he died a few months before I moved to Minsden.' She tickled her new canine friend under his chin, admiring his blue silver-buckled collar. Giving a sigh of contentment, she diverted her attention away from Duke, taking in her surroundings.

'This place is *so* beautiful,' she remarked softly with a quiver of emotion running through her voice. 'I don't know why, but it feels as if I've been here before.'

Oscar looked around him with a tinge of sadness. 'My wife must take all the credit for this - she's the one that planned out all the décor and the furnishings and helped make this cottage into a real home.' He rubbed his hands together in thought. 'Hey, why don't you sit yourself down? Do you fancy a tea or a coffee? Or maybe you'd prefer something a little stronger?

'Coffee will be fine,' Laura insisted as her eyes followed him entering the adjoining room where Duke had just moments appeared from, realising now had to be the kitchen.

She sat down on the softly upholstered sofa, placing the cushion to the side of her. Maybe she could have gone for something stronger like a glass of wine, she thought with amusement; after all this was only a dream and was highly unlikely to get drunk or do anything to make her migraine worse. Blinking in astonishment, Laura touched her fingers to her temple, to her great surprise, realising for the first time that her migraine had vanished without a trace.

Listening to the sound of crockery being moved as Oscar

busily prepared their drinks, decided to take advantage of her moment alone. Seeing this as her perfect moment to take a quick snoop around, stood up, stepping carefully over Duke who'd made himself comfortable on the soft rug peering at her with curiosity. Brushing her long hair behind her ear, once again waist-length as in the previous dream, immediately fell in love with the simplicity of the sitting room with the neutral tones of the magnolia walls, hung with a few framed oil paintings. Taking a closer look at one of a woodland scenery in autumn displaying trees with leaves in an array of rusty orange and gold shades, the fallen leaves creating a colourful carpet on the ground below; another close by of a seascape with a large full moon appearing to hang low in the cloudless night sky. Its bright, glowing orb reflected its radiance onto the large dark inky-blue waves of the ocean, crashing fiercely against some rocks on the shore. Almost certainly these must have been painted by Oscar, she guessed correctly. Judging by his work could see he was clearly a very accomplished artist and hoped one day to see some more of his work.

Returning to the fireplace, she gazed up to the large wooden-framed hexagonal clock hanging above the paintings; its black metallic hands spread over the Roman numerals showing the time to be five o'clock. Narrowing her eyes, took a closer look, realising the second hand wasn't moving. Giving a small shrug assumed the timepiece had either broken down or the battery must have simply run out and Oscar just hadn't got around to changing it.

She gazed fondly at Duke now lying on his side with eyes firmly closed, clearly fast asleep on the floor as she ventured over to the large bay window; draped with long curtains patterned with reds and golds, making the perfect setting to overlook the large front garden outside that only moments ago she'd been walking along. This place was so peaceful and tranquil, she thought wistfully, just the kind of place she would love to live one day.

Her moment was broken as the door creaked opened with Oscar holding a tray laden with two cups of coffee and a plateful of custard creams.

His eyes followed her as she joined him on the sofa, taking a sip of her coffee, giving out a small sigh of contentment.

'That's the best coffee I've drunk in *ages!*' she admitted. 'You've made it exactly the way I like it, strong but not too strong, and with one sugar!' Quickly helping herself to one of the biscuits, took a small bite. 'And it just so happens that custard creams are one of my favourites.'

He gave a cunning smile. 'Well, that was one lucky guess - looks like I'll need to get a steady supply of those from now on!' His smile disappeared, studying her intently. 'Oh Laura, I *have* missed you! How is everything?'

She looked into her coffee cup, considering his question. 'Well, I guess I can't complain - not really.' Taking another bite of her biscuit, confessed, 'To tell you the truth I've missed you too, but...well as you know, there isn't really any way of contacting you. To be honest I really didn't expect to meet you again, let alone be sitting here with you over coffee!'

His tender smile melted her heart. 'Well, I guess the most important thing is we *did* meet, and now here we are together!'

Feeling confused, she placed her cup gently on the tray as she peered around the room. 'But where exactly is *here*? As far as I'm aware this place doesn't exist outside of my imagination!'

He watched her thoughtfully through narrowed eyes, looking philosophical. 'Is that what you think? That all what you see here isn't *real*? Can't you *taste* the coffee you're drinking? Or the sweetness of those custard creams you've been tucking into?'

She paused for a moment to consider, then nodded reluctantly. 'Yes, you're right, I can taste *everything*.' A troubled frown creased her forehead. 'And when I was outside of the cottage, I could really feel that chilly breeze and smell the scent of the freshly cut grass - how's any of that *possible*?'

'Well, try not to think to overthink it,' he suggested giving a firm shrug of his shoulders. 'What's important is that here we are, together again.'

How she loved the simplicity of his logic, even if happened to be just some amazing fluke that made this possible.

Taking a sip of her coffee, flinched as the hot liquid flowed inside her mouth, painfully burning the tip of her tongue. Just *how* was it possible to experience all these sensations in a dream?

Oscar chuckled as he relaxed, leaning back on the sofa, watching her intently as if reading her thoughts. 'Oh, and by the way, congratulations on being nominated for *Most Loved Manager*!'

'Should I ask how you knew?' she asked, with a wry smile, completely taken by surprise, only too aware just how ridiculous her own question sounded. 'I guess none of this is making any sense - but thanks anyway! It might not be for the Nobel Peace Prize, or anything that grand, but I've got to say it meant so much being chosen by my colleagues - even if I don't get to win, well it was nice just to be considered.'

'Well you *deserve* to win, because you're a lovely person,' he insisted, 'Even if I happen to be just a little biased!'

Finding his optimistic outlook heart-warming, realised it had been some time since she'd genuinely felt this happy. If she really was completely being honest with herself she really hadn't felt this good since…

'A penny for them,' he smiled teasingly, rousing her from her own deep thoughts.

She gazed into those smouldering dark eyes that seemed to penetrate her soul, causing her heart to flutter. 'Oh, sorry, for a moment I was lost in my own small world! I've got to admit there've been times when there's not been much to smile about. I won't bore you with all the details, but there's been a lot happening at work, not to mention thumping migraines from hell that won't leave me alone.'

He looked more than a little concerned at her news. 'I'm really sorry love, and I promise you're not boring me. I take it you haven't got things checked out with the doctor?

She shook her head. 'Migraines just happen to be the family curse inherited from my mum's side. Not much you can do about them, but I've pretty much learned to live with them for the past few years.'

'Just make sure you take it easy and don't go stressing yourself with work,' he urged gently squeezing her hand. 'Promise me.'

'I promise,' she assured him placing down her cup on the silver tray and decided to change the subject. 'So, how's everything in Oscar's world?'

He gave a throaty chuckle as he brushed his hand through his hair, ruffling it further. 'Mustn't grumble. In *Oscar's World* I get to do all the things I enjoy - spending time with Jessica, and doing my paintings. Just so happens she's a budding artist - takes after her dad in the respect… and her mum come to that,' he informed her proudly. 'I've got to admit there are times I do get a little lonely, but thankfully I have my little girl and some good friends around me to keep me company.'

'How long have you both been on your own for?' she gingerly asked, wondering if she might have overstepped the mark trying to find out about his wife.

If those were his own thoughts, Oscar gave no indication, but his face turned grim as his mind wandered back, pondering for a few moments before giving her an answer, as if choosing his words carefully. 'It's been some years since Jessica and me have been on our own. We do miss her mum, but sadly that's the way things turned out.'

Realising just for now she wouldn't get any further in learning what had happened to Oscar's wife, had just one question she needed to ask. 'Where's Jessica at the moment?'

He paused for a moment, as if gaging her reaction. 'Actually, she's in her room doing some homework. It would be nice for her to meet you, but I don't feel now is quite the right time.'

She nodded her head in agreement, but not certain if she really understood. 'Well, I'm sure you must both be very happy here - this strikes me as being such a peaceful place to live and from what I've seen so far of the village too.'

'You're right,' he confirmed, strolling leisurely over to the bay window, gazing at the garden outside. 'Apart from the fact this home is missing one special person to fill that void, then everything is about as perfect as it can be.' Stirring from his own thoughts turned his attention back towards her, looking more upbeat. 'Hey, one day I'll have to show you around our beautiful village - I'm sure like everyone else around here, you'll soon fall in love with the place.'

'Hey, how can you be so sure I'll be coming back?' she asked sceptically, but secretly hoping he was right.

'Oh, you'll be *back*,' he assured her confidentially, 'Why do you think I mentioned earlier that I'll need to be getting in a steady supply of custard creams?' Seeing she looked more than a little pleased at the prospect of returning, added encouragingly, 'I'm sure today will be the first of many visits to Rose Cottage.'

Despite her excitement, she tried to stifle a yawn, realising for the first time just how tired she was feeling.

Returning to the sofa to join her, he gently took hold of her hand. 'Just relax and make yourself at home, sweetheart -

you've been through such a lot lately one way or another. Just for once try to take things easy.' He watched on as she leaned her head back on the sofa, her eyelids beginning to feel very heavy. 'That's it darling, just close your eyes and rest.'

Laura did as Oscar suggested and felt all her muscles untensing as she relaxed; her eyelids closing as tiredness quickly washed over before finally drifting off into a deep sleep. Losing all sense of time, she finally opened her eyes again, only to find herself back in her flat, lying uncomfortably on her hard leather settee.

CHAPTER SEVEN

The following nights where her dreams had failed to take her back to Rose Cottage, Laura did everything within her power to take her mind away from the captivating Oscar Devereux. On the Saturday after a particularly demanding week at work, the best part of her day was spent cleaning the entire flat from top to bottom, with no place left untouched. Finally, with a deep sigh, feeling hot from all the exertion, realising there was nothing left to clean, slumped down onto the sofa with a bottle of chilled mineral water taken from the fridge.

Giving a yawn, she picked up her mobile from the coffee table, deliberately left in silent mode. Peering at the display, felt more than just a stab of guilt at all the missed calls, voicemails and text messages that Karen had left, with not a single one having been replied to. As she scrolled down, reading some of the messages, it was clear to see that her friend was clearly frantic with worry at not having received a response. Just as she was about to call Karen to quickly put her mind at rest, the loud sound of the intercom buzzer startled her. Knowing only too well who the caller would be, Laura pressed the button to allow her visitor to enter.

Karen watched her sternly as she entered the living room, clutching a bottle of white wine; but despite her cheeks flushed with anger, was plain to see she was deeply concerned. In frosty silence, she walked into the kitchen, taking two wineglasses from the cupboard before returning and offering her one of the two, each of them filled close to the brim.

Laura placed herself down on the armchair, sitting upright, nervously biting her bottom lip, feeling like a naughty schoolgirl caught smoking behind the bike shed. Rubbing her hand over her face, took a long sip and sighed deeply. 'I'm so sorry for being such a selfish bitch.'

Karen sat down on the armchair opposite, peering at her with disbelief. 'Laura, what on *earth* is the matter? For the past few hours I've been worried out of my mind over you! Ignoring calls and texts is just so not you. To be honest with all these headaches and being stressed, well I was beginning to imagine the worst - the least you could have done was send me a quick text!'

Laura smiled at her sheepishly. 'Well, as you can see I'm definitely alive and kicking!' She gazed briefly towards the cleaning cloth and bottle of *Flash* placed on the coffee table.

'I decided to have a quick tidy-up and ended up cleaning the entire place to an inch of its life - you know what it's like with me being busy at work, I kept putting it all off and the place was beginning to look like a tornado had ripped through!'

But judging by her friend's disgruntled expression was quick to see she clearly didn't share her amusement. Feeling thoroughly ashamed at her own selfishness, leaned back on the sofa, rubbing her weary eyes, before letting out a sigh. 'But yes of course you're absolutely right, it's no excuse to ignore your calls - it was rude and thoughtless and I'm so very sorry.'

Karen's face softened. 'Hey, it's ok, I didn't come here to read you the Riot Act and look for apologies. To tell you the truth I'm just *so* worried about you! I've noticed over the past few days that you've seemed lost in your own world.'

Laura looked vacantly into her wineglass. 'Well, it was a pretty full-on week with those interviews - didn't help having time wasted with those no-shows. Looks like I'll be spending a big part of next Monday looking for some more applicants to call - happy days!' She took a deep breath, deciding she owed her friend the truth. 'I wasn't going to say anything, but I guess I might as well tell you while you're here. I dreamt about *him* again.'

She blinked her eyes in astonishment, almost spilling some wine from her glass. 'I take it that the *him* you're referring to is Oscar?'

Nodding in confirmation, Laura told her in as much detail as she could remember about how she revisited the cottage in the dream, and her encounter with Oscar and what they discussed.'

Karen sat there for a few seconds in thought, contemplating her friend's surprising news. 'Well, I really don't know what to say - I mean, that first dream you had about Oscar and those friends was pretty amazing in itself. But to dream about that cottage that you sketched and then going *back* and your dream guy there...wow!'

Bringing out a glass bowl filled with Thai Sweet Chilli crisps from the kitchen, Laura joined her friend on the sofa. 'The worst thing is that ever since that night I literally *prayed* that when I go back to sleep, I would return to the cottage and see him again. But it's just not happened. Most the time I can't even remember my dreams when I wake, but I know I would definitely have recalled any further ones which included *him*.' She looked pleadingly at her friend. 'Oh Karen, what's it coming to when I'm yearning to see some gorgeous guy who doesn't even exist outside of my imagination?'

Her friend, watched her with tenderness, giving her a gentle hug. 'Oh hon, you mustn't beat yourself up over this - you're simply feeling a little lonely. You just need to get out there a bit more and give yourself the chance to meet someone special - you're a beautiful person and deserve so much better than a life just focused around work and coming home. Any man would be so lucky to have you.'

Laura wiped a tear away from her eye. 'Now you're making me all sentimental. I can't really complain - after all I have a nice flat, not badly off financially and a job I enjoy, and not to mention this awesome friend called Karen who always looks out for me!'

Karen grinned. 'Oh yes, I know that friend of yours is awesome and you're without a doubt brilliant at your job. But sometimes that's not always enough. What you need is somebody special, other than a man who only exists in your dreams.' Pursing her lips, she gazed at her thoughtfully. 'So, how's everything going with the online dating?'

She felt after already upsetting her friend that honesty was the best policy. 'To tell the truth with everything going on with work and...Oscar, I hadn't given it another thought,'

'Oh, what are you *like*! Come on, get that laptop fired up and let's see if Julian or anybody else has been in touch.'

Karen put on her reading glasses in eager anticipation as Laura logged onto the dating site. 'You've got some messages,' she informed her excitedly looking at the inbox. 'Looks like Julian is keen as three of those are from him.'

Laura read through these to herself as her friend discreetly looked away. 'Well, in the first one he mentions he's interested in meeting up and was a bit worried in the other two messages why I hadn't replied. He's suggested getting together for a meal and he's given me his telephone number.'

'It looks like you're not so sure.'

'I just feel things are moving a little too quickly for my liking,' Laura admitted with a sigh. 'I think I would prefer to get to know a little more about him before I decide. To tell the truth it feels a little weird meeting up with someone I've never met before - for all I know he could be some psycho.'

Karen nodded thoughtfully. 'I completely get your point - we should always be very careful. But really the same could be said if you met some guy at a club where there was an instant chemistry and you went out on a date. The chances are he would be ok, even if in the end he turned out not to be your type. In both scenarios, there's always an element of risk.' She topped up their glasses with some more wine. 'But if you never took any chances in life always assuming the worst, you would never leave your front door.' She had an idea. 'Look, why not call him or send a text first if that makes you feel any better. Just take your time getting to know him a little better, then you can decide whether or not to meet up. I would be more than happy to come along and blend into the background to keep an eye on things if it makes you feel any better - that way you would be completely in control.'

'*Maybe*,' Laura agreed grudgingly with a shrug, unable to share her friend's enthusiasm. 'He does seem quite attractive, but I can't say at the moment that I feel any spark as with...'

'You mean as with Oscar, that handsome guy that only exists inside your head?' Karen finished off cynically, peering over her spectacles.

'Point taken. Ok, I'll send this Julian a text when I feel ready and take things slowly - I don't see the need to rush into anything.'

Laura continued reading the other two messages on the website. 'Well there's Anthony from Bristol who thinks I'm gorgeous and would like to get to know me better.' Her nose crinkled in distaste. 'I'm not so sure I can say the same about him - call me shallow if you like, but that greasy looking hair does nothing for me. I'll move on to the last message.'

Karen gave a chuckle. 'I just think he's overdone the hair gel a bit. Perhaps he's got an amazing personality or something else going in his favour.' Realising that something had grabbed her friend's undivided attention on the website took a closer look at her source of interest. '*Wow*, who's that guy?'

'Yes, he's pretty hot,' Laura agreed, studying the photo of a man who at a guess was in his late thirties to early

40's, with a shock of thick black hair and the most amazing pair of smouldering dark brown eyes she had ever seen. 'He's definitely more pleasing to the eye than Anthony - or even Julian come to that.'

'I should say so,' remarked Karen, her interest clearly aroused. 'Read on, what does he have to say about himself?'

'He says his name is Michael James and he comes originally from the US. He's a widower with a son called Kelvin and a civil engineer working on a contract in Lagos, Nigeria. He's looking for the love of a good woman and came across my profile which he found totally enchanting and would love to get to know me better.'

'*Whoa!*' Cried Karen quickly removing her spectacles. 'Don't even go there!'

'Why not? You think he could be a scammer?'

'*Think? I know!*' Seeing the look of confusion on her friend's face, went on to explain. 'Surely you must have heard of all those Nigerian romance scams - there's been enough mentioned about them in the news. Usually come in the guise of American or English profiles, or from just about any other European country.'

Laura studied the handsome man on the profile picture, with the radiant smile, displaying the most perfect set of white teeth, probably thanks to some high-cost cosmetic dental work. 'But surely there must be Europeans and Americans working in Nigeria who might be looking for love just like everybody else?'

'I'm sure there are. But *believe me* when I'm saying when you see photos men as hot as him looking for a relationship on a dating site, that it's most unlikely the man or even woman has any connection to the person behind the profile.' Karen zoomed in on the photo of the strikingly handsome man to take a closer look. 'If we Google-reversed his image, I'm sure this photo would come up on dozens of modelling agency sites or something of that nature. Those criminals are very clever and good at pulling at the heartstrings of lonely people.'

'Lonely as in people like me?' Laura interjected.

'Just about *anybody* who is looking for love or a way to fill some gap in their life,' Karen explained with sympathy. 'They know all the ways to have you falling madly in love with these images, and before you know it, you will be asked to send your hard-earned cash for some crisis that has suddenly arisen!'

Laura gave a wry smile. 'I guess you're right – let's not to even go there! Just hard luck on all the good people of Nigeria and those *really* working over there looking for true love.'

'Well, I guess it is, but that's not *our* problem - all we need to concentrate on is *your* love life, or lack of it!'

Laura reluctantly picked up her mobile from the coffee

table. 'Well, I certainly don't have any intentions of sending my hard-earned money to Nigerian criminals, so I guess my best bet is Julian.' Biting her lip, she stared at her phone. 'What do I text? I'm just *so* out of practice - *what* do I say?'

Karen gave a shrug 'Talk about the weather, or world politics.'

Grinning and looking at her friend as if she was completely crazy, Laura began to text.

Hi Julian, this is Laura. Hope everything's well. Received your message. Yes, it would be nice to meet up for a meal or a drink some time. Look forward to hearing from you soon. Laura.

Karen looked at the message on the display, giving a nod of approval. 'Looks good to me - comes across as friendly but not desperate. Yes, send it!'

Laura, closed her eyes and took a deep breath as she pressed the Send button. Slowly breathing out she opened her eyes, looking at her friend in desperation,

'Heavens, what have I just done?'

'What you have just *done*, Laura Winters, is took the first positive step that you've taken in a long time - you're much too lovely to be stuck at home on your own and become one of those crazy cat ladies.'

She glanced at her smartphone, her hands feeling suddenly clammy. 'He probably won't reply and already has some hot date lined up.'

'*Maybe* he has, but I'm sure none of them will be as amazing as you!'

Laura looked at her friend and burst out laughing. 'Now why can't there be a *male* version of you? Then all my prayers would be answered.' She looked at Karen apologetically. 'Oh, don't worry, I haven't changed my sexual orientation - we wouldn't want Andrew getting worried!'

Laughing, Karen steadied her hand, narrowly avoiding spilling some wine onto her top. 'Oh, you do crack me up! I'm pretty sure he realises he has nothing to worry about there.' Giving a wink, she had a thought. 'On second thoughts, the idea would *probably* excite him!'

Their peals of laughter ended abruptly as Laura's phone suddenly sprang to life with the loud ringtone.

Biting her lip nervously, Laura cried out, 'Oh my God, that has to be Julian! There's no name coming up because I haven't added him to my contacts and...'

'Don't you think you'd better answer it?' Karen prompted gently.

Taking in a deep breath, Laura took the plunge, pressing the green button on the touchscreen.

Noticing her friend's face turn a deep shade of red, Karen discreetly went into the kitchen equipped with a magazine lying on the coffee table.

After about ten minutes, but to what seemed to Laura an eternity, joined Karen in the kitchen who peered at her over her reading glasses, eagerly awaiting the outcome. '*Well?*'

She gave a shrug. 'Well, he sounded nice enough - he took me a bit by surprise when he said about meeting up this evening for a drink. But I didn't want to come across as desperate and suggested next Wednesday at the Cow and Moon - so much for my idea of taking things slower.'

Karen nodded approvingly. 'That sounds fair enough and you're right about not coming across as too keen - The Cow and Moon's only around the corner from here too.'

The look of regret registering on her friend's face wasn't lost on her. 'Look, I know you've been off the dating scene for some time and you're feeling a bit out of practice, I completely get that - I can tell you first hand it can feel a little daunting meeting somebody for the first time that you've met online.'

'Yes, that's my biggest worry to tell the truth. You hear all these stories about people not being who they claim to be.'

Karen smiled sympathetically. 'That's completely understandable and I totally agree that the sensible thing is to play things safe. Ok, as I mentioned earlier, I'll be your emergency backup and hover in the background. If you want to escape with an excuse, then I'll be there on hand.'

Laura let out a huge sigh of relief. 'Would you *really* do that for me? Oh, Karen, I really owe you one. I'm just completely terrified of the unknown, just in case he turns out to be some lunatic.'

'I'm sure he'll be just fine and it'll be your chance to get to find out a bit more about each other in a safe environment.'

After a busy three days at work, Laura eagerly prepared for her date. She finally decided on what to wear after having changed her mind about twenty times in between. Finally, she opted for a pale blue shift dress that had been left hanging in her wardrobe having only been worn a couple of times. Once applying her make-up, carefully studied her reflection in the full-length mirror and decided she looked as good as she was ever likely to look for her age.

As she strolled into the living room, Karen who'd been sitting comfortably on the sofa watching a quiz show on TV, promptly switched off the programme with the remote control. 'Wow, you look *amazing*! Had I been a man or that way inclined, I would be proud to have you on the end of my arm for a hot date!'

Laura couldn't help but laugh. 'You don't think I look a

little too over-dressed for a drink at the local pub?'

'*No way* - for a first date, it's important to make a good impression. I really made the effort for Andrew and he was full of compliments when we met for the first time.' She placed the remote control gently onto the coffee table. 'I remember feeling so nervous, believing he might be disappointed with what he saw - that I was too fat or not the woman he imagined me to be.' A dreamy smile spread across her face as she reminisced. 'But now we just feel so comfortable together. Don't get me wrong - I haven't let myself go and morphed into some bag-lady, but on the other hand, I don't feel the need to keep looking at my very best under a ton of make-up.'

Adjusting the silver bracelet hanging loosely on her wrist, Laura gave a deep sigh. 'I don't know, but this dating game just seems too much like hard work - it's not easy putting yourself out there.'

Karen agreed. 'It's not easy - that I do know having spent years of being single on and off and getting my heart broken in between. All I can really advise about this evening is make it all about just enjoying yourself and most importantly to simply be yourself. He's clearly very keen, calling and texting you every day as he done has since arranging the date, so the signs look promising.'

'I know, but...'

'No buts,' she chided. 'You'll not be in any kind of danger - I'll be hanging around in the background having a drink on my own like Billy No Mates, making sure you don't come to any harm.'

After checking her handbag one last time, Laura peered at her watch. 'I suppose we'd best make a move and get there a little early. Don't want him seeing I have my best mate checking up on us.'

While Karen sat and made herself comfortable in the pub drinking a refreshing spritzer, Laura patiently waited outside the entrance to the building. Feeling more than a little foolish at standing there on her own, the time on her watch indicated he was now ten minutes late. Briefly opening the door, she glanced over her shoulder towards her friend who was looking equally as puzzled taking a look at her own watch, shaking her head. Laura gave a shrug with Karen miming to give him a call.

After a further ten minutes of waiting with people giving her curious looks as they left the pub, Laura resigned herself to the fact that she'd been stood up. Besides the humiliation of having to stand around like some lemon, there was one thing she hated in life and that was people being unpunctual for no good reason. But to simply not show up without explanation, considered this the height of rudeness. Just as she was about to head back inside, feeling the first few spots of rain, a man walked towards the entrance with his eyes fixed firmly on her.

She gazed at the short, rather plump looking man with a puzzled frown, thinking at first, he might have lost his way going somewhere and wanted some directions, feeling even more surprised he said her name.

'Laura...?'

She blinked, her face turning pale as a look of recognition crossed her face. '*Julian*...?'

He gave a broad smile, making her very much aware he had a missing front tooth, then gently cupping her face, he kissed her full on the lips, making her shudder as she detected from his breath that he'd already been drinking alcohol.'

His face still too close for her liking, he looked at her with a hint of lust. 'You look absolutely gorgeous - a real knockout! Those sexy green eyes are amazing and make you look like a gorgeous pussy cat just waiting to be stroked.'

Giving an involuntary shudder, Laura realised she had probably made the biggest mistake of her life. Trying her best not to look at him with distaste, could see he was undoubtedly the man in the photo, but looked at least a good ten, maybe fifteen years older and quite a few pounds heavier. That amazing dark hair that had attracted her from his photo on the dating site profile, now mostly grey and receding at the temples.

Misreading her expression of disappointment, looked at her apologetically. 'I'm really sorry at being late babe, but I got stuck in traffic - looks like there'd been some accident and I couldn't very well use a mobile when driving. Well, at least not with all the cops that were hanging around!' he added with a knowing wink.

Laura gave a shudder, not liking the look at all of this man who'd made no effort to impress with his unkempt appearance; his shirt creased clearly never having seen an iron with the buttons straining over his large, rounded stomach. The worn grey jacket he was wearing certainly looked as if it had seen better days.

He placed his hand on her cheek, causing her to flinch. 'I can see you're feeling a little cold - let's step inside and get a drink.

She felt relieved to be inside the pub lounge which was thankfully not too busy being a Wednesday and got to a table as close to Karen as possible. While Julian went to buy their drinks at the bar, Laura looked towards her friend, her expression showing she was clearly horrified and giving a thumbs-down sign. They had already arranged if necessary to cut short the date by her going to the toilet and sending a text to Karen to give her call her from outside so she could leave due to some *unforeseen emergency*.

Bringing over their drinks, Julian placed his own pint of beer on the table, with some of the contents spilling onto the table top.

Laura, her nerves now getting the better of her took a long sip of her white wine, making Julian chuckle.

'Hey, no need to rush it down babe - don't think there's any chance of us dying of thirst here!' She promptly placed her glass onto her beer mat, realising getting drunk wasn't the most sensible thing to do and would immediately put her at a disadvantage. He quickly changed the subject as he studied one of the menus. 'I'm sure that bird sitting behind you has got the hots for me.' He discreetly nodded his head, encouraging her to look behind to Karen who noticed she had caught his attention and quickly pretended to be messaging on her mobile.

'Saw that one staring me at the bar - can't take her eyes off me. She's either got stood up or she's here on the pull!'

Seeming to spend more time gazing at her cleavage than her face, he wiped the froth of beer from his lips.

'So, what's a lovely girl like you doing on her own?'

'It's a long story,' she replied not wanting to give too much away about herself to this unpleasant man.

'Yep, it usually is a long story,' he agreed. 'I was married - had a beautiful wife and three kids. Thought I had it all, with a well-paid job as a sales director.' He took another long sip of his beer followed by a loud belch. 'Then one day I came home early from a conference and thought I would give her a surprise. Not sure who had the biggest surprise when I found the bitch in bed with the neighbour!' His face became solemn as he looked back with sadness. 'My heart was broken, I gave that woman everything - she couldn't want for *anything*. Didn't realise she had it all - a loyal and loving husband who put her at the centre of his universe and that is what I got in return!'

'Yes, life can be very cruel,' Laura replied, not believing a word of what she felt was a well-used script he practiced on all his online conquests.

'So, tell me what happened to *you*?'

She shook her head. 'I would rather not discuss now. I...'

He undid the top button of his shirt. 'It's getting hot in here - do you live close by? Perhaps we could go back to yours.'

Beginning to feel real panic setting in, Laura almost forgot about her friend sitting close by. 'No! I mean, no it's not possible - I'm in the middle of decorating and the place is in a real mess!'

Julian gave a loud chuckle. 'Do you think I'm going to be *bothered* about a few cans of paint around the place? I can buy a bottle of wine from the bar and I'm sure we'll find a way to make ourselves cosy!'

Feeling her heart race as he was about to make his way to the bar to buy a bottle, Laura quickly stood up. Seeing his puzzled frown, she explained. 'I have to go to the toilet...' She was about to go there and text for Karen to call her so she could leave, when she gave a start as the entrance door slammed loudly causing everyone in the lounge to look towards the source of the noise.

She watched, her own worries forgotten for a moment as a middle-aged woman of ample proportions and long curly auburn hair came storming across, looking directly at Julian with her face deep red with rage.

'*So*, this is where you turned up!' she spat out accusingly, her loud, shrieking voice causing a silence to fall as the pub-goers watched on with interest at what was about to unfold.

The older woman looked towards Laura accusingly, her green eyes hard and piercing. 'So, this is where you turn up when you said you were going to visit John - out seeing this *slapper*!'

Julian's face having turned a distinctly paler shade, stood up. 'Verity! Of course, I was going to see John! I just popped here to buy him a bottle of his favourite malt whisky that they do here! I just bumped into an old friend from school and we got talking!'

Laura felt her face burn with humiliation, peering behind

to Karen who also stood up, looking very concerned about how the scene was unfolding.

'Like hell is she an *old school friend*!' Verity shouted nastily. 'Again, I catch you out with yet another tart you've picked up from that dating site!' She glared at him with triumph, her cheeks an angry shade of red. 'Oh yes, I *know* all about that blasted dating site - you're so thick you don't even have the sense to clear the browsing history!'

Laura and Karen looked towards each other in shock, their pretence at being strangers long-forgotten. But Verity had more to say.

'Yes, my dear, I'm afraid to say you're not the first,' She glared at Laura, her voice thick with sarcasm and rage. 'I bet he's not got 'round to telling you that he had to step down from his job for screwing the secretary who was married to the director. So, while he's been jobless for the best part of three years, I've been the one working my backside off to help pay the mortgage and take care of our five kids!'

The whole room was in complete silence as everybody listened with interest, their attention firmly fixed on to the drama unfolding before them, more entertaining by far than anything they had seen on TV of late.

Laura wasn't prepared for what was to come next, when the woman suddenly slapped her hard across the face.

'That'll teach you to steal other women's husbands, you bitch! What is it that so attracts you to married men? *Tell me, is it the thrill of the chase?*'

Just as the landlord was about to intervene, she left abruptly, her face now a deep shade of red with Julian following meekly behind.

Everybody in the pub started talking again, realising the episode had come to an end, with some watching Laura with unconcealed disgust as she touched her cheek stinging painfully from the slap, causing her eyes to water.

Karen quickly came over. 'Are you ok, sweetheart? I'm so sorry - I just never dreamed anything like this would happen.'

Laura nodded, feeling both angry and humiliated. 'I'm ok, but just remind me not to have *any more* to do with online dating *ever* again!'

CHAPTER EIGHT

L aura sat at her easel, her bare feet feeling the coolness of the wooden laminate of the bedroom floor. Eager to express her mixed up feelings in some way on paper, but not quite knowing what to sketch, thought back to earlier after returning the short distance home with Karen. Her first reaction had been to feel annoyed with her friend; for much against her own better judgement, had finally persuaded her to try online dating, and even angrier at herself for going through with it, knowing in her heart this wasn't for her. But with her eyes welling with unshed tears it was plain to see that Karen was full of remorse as she expressed how sorry and responsible she felt for what had taken place. How could she possibly stay cross when her friend had only acted with the best of intentions?

Once they returned to the flat, Karen applied a cold flannel to Laura's cheek, reassuring her the bruise didn't look so bad and would be gone within a couple of days.

They sat together for a while on the sofa, each nursing

a glass of white wine, as they reflected upon the evening's events. Laura admitted her disappointment wasn't so much down to the fact that Julian had turned out to be a balding middle-aged man with a paunch; because after all, everybody's looks would fade with time. As far as she was concerned a good personality and a kind heart were by far the most important attributes. It was the fact he'd told so many lies, misleading her with old photos, allowing her to believe he was a much younger man, but worst of all, pretending to be unattached.

Karen admitted that although dating sites did their best to sift out the players and the scammers, sadly a few would always slip through the net before their accounts were finally closed down. Both agreed it was very likely that Verity would forgive Julian as had probably cheated on her countless times before.

As much as her face stung by the hard slap delivered by Verity, Laura was certain in her shoes she would have reacted in pretty much the same way; by literally hitting out at the other woman in anger and frustration who she saw as another notch on her husband's bedpost.

How was it possible to want to remain married to a man who was a serial cheat? More to the point, the woman must have still loved him as this was the only explanation to have tolerated all his infidelities. Or maybe at her time of life was simply too afraid to start out on her own. Perhaps it was a combination of both. Although Verity might be described as a lady of mature years she mused, could easily see in her younger days had probably been quite an attractive woman with that flame of auburn hair now frizzy and neglected. With a little more attention to healthy living and to her general presentation, felt certain could still look quite stunning.

Realising Karen had already cancelled her night out with Andrew, Laura quickly assured her she would be fine and to go and spend what was left of the evening, with her man.

Placing her pencil on the stool, let out a deep sigh, as she walked over to the large mirror hanging on the wall, cringing as she studied her reddened cheek now feeling very sore, hoping desperately this would fade by the time she returned to work on Monday.

The room would have been unbearably silent had it not been for the sound of the clock ticking steadily on the wall; a grim reminder that she had never felt so alone as she did at that very moment. Undoubtedly, Karen would be cuddled up on the sofa with Andrew watching some late-night film before making their way to bed probably to make love. It only took a small stretch of the imagination to visualise Julian and Verity practically murdering one other with every likelihood of keeping the neighbours awake with their loud and angry words.

Many single people like herself would argue it was better to be lonely than be with somebody that made you feel unhappy and worthless, she thought, wrapping the pink dressing gown around herself as a shiver ran down her spine. Yes, maybe that was true, but surely any love was better than no love, she contemplated with weary sadness.

With the seeds of an idea beginning to form in her mind, stirred herself from her dark thoughts. Returning to her easel with pencil in hand, stared vacantly for a moment at the blank sheet of paper in front of her, before beginning to frantically sketch away.

After a couple of hours of almost relentless drawing and painting with water colours, Laura finally stood back to study her latest composition. As she gazed at the portrait of the man, looking longingly at the dark, slightly tousled hair with a small hint of grey, to the twinkling brown eyes that sparkled as brightly as the distant stars in the night sky, simply imagining his warm smile was exclusively for her, felt she had manged to capture the very essence of Oscar Devereux on paper.

Giving a long yawn, as tiredness suddenly swept over her, placed down the paintbrush alongside the rest of her colours. There was still more work to be done with detail she knew, particularly to the blue shirt she remembered him wearing in the dream inside of Rose Cottage. But that could wait for another day.

Why did fate have to be so cruel, she thought with more than just a tinge of sadness and frustration. To introduce her to a man so right for her in every way, but only existed inside of her head! If only it was possible for him to be transported to her real world, along some much-needed love and happiness!

Only too aware that was never going to happen, climbed into her large empty double bed. Despite her solemn thoughts, after reading a few pages of her latest read, succumbed to her tiredness, finally drifting into a deep sleep.

Opening her eyes after what could have been minutes or possibly even hours, Laura found herself standing at the gate of Rose Cottage; only this time, almost everything around her was engulfed by a dense fog, making it difficult to see the dwelling ahead. Giving a small shiver, was grateful for the cardigan she was wearing, pulling this firmly around her, providing at least some protection from the dampness of the cold air. Peering at the light of the large full moon above, watched in fascination as its pure white light emitted through a brake in the clouds of the night sky, painting the cottage with an almost eerie, shimmering glow.

Laura glanced over to one of the bedroom windows of the cottage, noticing the hint of a faint light from within. Frowning in concentration, thought she could make out the silhouette of a person standing there, looking out the window in her direction; the heavy fog made it difficult to distinguish if this could be Oscar, who might well be expecting her. Reluctantly, she opened the white wooden gate, making her way slowly down the pathway, feeling almost as much apprehension as she did on her first visit.

As she approached the cottage, her heart began to race faster with eager anticipation. With the sheer excitement at the thought of seeing the very man through a single dream had managed to completely turn her world upside down by injecting a spark of happiness, lighting up the mundane life she had led, engulfed by an impenetrable darkness for much too long. Did it *really* matter if this was all just a dream? She was here, now and with her skin tingling from the cold, damp night air, feeling more alive than she had done in a very long time. Surely that's what counted.

Her confidence lifting immediately, eagerly made her way towards the cottage, knowing with certainty that Oscar was there waiting for her, with every chance they would share their first kiss. As she stopped at the entrance, about to knock at the door, woke up suddenly, lying in her bed, with an overwhelming feeling of disappointment sweeping over her.

By Monday the red mark had all but vanished from Laura's cheek, so decided to put on some foundation in an attempt to conceal what was left to remind her of Saturday night. As a rule, she wouldn't have even contemplated wearing such heavy make-up, reserving the more high-maintenance look for a night out. But the thought of opting for her more natural appearance, attracting all the questioning looks from her colleagues was more than she could bear. Most would have been too polite to ask she knew, but undoubtedly would be debating behind her back the possible causes for her battered face.

After applying a small touch of blusher to her cheeks for some added colour over the pale concealer, felt reasonably satisfied that nobody would be any the wiser. But there was no fooling Karen, who paused updating her spreadsheet on her PC, to peer over her spectacles.

'Oops, so it didn't quite disappear?'

Alarmed, Laura put a hand defensively to her cheek. 'Does it still show?'

'No, but I can see you're wearing foundation.'

With a momentary feeling of relief, looked around discreetly to see if any of the others in her team had noticed, but saw Charlotte working away as normal, seeing to the post and the others either staring at their computer screens or busy on a call. Just as she was about to sit at her desk, her attention was caught by Edwina in the distance, peering over in her direction. Laura looked on grimly seeing she was engrossed in conversation with Stuart Chatsworth, one of the directors who was apparently paying an unscheduled visit from head office.

'That's looking a bit ominous,' she murmured. 'One of the big bosses coming down without any warning,'

There was one thing she had soon learned about her boss and that was she never missed a thing. As far as she could recall, nothing had been mentioned about Chatsworth paying a visit and only hoped she wasn't about to receive lecture or something even worse about allowing her personal life to spill into the workplace. That was *just* what she needed on top of everything else.

Karen shrugged, taking a quick sip of her coffee. 'Nothing to worry about, I'm sure. Probably just slipped Edwina's mind - it happens to us all.' Watching her gingerly, placed the mug back on her desk. 'Am I forgiven for last Saturday?'

Seeing she was clearly worried that she hadn't been in contact over the weekend, Laura managed a small smile to reassure her. 'There really isn't *anything* to forgive. How could you have possibly foreseen what was about to happen?'

'Well, I hope you're not going to let that unfortunate episode put you off of dating, because it would be such a shame.'

Laura pressed the keys firmly on the keyboard as she logged onto her PC, glaring at her friend with bemusement. 'I hope you're not suggesting giving online dating another try, because I can promise when I get home this evening I'll be deactivating that account!'

Karen shook her head. 'No, but there's something I want to discuss with you later.' She paused, looking past her, appearing distracted. 'Oh, looks like Edwina's heading this way with our illustrious director. I'll tell you the rest over lunch.'

What's going on? Laura wondered with a frown of confusion creasing her forehead, as Edwina came along in her direction clutching a carrier bag. She watched on as the older woman invited the whole department to come over to the Investments Solutions team. Judging by the bright smile on her boss's face, was now certain this gathering wasn't about giving her a public dressing down about her personal life.

The whole room fell into complete silence as Edwina began to speak.

'Well, as I'm sure you're all aware by now from the posters around the walls and all the news on the intranet site, that the Global Life Employer awards ceremony will be taking place very soon!' A few murmurs of approval rippled through her audience. 'With this in mind, the committee have at last selected our finalists from all of the many very deserving nominations that have been received this year.' Edwina smiled, shaking her head in mock despair. 'And I've got to say from *all* the amazing emails we received, has made this a particularly difficult job.' Quickly, rummaging through the carrier bag, took out one of the miniature version of the prestigious Global Life award trophies that were awarded to the finalists.

With the smile fixed firmly on her face, handed this to Chatsworth, tall and dark suited. 'I'm sure you'll all be delighted to know that our first award goes to our lovely Investments Solutions Team Manager, Laura Winters who is now officially declared a finalist for the *Most Loved Manager* category. Very well deserved, I've got to say too!'

Stuart Chatsworth came over, wearing a beaming smile, treating her to a view of his large, veneered white teeth. Giving her a firm handshake, handed her the much-coveted trophy, along with a gift voucher of £40.00. The whole department erupted into a huge round of applause, cheering loudly, as Edwina captured the moment with her small digital camera.

Maybe wearing foundation wasn't such a bad idea, she thought with some amusement, knowing her face would have turned a bright shade of red. Thank goodness, she decided to wear her smart black shift dress too. Although feeling slightly embarrassed at being the focus of so much attention, was absolutely moved and delighted that so many of her colleagues at the company had felt her worthy of such an award and taken the trouble to nominate her. Who would have guessed when she came to Minsden three years ago, leaving her former life and job behind that she would climb the ladder along a completely different career path? Her day was made even brighter when Charlotte also received a finalist award for *Most Loved Employee*.

After having experienced what proved to be a thoroughly miserable weekend, to know how everybody was so genuinely pleased for her and also her young apprentice's hard work having been officially recognised, was such a heart-warming feeling. It felt as if nothing or nobody else could spoil her perfect moment.

'Definitely looks like you'll be needing to go and buy that dress now, so no excuses!' Karen remarked with a grin. Watching her friend intently, her face became more serious. 'Joking aside, it's about time you had some luck after everything that's been happening of late. On the subject of happiness, I think I have the perfect date for you.'

Laura's rolled her eyes to the ceiling in despair, 'Oh *please*, not the *Dynamic Don* our illustrious CEO again - I thought we'd already drew a line under that one. Yes, I know he'll be attending and you say he's got the hots for me and yes, I've got to admit he's rather pleasing to the eye - but he just happens to be married to the beautiful daughter of a multimillionaire businessman, so he definitely *won't* be interested in the likes of me!'

Laughing seeing her friend was on a tangent, Karen was quick to put her into the picture. 'Look, I know exactly what you must be thinking and no I've *no* plans to match you up with Donald White, but I want you to hear me out before you dismiss what I've got to say. I'll fill you in when we go to lunch.'

'Ok, so he's divorced with two kids and a lifelong friend of Andrew's,' Laura repeated after her friend discussed details about her next prospective date. As they sat at a table in one of the town centre cafés, both eating a chicken wrap with a coffee, gazed at her cynically, before wiping her hands with a paper napkin. 'Hmm, *divorced* - those famous last words from Julian that I recall so well.'

'Well, I can promise you that Dan is definitely unattached!' Karen replied indignantly. 'Actually, he's been divorced for about three years but was in a long-term relationship for just over a year until about six months ago.'

But Laura remained sceptical. 'So, I guess it ended because he did the dirty and played away behind her back?'

Karen gave a chuckle. 'My, you *do* have a very low opinion of the entire male population since Julian!' She stirred her Skinny Latte thoughtfully with a plastic spoon. 'Actually, I have met him a few times. Not bad looking as it happens, but I guess like a few of us he's just been unlucky in love.' Placing her spoon gently back on her saucer, she continued. 'From what Andrew's told me, his wife went off with the French teacher at the school she worked at - he was really in bits at the time.'

'Not a nice thing to happen,' Laura agreed. 'But perhaps his wife had her reasons for leaving him. So, I guess the other lady in question also felt the need to part company.'

'Not exactly,' replied Karen, her expression grim. 'She died.'

Laura felt her face burn with shame. 'Now I feel *terrible*. Poor Dan, it couldn't have been easy for him.'

'It wasn't, she had leukaemia - it turns out she'd already been suffering from it before they met. So, he kind of knew what he was letting himself in for. The last few months were particularly difficult for him as most of those she spent at a hospice.'

Laura put the half-eaten chicken wrap on her plate,

feeling more than a little ashamed of her unkind thoughts for a man she hadn't even met. 'It certainly sounds like the past few years haven't been kind to him. What gets me is why there are those who don't give a damn how they treat others, everything seems to go their way - yet the ones that are kind and caring always get dished with all the bad luck!'

'Tell me about it!'

'Don't you think that perhaps with it just six months since his girlfriend passing away, is just a little too soon to be thinking about dating?'

Karen's face lit up with a warm smile, feeling encouraged as she detected the first flicker of interest from her friend about the possibility of another date. 'Not at all! There's no set time for grieving then moving on. You remember I told you about my dad when he died suddenly after 20 years of marriage? Mum was beside herself with grief and to tell you the truth I thought she was destined to spend the rest of her days on her own. Then along came Ted two years after and they've been happily married to this day!'

'That's so lovely and heart-warming,' Laura agreed. 'I feel very strongly that those who leave us behind wouldn't want us to grieve for the rest of our lives.' Suddenly without warning, she felt an overwhelming feeling of sadness and began to weep.

Feeling very surprised at her friend's sudden emotional outburst, Karen quickly offered her a tissue. 'Sweetheart, I'm so sorry! If I have said...'

Quickly wiping the tears as she saw the bemused looks of people sitting close by, shook her head. 'It's ok...really. It's just that with Dan...'

'Hush, it's ok - there's nothing to explain. You've been through so much these past few days and it's no wonder that your head and heart are all over the place. Look, if you don't feel ready for another date so soon, I will...'

Wiping away the tears, Laura managed to compose herself. 'Really, I'm fine. Yes, there *has* been a lot going on. Not helped by the migraines from hell, along with a date coming from the same place!' She placed the crumpled tissue inside her handbag. 'So, based on the fact that I'm never going to meet Oscar Devereux for real, then *yes*, I would like to meet Dan.'

'*Really?*'

She confirmed with a nod of her head. 'Yes, *really* - but only as long as we make up a foursome with you and Andrew.'

Karen couldn't help but show her pleasure. 'That's a deal! I'll speak to Andrew tonight and then we can arrange a night to suit everybody.'

'Sounds good to me.' Laura got up from her chair. 'I'd best

pop to the ladies and sort my face out - tongues will be wagging if I return to work with mascara streaked down my face!'

After returning home and eating a light salad for her meal, got down to work on her portrait of Oscar. After applying the final details to his features, including some extra sparkle to those warm brown eyes that she remembered so well, took a step back to see what other detail might need to be added. She gave a start as her mobile rang loudly, breaking into the silence of the room.

Picking up the phone from the small occasional table where she laid her pots of paints, looking with dread at the display, seeing it was her mum. Reluctantly, she answered the call.

'Laura, oh *Laura*, how are you dear?'

She swallowed nervously. 'I'm ok Mum. Really. I'm so sorry that I never got back to you, but there's just so much going on with work.'

'I've been *so* worried about you!' The emotion in her mum's voice was unmistakable and felt sure she was on the brink of tears.

Taking a deep breath to help calm herself, made her way to the bedroom and sat down on the edge of the bed. 'Mum, how are you? And how's Louise and little Toby? I can't believe how much he's grown!' She remarked, referring to the photos that Louise posted to her a couple of weeks ago.

Trying her best to sound more cheerful, her mum gave a chuckle. 'Oh yes, Toby's really growing up quickly. Mind you, he can be a real handful at times, but he's doing well at school and getting glowing reports from his teachers. Lou and Mike are so proud of him!'

'What about Brenda and Alan?' she asked referring to her mum's next- door neighbours.

Her mum's dark mood seeming to be lift, laughed warmly. 'Oh Alan's still driving her mad with his snoring. Brenda's forever moaning about having to move to the spare room to get some sleep.'

'Is everything going well with the Women's Institute?'

'Oh, you know always plenty there to keep me occupied. The recent village fete was a huge success - we'd managed to raise three thousand pounds for cancer awareness, would you believe, thanks to some wealthy donors!' There was a long pause before her mother broached the next subject. 'I was just wondering if you were free next weekend?'

Laura was prepared for that question and had her answer ready. 'Oh mum, I'm really sorry but I'm going to be pretty tied up helping Karen spring clean her house.'

There was silence as if she knew her daughter was lying.

'Really? Isn't the woman capable of doing her *own* housework?'

'Oh mum, she's very hardworking, but at the moment she's got a lot on her plate with her daughter going off to university. I'm just returning the favour as she was kind enough to help me tidy up the flat.'

There was more silence and Laura knew without a doubt that her mother didn't believe her lame excuse. 'Well, I suppose you can't really let her down if you've made a promise. Perhaps the following weekend me and Louise could drive down to yours? I know Toby would just love to see his Aunty Laura!'

Laura closed her eyes, taking in a sharp intake of breath. 'Oh, Mum that would be lovely, but at the moment I'm having to work a few weekends - I know only too well while I'm so tired I won't make the greatest of company.'

Her mum gave a sigh knowing she wouldn't get any further with this. Laura couldn't help feeling mean knowing she was clearly disappointed. 'Oh well, I guess it can't be helped - it seems these bosses want more and more out of us these days.'

'Yes, that's very true. But I guess with how things are I'm just glad to be in work.'

'Absolutely! So, has there been anyone special you've been spending time with?'

Taken aback by her mum's direct question, gave a chuckle. 'I take it you mean as in a guy? Mum, you're so *subtle*! No. No, there isn't been anybody special apart from a disastrous date that I wouldn't care to mention!'

'That doesn't matter, there's always plenty more fish in the sea! It's just good to see you dating again after...well you know. Well, as us ladies say, that we have to kiss a few frogs before finding the prince!'

'That's true, but I think I'm quite happy just to be on my own.'

After finishing their conversation with Laura promising to call the next time, placed the phone gently on the bedside table. Giving a deep sigh, rubbed her eyes as she stood up from the bed. Had it really been three years since she had last seen her family and left behind all those that she loved?

Walking over to the dressing table underneath the bedroom window, her attention focused on the bottom drawer. As she pulled on the handle found this to be a little stiff, but with a gentle tug pulled out with ease. She took out a photo album with the collection of photos her mum had sent to her after she moved away from Dorset. Opening the album carefully, studied the first photo of a very young Toby with a large smile, sitting on her sister's lap. The Toby she remembered so well just before she had to move away. Her sister looking lovingly towards the camera, the picture she recalled had been taken by her husband Mike.

People often commented how alike the two sisters were in looks, only Louise had hair dyed ash blonde and was taller and with a lot more self-confidence.

She turned the page of the album, to other photos of Toby standing in his inflatable swimming pool with her mum sitting on a deckchair drinking what looked like her favourite tipple of gin and tonic, dangling her feet in the water to cool off on a hot summer's day.

Slowly moving forward to the next page of the album, came to a picture of her mum holding her grandson, the look of love in her eyes unmistakable. Toby smiled towards the camera, the picture probably having been taken by one of his parents. But the strain on her mum's face was very plain to see, her eyes appearing sunken with dark shadows underneath, the many nights of lack of sleep having taken their toll.

Peering at another photo, gave a smile seeing Toby standing proudly in his school uniform ready for his first day of school, carrying his lunch box. Another showed a selfie that Louise had taken of them in the car, no doubt of the very first school run. Louise smiling proudly with Toby belted up in one of the rear seats behind also smiling but clearly looking a little nervous about what was to be one of the biggest days of his life. No doubt her sister would have posted the proud moment on social media. Of that, Laura was certain, although she had closed her own accounts long ago.

With a tear that escaped from the corner of her eye, slipping slowly down her cheek, gazed longingly at photos of all the birthday parties she had missed, all the family events including Christmas where Louise would invite their mum for the holidays. Family events where she should have been, watching with love, seeing tiny young hands excitedly ripping off the wrapping from presents delivered by Santa Clause. She should have been there with her family, with all those most dear to her heart embracing every second of their time together. Her attention turned to the other album, large and white, her hand trembling as she prepared herself to open to the first page. Her heart raced feeling a wave of nausea as the blood rushed to her head. Knowing she could continue no further, quickly, placed both albums in the drawer before breaking down and sobbing uncontrollably as she sat on the bedroom floor.

CHAPTER NINE

L aura slowly opened her eyes, rubbing them, as reality cruelly hit her with memories quickly flooding back from the night before. Oh, how she wished she hadn't looked at those photos; a painful reminder of the life she had been robbed of, her family and all those precious moments that had been and gone in the blink of an eye! Just *why* did she have to be so stupid she reflected, reopening old wounds and trying to relive a life that would never be hers again?

Feeling both hollow and deflated with no more tears left to shed, sat up slowly taking in her surroundings, as sudden realisation emerged that she was no longer lying on the bedroom floor where she'd cried herself to sleep, but on the comfy sofa inside of Rose Cottage. As she roused herself from the last remnants of sleep, her attention wandered to the paintings she'd seen on her last visit, hanging on the magnolia painted walls and to the dark wooden beams running across the low ceiling. With a wry smile she noticed the clock hanging above the fireplace with its hands still set firmly at 5 o'clock, telling her that time-keeping clearly wasn't high up on the list of Oscar's priorities.

Duke who'd been peacefully napping on the rug near the fireplace, his interest immediately roused at seeing he had some company, came rushing over hurriedly as his short tail wagged with excitement, rewarding her with a gentle lick to her hand as she stroked the top of his furry white head.

She gave a start as the door opened, with Oscar entering the room, carrying a tray laden with two cups of coffee, the aroma of the beans strong and inviting. Her heart seemed to skip a beat as he studied her with those warm brown eyes and a smile that would melt the largest of glaciers.

'Hello, sleepyhead,' he greeted her. 'Thought you might like this, knowing how much you enjoy your coffee first thing.'

He watched her with amusement, studying her wide-eyed look of surprise at naming her favourite morning beverage. She let out a contented sigh as she took a sip of the hot drink. 'Oh, this is just so *delicious!*'

Oscar gave a chuckle. 'I aim to please! Taking a wild guess, I think you *just* might like some porridge with plenty of blueberries?'

Placing down her coffee cup on the table couldn't help but smile. 'Now *why* shouldn't it be such a surprise that you just happen to know porridge is my favourite breakfast? Especially porridge with blueberries?'

He answered back as he walked into the kitchen. 'Oh yes, and for the record I know how you like it like it with *plenty* of milk.'

She stood up from the sofa giving a relaxing stretch of her arms before following him into the kitchen.

As she entered the room, she was immediately enchanted by the small but quaintly furnished kitchen with its light pinewood cupboards and shelving; such a pleasing diversion from all the harsh whites and stainless steel of her own back at the flat. The small window overlooking the enamelled sink, draped with curtains in shades of soft peach, added a quaint charm to the small room. Finally, her attention wandered to the large pine table, surrounded by four chairs, each plumped with cushions in the same shades as the curtains, the arrangement making this the perfect centrepiece to the room.

'This is just *so* beautiful,' Laura sighed as she glanced at all the homely touches of hanging potted *begonia* plants seemingly placed in a random manner here and there, their vibrant petals in shades of pinks and yellows with their green foliage making a dazzling contrast against the walls painted in a neutral shade of magnolia. She wandered over to the large Aga in a shiny cream so in character with the cottage, caressing her hand lovingly over its smooth surface. 'I've *always* wanted one of these,' she admitted, 'but sadly this would be just so out of place in my flat.'

Oscar smiled, as he watched her take the wooden spoon from the saucepan of porridge heating away on the stove, gently stirring the contents as they simmered away. 'I've got to say I would never be without it. It serves so much more purpose than just be a cooker – it keeps the place so toasty warm in the winter too!'

Laura peered over her shoulder towards the window, enjoying the view of the picturesque garden with its smooth well-manicured lawn. 'I know this is all a dream, just something that exists inside my imagination, but this is simply the most beautiful place I have ever seen.' She gave a small shrug as she tried to express her thoughts into words. 'And to tell the truth, this cottage is just *exactly* the kind of place I have always wanted to live.'

As Oscar came to join her at the window, standing closely by her side, an overwhelming feeling of familiarity enraptured her, a sense of déjà vu, as if a similar moment had happened many times before. To be close by his side in this agreeable silence as they enjoyed the view outside felt so completely natural. 'It's a wonderful place to live,' he agreed. 'More importantly Jessica's very happy here too - she's made so many friends at the local school and sometimes enjoys sleep-overs with a few of them.'

For a moment he became silent as his face turned solemn, his expression telling her he was lost in his thoughts. 'It wasn't easy to begin with, I've got to say,' he finally confessed. 'When we first came to the village, there were so many huge changes to contend with - unsurprisingly, to be suddenly away from her mum didn't come easy to her.' He turned to her, his eyes filled with sadness. 'I have to be truthful, it was very hard for me too. But with thanks to all the love and kindness of the good people around here, we have somehow got by.'

Trying to lighten the dark moment that had developed, he gave a watery smile, doing his best to reassure her that life was now good. But that faraway look in his eyes told her otherwise; but not quite understanding what he was trying to say, felt certain there was more to this story than what he was revealing. But she wouldn't press him any further she promised herself, feeling that following her own instincts was the best thing, and he would tell her more when the time was right.

Determined to keep the momentum on a more positive keel said, 'I know I haven't met Jessica, but what I do know for sure is that she has the greatest Daddy ever who'll always be there for her no matter what!' Much to her relief, a warm smile spread across his face making her heart turn over.

'Come on, let me give you a hand with that porridge,' he muttered, giving her a small wink of the eye. 'I don't know about you but I'm getting quite famished!'

In next to no time they were sitting at the large wooden table each with a cereal bowl in front of them filled to the brim with a generous serving of the oat breakfast, sprinkled with fresh blueberries along with a rack of toast on the centre of the table to share between them.

Laura gave a contented sigh as she took a taste of her porridge. 'This is just *so* delicious - much better by far than anything I zap in the microwave.'

Oscar watched her clearly taking pleasure at seeing her eat with such relish. 'I guess with rushing to work in the mornings you don't always have the time to warm up porridge over a stove.'

She gave a sigh. 'I wish! Life these days is so fast-paced - sometimes it just seems we live to work and not work to live.'

He looked at her with what she could only describe as sympathy with perhaps a hint of pity. 'You're not wrong there - I remember back in the day when I was a wage-slave working for a large corporate company. Quite often it felt I was giving my all, for a relatively small reward from an employer who had little appreciation for me as a person.' He gave a contented sigh. 'I'm just so glad I finally took the plunge to become self-employed. I won't lie, it wasn't easy to begin with and there was a lot of blood, sweat and tears along the way - but I'm really glad I took the courage to believe in myself and to follow my heart.'

Laura stirred the spoon into her porridge in thought. 'I just wish I had the nerve to be as brave as you. Don't get me wrong, I love my job and getting nominated as *Most Loved Manager* by my colleagues is a fantastic boost.' She placed the spoon back in her cereal bowl with a grimace. 'But somehow as lovely as it is, I feel there's a huge chunk of my life that's missing. Not sure if that's necessarily down to wanting to be my own boss - it's very hard to define...'

He helped himself to a slice of toast, watching her with such tenderness she could see without a doubt he shared her pain. 'I know what you mean, life can present us with more than its fair share of challenges - that much I know, when it seems that just about everything goes against us.' He broke his toast in half, his face solemn as he studied her. 'You've had a very difficult time of it over the past few years, haven't you?'

Much to her own surprise she could feel the tears spilling from her eyes, as she gave a nod of her head as long forgotten memories buried deeply, resurfaced dangerously to the fringes of her mind. 'It's been very hard,' she admitted. 'When *things*...

happened, I was in a complete state of shock...total disbelief.'

Oscar watched on patiently, waiting for her to continue, noticing how pale and fragile she appeared as her mind regressed back to the very reasons that had brought her to Minsden. 'Well, to cut a long story short, everything that I loved and cherished had suddenly been...taken away from me.' She had no desire to elaborate. She *couldn't* elaborate! 'I just thank God that I discovered Minsden... for meeting Karen and for Edwina taking me on. Global Life literally saved me and the people there have been my therapy.'

Oscar blew gently on his coffee as he suggested, 'Perhaps a kind of extended work family?'

'Oh, without a doubt! If it hadn't been for their support heaven knows where I would be today.'

Noticing that she didn't wish to go into further detail about what had proven to be the most difficult time of her life, he tactfully changed the subject.

'Well, I thought with the weather being so pleasant today...perhaps you might want to join me on a picnic?'

Laura gave a blink of surprise at the unexpected invitation. 'A *picnic*?' she repeated as if she had never come across the word before. 'Well, I really don't know what to say.' Her lips turned up into a small smile as she contemplated his invitation. 'It's been quite some time since I've been on one, let alone in a dream!' Giving a shrug of her shoulders, her mind was made up. 'So, I guess the answer has just got to be *yes!*'

With a boyish grin on his face, walked across to the larder, swinging the door open. 'Well, that's good to know, because here's one I prepared earlier! With that he retrieved a large wicker basket from the shelf, covered over with a bold red and white checked cloth, undoubtedly filled with a variety of goodies to make the perfect picnic.

Oscar couldn't help but chuckle as he noticed the undisguised amusement written on her face. 'Ok, maybe I was being a little presumptuous, but to tell the truth I'm really in love the idea of spending some quality time with you.

Gazing at the basket which she was certain had been lovingly prepared, gave a gentle smile. 'In that case, how could I possibly refuse? Yes of course, Oscar Devereux - I would *love* to spend some time with you!'

Together, for the very first time they left the comfort of Rose Cottage, walking along the pathway until they came to a nearby meadow; the grass wild and long, scattered with the blush of red poppies, such a vivid contrast to the deep blue of the cornflowers and the bold yellow of the buttercups that all grew in abundance.

She took a deep intake of breath, savouring the sweet fragrance of the countryside, enjoying the sensation of the gentle breeze brush against her skin.'

'Wow, this place is just so *beautiful*,' she sighed. 'It's so rare to see meadows like this these days, where everything is either ploughed up to grow crops or to make way for building hundreds of houses or flats, one on top of each other.'

Together they made their way towards the top of the field, searching for the perfect spot to share their picnic, and decided upon a space located on the edge of the meadow, offering the welcome shade from the bright sunshine, thanks to some low hanging branches of a large oak tree. Laura carefully helped Oscar to unfold and place down the blanket that had been tucked firmly under his arm, spreading out all the food from the basket. Finally done, she gazed at the tempting sandwiches, crackers, grapes and fairy cakes just waiting to be eaten.

Oscar smiled as he poured some chilled chardonnay wine into their glasses, causing her to gaze at him questioningly at the reason for his sudden amusement.

'It's ok,' he explained. 'Just to see you looking so happy has completely made my day.'

She sighed contentedly after taking a sip of the cool wine. 'Yes, I *am* happy. What's not to love about this beautiful place?' He followed her gaze as she took in the sights of the meadow which gently sloped downwards towards the road they'd just come from, glimpsing the wild flowers scattered along the way, softly swaying in rhythm with the breeze, and the background sound of bees buzzing as they busily collected pollen to take back to their hives. The chorus of birds happily singing from the surrounding trees was music to her ears. 'This is pure heaven,' she sighed.

He studied her thoughtfully as he helped himself to a chicken sandwich from one of the many plates laid out on the blanket. 'Yes, I guess it is! As you've now probably worked out, although our cottage is just on the edge of the village with all these fields and woodlands close by, we're actually not at all far from civilisation! If we'd walked a just few yards in the opposite direction we would've found ourselves right in the heart of the village.' Wiping his hand on a paper napkin, screwed it up firmly into a ball. 'I'll have to take you on a tour some time and introduce you to the locals - I'm sure you'll come to see why we love it here so much!'

Together they talked about their lives, at least mostly about Laura's over the past three years since working at Global Life. Oscar quietly listening as she told him about the time she moved to the town of Minsden and how the kindly customer service manager, Edwina Charlton had offered her a job. She shared with fondness about her special friendship with Karen, filling him in on just about everything, since moving to her adoptive town. Everything that is, except for the very reason that brought her there in the first place.

'What about the family you left behind?' Oscar probed gently. 'How's Angela?'

Her face turned pale when he referred to her mother by name; but she guessed because after all this was just a dream that nothing should really should come as a surprise to her about this situation.

'Mum's ok,' she replied, dusting off some imaginary crumbs from her dress trying her best to mask her surprise.

'What about Lou and Mike…and of course little Toby?'

She nodded, blinking rapidly, feeling more than a little overwhelmed as he referred to all the immediate members of her family. 'Yes…yes, everybody's fine. Toby's doing very well at school and has made loads of friends.'

The look of concern on his face was unmistakable as she guiltily admitted the truth. 'I guess I don't need to tell you that I haven't seen my family since… I went away.'

He took hold of her hand tenderly, immediately causing a shiver of delight to run down her spine, gladly welcoming this much-needed lifeline of comfort. Somehow the touch of his hand felt so familiar, so *right*.

'You know your mum's worried about you, and Louise too.'

She clung to his hand as she nodded guiltily. 'I know and I feel so bad about everything - it's just that there are things back home I find so difficult to face.'

He slowly rubbed his thumb on the palm of her hand as he looked tenderly into her eyes. 'I know, sweetheart, but your mum and Lou are just missing you so much.'

A tear slipped down her cheek, which Oscar gently brushed away with his finger before she made her confession that she'd never shared with anybody before, not even Karen, because she felt too ashamed.

'There was a time when mum and Lou paid me a surprise visit,' she began, taking a long sip of her wine, as she glanced over towards the meadow ahead before summoning up her courage to explain. 'It was about nine months after I'd left. I was making my way back from the *Tesco Express* close to where I live because I'd run out of milk, when just as I was coming around the corner, I saw Lou's Range Rover parked outside the flat.' She gave a bitter smile as she thought back to that day. 'Lou was frowning as had been ringing the intercom and getting no reply. Mum was standing next to her, her face so drawn and pale as she held onto Toby - I just stood around the corner, hoping I wouldn't be seen. For a brief moment, I thought mum had spotted me, but then her attention focused on Toby when he started to cry over something.'

She turned to Oscar who looked at her with undisguised pity. 'Instead of coming over to them, the family I love who came miles just to see me, I took the coward's option - I walked back in the direction I came and took a bus into the town centre.' She looked up to his face in shame as she dabbed her nose with her napkin. 'They called me countless times on my mobile, but I just ignored all their messages and called them back later with some lame excuse about popping to Karen's and leaving my phone at home. To this day they've never come back on any more surprise visits.'

The look of sorrow was etched clearly on his face as he gently turned her head towards him; his touch so warm, so comforting as he kissed her tenderly on the lips. To wrap her arms around him and allow him to hold her closer still felt so right as if being held in his embrace was the most natural thing in the world. As she wept, he placed a kiss on her head, gently stroking her hair, long again as in the previous dreams.

'Hey, it's ok,' he whispered softly. 'Your mum and sister understand far more than you realise - that you've been through such a lot and that's why they'll never push you into something you're not ready for.'

Laura looked pleadingly into his eyes. 'But surely after three years I should be ready?'

He placed his finger gently to her lips. 'There are *never*

any timescales set on how long it should take for us to heal when we've been through some difficult times - only *you* will know the answer to that question. But perhaps the fact you're able to discuss this with me gives an indication that the time might now be approaching.

For a while they sat in companionable silence as she rested her head on his lap while he playfully fed her with a bunch of grapes dangling above her face teasingly from his hand.

Giggling, she picked a grape, quickly placing one playfully into his mouth.

As he chewed, studied her through eyes narrowed with suspicion. 'Now, when I see you with that thoughtful look on your face, I just know there's bound to be a question coming up.'

She gave a shrug. 'Not really, but I guess I'm just a little curious about what happened to Jessica's mother.'

Seeing his expression immediately turn grim, instantly regretted her words, wishing she could take them back. 'I'm sorry, I shouldn't have asked...'

Holding her closely, once again he gently brushed his finger across her lips. 'Hush, hush, it's ok! Really.' Letting out a long sigh, he held her closer as he gathered his thoughts.

'Let's just say that matters were taken out of our hands

when me and Jessica had to part company with her. The situation was kind of *forced* upon us...something that took us all by surprise.'

Sitting up, Laura gave a puzzled frown as what he said didn't really make any sense, but felt she shouldn't press any further as could see he was clearly finding this difficult to discuss with her.

'But despite everything, Jessica knows without a doubt that her mother still loves her very much,' Oscar explained with a wry smile. 'Things didn't turn the way they did through choice, but because of circumstances, and she's aware of that.'

She gazed up towards Oscar. 'Does Jessica ever see her mother? Do *you*?' Her curiosity got the better of her and couldn't help but ask.

He kissed her lightly on the cheek. 'All the time, Laura. *All the time.*'

A sudden pang of jealously stabbed through her, which was ridiculous when this all was nothing but a dream. Prising herself apart from Oscar, glared at him accusingly. 'You still love Jessica's mother, don't you?'

His expression was one of both a mixture of surprise and pity. 'Laura...sweetheart, you don't understand...'

Feeling her face burn with unashamed humiliation, she gave a snort. 'Oh, I think I do, Oscar! It kind of sounds like your wife left you for another man… leaving you to look after Jessica. And yet you *still* have feelings for her!'

He gave a weary sigh, shaking his head in frustration as if she was clearly missing the point.

'Then please *explain*, as none of this is really making any sense.' she demanded. 'From what I understand, it sounds like see she possibly left you for somebody else, yet it seems you still have feelings for her.' She would have preferred if he got mad at her constant probing and told her to mind her own business instead of this looking at her in what only could be described as pity. 'Do you feel there's still a possibility of reconciliation? After all, she is the mother of your child.' she knew she came across as an insanely jealous woman, especially as they hadn't long met but felt she had to know the truth.

'Laura darling, I know at the moment none of this is making any sense to you - but believe me I'm not lying when I say you really do mean the world to me.'

Giving a deep sigh she felt her eyes filling with tears. 'I'm sorry. I know I shouldn't be having a go at you - I know how complicated relationships can be.'

He nodded grimly in agreement.

She felt compelled to make a confession to him, if for any reason other than to make him feel as jealous at the way she was feeling at that moment

'I have a date coming up soon,' she revealed.

'Oh, you do?' he asked, trying to sound surprised.

She looked up to the trees above in despair. 'But I guess you already know that?'

Oscar's coy expression and silence confirmed her suspicions.

'Is that what you want? To meet someone else?'

She waved her hands in despair. 'Oh, I *just* don't know Oscar. I'm just not sure what I really want anymore. Karen seems hell-bent on fixing me up with somebody. Not satisfied that online dating didn't work out for me with that loser Julian, now she wants to fix me up with Dan.'

'*Dan* whose girlfriend died of leukaemia,' stated Oscar with a wry smile.

She noticed although he showed no outward signs of being jealous, he did appear to be lost in his thoughts, which irritated her slightly.

'I said I *would*,' she told him with more conviction than she actually felt.

He took hold of her hand, kissing it lightly. 'You must do what you feel is right for *you*, my love. Not what Karen wants - nor me come to that!'

Considering this was just nothing but a dream, felt ridiculously disappointed with his reaction.

She dabbed her face with one of the paper napkins. 'Sometimes after everything that happened, I feel I could never love again, that nothing will ever come as close. But for some time, especially after those headaches got worse, there are times I feel that it would be lovely to have somebody to come home to after a busy day at work.'

He listened, studying her face deep in concentration as she contemplated all that had happened.

Stirring from her thoughts, she glanced over to him, screwing up her napkin and tossing it onto her empty plate. 'For a brief moment, I felt sure I was meeting my dearest friend Becky for her birthday, where I met this amazing guy called Oscar Devereux - that special connection we made felt so incredibly real, until I realised my friend and the amazing guy only existed in my dreams.'

Oscar looked at her with a hint of sadness written on his face as he refilled their wineglasses. 'I'm so sorry that things are this way, sweetheart - if I had the power to change things, I would gladly wave my magic wand and would do exactly just that! Go on your date, my love, enjoy yourself - life is for living. One day everything will work out just fine for all of us - you have my word.'

Laura smiled weakly but not sharing Oscar's optimism about the future. 'That's one big promise to keep!'

He gave a long yawn as he stretched out his arms. 'As lovely as this has been, I think it's time for us to head back. Jessica will be coming home from school any time and I wouldn't want to make Mrs Lock cross!'

She frowned with a puzzled expression crinkling her forehead. '*Mrs Lock*?'

'Mrs Lock from the primary school in the village,' he explained. 'She's a teaching assistant there and when we... arrived, she took Jessica under her wing and really took care of her.'

Much to her shame, Laura felt another stabbing pang of jealousy, this time over Mrs Lock, imaging her to be some glamourous widow or divorcee, trying to impress Oscar with her amazing maternal skills!

'Would you like to meet Jessica? he asked, studying her carefully as if trying to gage her reaction.

She was taken by surprise with his question, but paused for only a split second before her curiosity got the better of her, saying she would love to.

After gathering up all the picnic items, made their way across the long flowery meadow back to Rose Cottage. This time they walked together, hand in hand.

Laura realised she couldn't have been more mistaken with her assumptions of Mrs Lock, as she entered the kitchen; instead of the young glamorous divorcee she'd visualised, stood a short, stocky matronly woman with snow white hair tied up into a bun at the nape of her neck, wearing a dark green jumper and tweed skirt draped with a long white apron over her generous curves. Hearing the sound of footsteps on the floor, Mrs Lock glanced sternly over her shoulder towards them, peering over the wire-framed spectacles perched on the end of her nose, as she busily stirred a hot mug of cocoa on the kitchen worktop. At a guess, Laura would have said the elderly lady was at least in her early seventies.

With his arm, gently placed around the small of Laura's back, gave the school assistant his most charming smile. 'Mrs Lock, I would like you to meet Laura.

The woman's face softened immediately as she gave the warmest of smiles displaying dimples each side of her full lips, giving her an almost girlish look. As she enfolded Laura's hand in her own plump one, gave it a firm shake. 'Hello my dear!' she greeted warmly in a high almost youthful voice that could have belonged to a twenty-year old. 'I've heard so many wonderful things about you. It's so good to finally meet you!'

Taken aback by the lady's kind words, Laura's eyes followed Mrs Lock who walked excitedly into the living room, stopping at the bottom of the stairs. 'Jessica dear, your cocoa is ready. You have a very special visitor waiting for you, too!'

For some reason, even though she was all too aware this was nothing but a dream, felt her heart beating faster in nervous anticipation as she heard the sound of small, footsteps rushing on the floor above, then bounding noisily down the wooden staircase. Without consciously realising, nervously gripped Oscar's hand firmly with her own.

Her anxiety so acute, Laura felt her heart would stop beating, when there before her was the most beautiful little girl of around ten years of age. Her pale pink school dress complementing her long, dark brown hair, tied loosely in a couple of plaits. Those large, almost emerald green eyes studied her so intently, stirring an emotion buried deep inside her that she couldn't comprehend. Both Oscar and Mrs Lock looked at each other with concern as the blood drained from Laura's face, making her look deathly white, as she stood back in shock.

Oscar held her across the shoulders clearly worried that she was about to faint. 'Laura...'

Trying to calm herself, she glanced towards Jessica and could see the child was clearly frightened. 'I'm sorry, it's just that...'

Before she gave herself a chance to finish her own

sentence, she rushed over to the young girl as if she was on autopilot, embracing her firmly as Jessica wrapped her small arms firmly around her waist, leaning her head on her bosom contentedly.

Oscar and Mrs Lock looked on with more than a hint of relief on their faces as they smiled their approval.

Despite feeling unsure and confused as to why she had reacted in this way to her first meeting with Jessica, Laura knew without a shadow of a doubt that she couldn't remember when she had felt this happy and complete in a very long time.

Suddenly, without warning, her entire body felt as cold as ice, causing her to shiver uncontrollably. A wave of nausea swept over her as she began to feel so dizzy that the room around her began to spin increasingly fast, making it impossible to focus on anything or anybody around her. Unable to keep her balance any longer, despite feeling Oscar's hands gently enfolding her waist, fell from his grip onto the floor, before succumbing to dark oblivion.

Opening her eyes after what might have been just seconds or even hours, found herself on the floor of the spare room where she had cried herself to sleep. With her body cramped where she had been lying uncomfortably contorted and coated by a sheen of cold sweat, returned to her bedroom, and climbed into bed.

After an hour of laying wide awake finally gave up hope of getting back to sleep and returning to Oscar and Jessica. With grim disappointment she made her way to the kitchen and prepared some tea, before finally retreating to the spare room to begin work on a new sketch.

CHAPTER TEN

Saturday night finally arrived when Laura pulled up in a taxi outside of the Robin and Rainbow pub to meet up with Karen and Andrew, with the company of their friend Dan. As far as she was concerned, she emphasised to Karen, this wasn't a date, simply just a night out with some friends.

Feeling more nervous than she cared to admit, opened the door to the pub with the sound of people chatting loudly over the lively music blasting through. Her forehead creasing in a frown of concentration she searched for her friends, quickly spotting Karen standing at the bar with Andrew looking her way, frantically waving her hand to gain her attention.

As she wove her way through the dense crowd, the couple each gave her a friendly peck on the cheek. 'You look lovely,' remarked Karen looking admiringly at the cream shift dress Laura was wearing.

She smiled modestly. 'Oh thanks - this had been sitting at the back of my wardrobe never seeing the light of day and thought the least I could do was give it one final outing.' Not wanting to admit that she bought the dress in a sale a few days ago especially for the occasion, felt she owed it to herself to make some effort for her night out.

'Thank goodness the rain never materialised that was forecast,' Karen said, secretly relieved her friend had turned up, with a worry nagging at the back of her mind after her previous disastrous date that she might cancel. 'I just hope I did the right thing in not bringing my brolly.' She glanced over to a fairly tall man who had been standing quietly next to Andrew. 'Oh Dan, I'm forgetting my manners! Let me introduce you to my best friend and work colleague, Laura.'

Holding a bottle of *Budweiser*, shook Laura's hand firmly with his free hand.

'Nice to finally meet you, Laura!' he greeted with a warm smile breaking out on his long slim face. 'Well I've got to say from everything Karen and Andy have been telling me, I feel we're already well acquainted!'

She laughed nervously. 'All good, I hope!'

He offered to buy her a drink, so decided on a small glass of Pinot Grigio.

With Karen doing her best to keep the conversation flowing between her two friends, desperate for them to get to know each other better, discussed recent events at work and asked Dan about his two sons. Andrew finally checked the time on his watch, suggesting they should make a move as the table at the Baba Indian restaurant had been booked for 8 o'clock.

Laura already had a fair idea of what to expect of Dan as during the week, Karen had shown a few photos of her prospective date on her smartphone. As she slyly glanced towards Dan, apparently a lifelong friend of Andrew, could see his brown short curling hair was perhaps more liberally sprinkled with grey and slightly more receding at the temples than what the photos had suggested, telling her the pictures had been taken some time ago. With his oval face and a slightly hooked nose, perhaps couldn't by any stretch of the imagination be described as Hollywood handsome, she mused, but could see by his twinkling blue eyes and engaging smile, that he came across as a kind person.

Together, they left the warmth of the large busy pub and much to Karen's dismay the weather forecasters made good with their promise as the rain poured heavily down with small puddles already forming on the pavements. Fortunately, Laura always prepared for any emergency, reached into her handbag for her foldaway umbrella which Karen gratefully shared on the short walk to the restaurant, with Andrew and Dan walking ahead, not too disgruntled about getting wet.

At the Baba restaurant and already well into their main courses, Laura sat directly opposite Dan, his hair still quite damp from the rain shower, finding him surprisingly easy to talk to and were soon engaging in stories about their work.

For a living, she discovered he was a manager for a builders' merchant where having been employed for the past twenty years, worked his way up from a forklift driver to his current position. He proudly showed her a couple of photos on his iPhone of his two teenaged sons who lived with their mother and her partner. Laura quickly realised there was already some attraction on his part, catching his lingering glances in her direction when Andrew shared an amusing story about an incident that had taken place on his delivery round during the week. She tried hard not to smile when Karen kept nudging her discreetly, clearly looking very pleased that the evening appeared to be a success, seeing how well she was getting along very well her partner's best friend.

To her own surprise, Laura enjoyed herself far more than she had anticipated and at least for a while her thoughts had been diverted from Oscar and his beautiful daughter, Jessica.

While the bill was being settled by Dan and Andrew, who insisted that this was their treat, the two women took the opportunity to freshen up in the Ladies.

'Well?' beckoned Karen, peering into the mirror while she applied her lipstick.

Laura studied her own reflection thoughtfully, as she combed her stylishly cut bob. 'Well, I guess he seems nice enough. We've exchanged phone numbers.'

Karen looked elated. 'Wow! That's awesome! Dan *is* a lovely guy, you know. I'm really not sure why I didn't think of him before I suggested online dating - maybe because he'd recently lost his girlfriend. But kind of looks like he's ready to move on.'

Laura's eyes narrowed in concentration. 'Well, if I'm being honest, I can't say he makes my heart race, but I can see he's a decent guy - I guess deeper feelings can grow with time.'

Taking one final look at herself in the mirror, Karen placed her lipstick back into her handbag. 'Precisely! When I met Andrew on our first date, I can't say it was love at first sight, but I knew within a short space of time I did feel there was a definite connection between us.' She pursed her lips in thought. 'To tell you the truth I don't *believe* there's any such thing as love at first sight. As for lust, well that's another matter altogether, but not really the recipe for a lasting relationship. I think if two people make each other happy, then that's an excellent basis for something to grow into something *special*.'

With a sigh Laura remarked, 'Maybe as we get older our needs change,' she gave a wry smile, 'He hasn't asked me for a second date yet, so perhaps we might be jumping ahead of ourselves - after tonight he might well have second thoughts!'

But it appeared that Laura was wrong, because after an hour of returning home, Dan sent her a text stating he loved meeting her and enjoyed her company, adding a smiley emoji. Her spirits soared as she replied, thanking him, also including a smiley to her message. His response came within seconds, when he suggested that perhaps they could meet up again soon.

Maybe it was the wine that was giving her some courage when she agreed it would be a great idea. He responded quickly by saying he would be in touch soon. This time, adding a couple of kisses.

She placed her mobile phone gently onto the coffee table, the smile fading from her face as she looked vacantly towards the window, the blinds open as she peered into the darkness outside. Karen was right, she *did* need to mingle more with the opposite sex; after all *she* was clearly very happy with Andrew who seemed so right for her. Lost in her thoughts, she walked to the spare bedroom, before preparing her water colours and brushes, to continue on her latest work of art. A portrait of Jessica.

Laura opened her eyes, expecting to be in her bed after working hard the best part of the night, on the painting; apart from a few minor details left to add, her portrait was almost completed. But instead of being in her bedroom, she found herself lying on the soft red sofa in the living room of Rose Cottage.

As she looked around, was taken by surprise at the sight of Jessica sitting cross-legged, yoga-style on the rug in front of the fireplace. The young girl held a sketch pad and a pencil, studying her intently with a smile spreading excitedly across her small, round face as Laura roused herself from the last traces of sleep. 'You're awake!' Jessica announced as if she needed reminding. She stood up, as Laura gazed at the pretty pink and floral dress the child wore, with her two pigtails tied with ribbons of matching colour.

Trying to stifle a yawn, Laura took hold of the drawing that the child proudly presented to her. Her eyes widened with surprise as she studied the sketch of a woman laying back fast asleep on the sofa. Unable to supress her smile, saw she had no need to ask the name of Jessica's chosen subject. Nodding her head in approval, studied the work in detail, realising without a doubt that Jessica was clearly gifted with artistic flair.

'That's *very* good, Jessica,' she praised with sincerity. 'I can see you have a special talent for drawing. Painting is something I happen to enjoy doing in my spare time.'

The child stood up from the rug, her eyes widening with excitement. 'Wow, *really*? I love painting too! I'm top of the art class at school! Daddy's always saying what a great painter Mummy is too! I want to be *just* like her!'

Giving a smile that didn't quite reach up to her eyes, Laura felt a sharp stab of jealousy course through her at the mention of Jessica's mother...Oscar's wife. Crazy really, when considering this was all just a dream.

The young girl watched her for a moment, the pupils of her large green eyes dilating as if she could read her thoughts. 'Daddy told me I was to keep quiet and not disturb you while you slept.' She gazed briefly towards the window. 'He's doing some gardening at the moment - I'll tell him you're awake!'

Without giving Laura a chance to reply, the child went bounding through into the kitchen, making her way out of the back door as she announced, 'Daddy, Daddy, she's awake!'

Laura tried to compose herself, running her hand through her now longer hair, hoping that she didn't look too much of a mess.

On hearing the back-door open with the sound of heavy footsteps striding across the wooden floorboards, quickly stood up, her eyes following Oscar clearly looking very pleased to see her, as he rushed over, casually dressed in a black tee-shirt and faded blue jeans. For a moment, time seemed to come to a standstill as she studied his dark hair looking a little windswept, with a tiny smudge of dirt marking his left cheek, but still managing to look devastatingly handsome. Holding her closely in his arms, for some reason felt the most natural thing in the world, as he placed a gentle kiss on her lips. At once that strong feeling of déjà vu ran through her body, so intense was the feeling that this had all happened many times before.

'Good morning, sleepyhead,' he greeted her affectionately. 'I hope Little Miss Trouble didn't disturb you too much.'

Before having the chance to reply, Jessica came running through into the living room, before stopping abruptly, glimpsing the scene before her. 'Oh yuck!' she protested, witnessing the adults having shared a kiss and covering her hands over her eyes in despair, and worst still, seeing them locked in an embrace.

They both looked over to the young girl, laughing as she sat down on the rug with a shrug of her shoulders and continued with her drawing as if nothing had happened.

Laura shook her head with a chuckle. 'No, she didn't disturb me in the least.'

He glanced over to Jessica, giving her a teasing wink before turning his attention back to Laura. 'We just didn't have the heart to wake you up. You looked so incredibly beautiful and peaceful lying there - just like the princess in *Sleeping Beauty*.'

Laura couldn't hide her amusement 'I'm not so sure about me being compared to *Sleeping Beauty*, but Jessica certainly has a great talent for drawing - it seems she takes after her mummy.'

The solemn look on Oscar's face didn't go unnoticed by her. 'Yes, that's very true - her mother is an extremely talented lady.' His dark moment lifted as he swiftly changed the subject. 'I'm not sure about you, but I'm feeling pretty ravenous. Do you fancy some breakfast?'

Within next to no time, to take advantage of the fine weather, the three of them sat outside at the table on the patio, Oscar and Laura tucking into their blueberry porridge and some *Cocoa Pops* for Jessica with a large plate of freshly warmed croissants in the middle of the table, their aroma extremely inviting for whoever cared to help themselves.

For the first time Laura was seeing the back garden and looked appreciatively over to the rosebushes with petals of reds, whites and yellows bordering the recently mown lawn, breathing in the scent of freshly cut grass. With the sound of the birds chirping happily from the branches of the nearby oak trees, and bees humming, busily collecting pollen from flower to flower, she felt that nothing could feel more perfect.

While they tucked into their breakfast, accompanied with some freshly squeezed orange juice poured carefully by Jessica from a large jug into their glasses, Oscar told Laura about the local school where his daughter had attended for the last three years. He explained since moving to the village, had settled in well at the local school and most of her teachers were pretty nice; even Mr Hughes the maths teacher, Jessica added, even though she wasn't very good at sums. After they finished eating, the young girl collected up all their plates and even offered to do the washing-up.

Laura was impressed. 'Wow, for a ten-year old she's very well house-trained!'

Oscar gave a throaty chuckle as he watched over his daughter collecting up and carrying the pile of plates and cutlery to take back to the kitchen, making sure she didn't drop anything along the way. 'She is, but I think today she wanted to make an extra special effort to impress *you*.' He swallowed some of his fruit juice before giving her a conspiratorial wink. 'But between me and you, I think this is her subtle way of giving us the opportunity to spend some time alone together.'

Laura couldn't help but smile, suspecting that was the

case.

He studied her thoughtfully, gazing into those sparking eyes that reminded him so much of green sapphire gems. 'So, how's life been treating you at the moment, Laura?'

She gave a small shrug of her shoulders. 'I guess as well as it can do - going ok on the whole this week despite the usual ups and downs.' A small smile curled her lips. 'Karen's such an amazing friend - we'll be going shopping next week to get dresses for the awards ceremony.'

He took hold of her hand before placing on it a gentle kiss. 'I can't think of *anybody* more deserving for the Most Loved Manager award - but then again I happen to be very biased!'

She laughed. 'It's very nice to know that you have so much confidence in me, but it's by no means certain that I'm going to win - I'm up against three other impressive people in my category.'

He gave her a sheepish grin. 'You'll win - believe me, *you will.* I feel strongly it's going to be a night to remember.'

'You think so? Then you know more than I do!'

He squeezed her hand gently. 'Yes darling, it's going to be your special moment. All you need to know is that afterwards we'll be here waiting for you.'

A puzzled frown knitted her forehead, not quite understanding what he was saying, but appreciated his optimism about claiming the Global Life award in her field. 'Well, whether or not I win, I want to make sure I'll get something special to wear for the occasion, just in case!' She narrowed her eyes in thought. 'I'm not quite sure what colour to go for. I usually end up getting something in the same old black to hide a multitude of sins - especially around the hips.'

Squeezing her hand, he looked lovingly in her eyes. 'Darling, there's nothing wrong with your figure, you've got nothing to *hide*. As far as I'm concerned, it's *perfect*.' He gently parted her fringe with his fingers. 'If my opinion counts for anything, I think something in emerald green would look sensational. To match those beautiful eyes.'

Laura bit the bottom of her lip in concentration. 'Hmm, that does sound rather nice actually. There are a few sales on in town at the moment, so will have to see what I can find.'

Her gaze turned back to Oscar seeing his look of amusement as she became lost in her own thoughts.

She decided to take the plunge. 'Actually, there is something I feel I think you need to know. I'm meant to be going out on another date in a few days.'

'With Dan?'

She nodded in confirmation, 'Yes, *who else*?' unable to hide her feelings of guilt, that she was somehow betraying him. 'After our night out, he texted me suggesting we get together again.'

He blinked rapidly as he contemplated the idea. 'Oh, well, it looks like you certainly made quite an impression on him.' His eyes seem to darken, losing their sparkle as he prompted gently, 'I know Karen means well and believes that where I'm concerned things are impossible, but is that what *you* want? Do *you* feel you would like to get to know Dan better?'

Laura let out a deep sigh, feeling a moment of despair, gently rubbing both of her temples. 'The truth is that I really don't know.' For a moment, she listened to the sound of crockery being moved in the kitchen, as Jessica busily washed away at the dishes in the sink, suggesting there wasn't a dishwasher installed at Rose Cottage. 'All I know is that as beautiful as this all is, I can't hope for something that can never be mine.'

'I understand what you're saying sweetheart,' he sympathised, his face filled with both a mixture of pity and understanding. 'You must do what you feel is right for *you*. Go on your second date and enjoy - life is a journey we must all follow through. Me and Jessica will always be here for you, no matter what.'

'A beautiful retreat where I hope I can always escape to - if I'm lucky,' she reflected with irony. 'By the way, nothing firm has been arranged yet. He's supposed to call me in the week and arrange something, but he might well get second thoughts.'

He placed a gentle kiss on her cheek. 'Of *course*, he'll call you! You are far too much of a catch to pass by. Dan *will* be in touch - that's a guarantee.'

Laura felt an overwhelming feeling of sadness and frustration with tears filling her eyes. 'I know this is all a dream, but I can't help feeling I'm betraying you and Jessica... that I'll be letting both of you down.'

Oscar watched her solemnly, his eyes seeming to penetrate her, with a sadness that mirrored the way she was feeling. He took her in his arms, as he gently stroked her hair. 'Hush darling, it's ok - you haven't got to think this way. Over the past few years you've experienced things that nobody should ever have to go through. I know more than anyone how difficult it is for you to look back on those dreadful episodes without feeling that your life is over.' He studied her intently, his eyes appearing to peer deeply into the core of her soul. 'One thing I've learned is that life's much too short not to make the most of opportunities. Have your date with Dan, and have a wonderful time with the blessing of both me and Jessica.'

The moment was broken as the young girl stepped outside, accompanied by an adult holding her hand. Laura's mouth opened in surprise as her gaze fixed onto Becky, the lifelong friend that she'd never had. As she watched Laura, her smile appeared as bright as the morning sunshine, the happy face she remembered from their imaginary schooldays when they first met.

Maybe, all these memories of their childhood days only existed in her mind, all the amazing times throughout their teens and into adulthood; treasured moments spent together, memories rich in their own unique history. But that didn't stop the waves of happiness at this moment rippling excitedly through her body, as she got up and ran into her arms of her friend as they firmly embraced.

'Hi stranger,' she greeted Laura with that roguish grin she remembered so well, her voice thick with emotion. 'Still looking as beautiful as ever I see. Oh, gosh, *have* I missed you!'

'Missed you too, Becks!' Laura peered at her with a watery smile. 'You're looking so great.' Glancing at the fair hair she remembered so well, only this time appearing longer almost down to her waist and a few shades lighter. Gone were the tell-tale signs of stress she recalled when her friend and husband Chris were setting up their hairdressing business. The dark circles that shadowed her eyes through lack of sleep and the permanent frown mark were no more, with her complexion looking positively radiant. Throughout most of her adult life,

Becky always chose clothes with vibrant colours and the long crimson dress she wore this morning was no exception.

Becky sat down on the chair opposite Laura, with Jessica sitting on her knee, giving a contented sigh as she studied Laura thoughtfully as if there was something she wanted to ask, but thought better of it. 'Sorry if I interrupted breakfast,' she apologised instead. 'Chris is out with a friend, and when I knew you were visiting, I just had to drop by!

Laura was curious. 'Are you still living in the town where I came for your birthday?'

Becky shook her heard. 'I haven't lived there for some time. For the past few years I've been here in this beautiful village.'

Laura raised her eyebrows in surprise. 'Really? What I've seen so far, this place *is* beautiful, but I wouldn't put it down as being somewhere you would choose to live. You were town born and bred as far as I remember - enjoying parties and clubbing. Just about everything life has to offer for the ultimate *urban chic!*'

Becky gave a chuckle. 'Well, all I can say now is don't knock country life until you've tried it - there's definitely still plenty of fun to be had around here too, I'll have you know.' She helped herself to the remaining croissant sitting on the plate, taking a small nibble. 'Well, as I'm sure you well remember, I grew up in a mid-terrace in the heart of town, with Mum and Dad and my two nightmare brothers, all pretty central to all the shops and pubs. Remember how we used to club? I knew it wasn't really your scene, because out of the two of us, you were always the quiet and sensible one, whereas I was the one that would always go in feet first!'

Laura was intrigued. 'So, *what* made you decide to move here?

Her friend watched her in a way which suggested she hadn't understood, closing her eyes for a moment in thought.

'Well, let's just say it was *circumstances* beyond my control that brought me here.' She gazed at the partly eaten croissant in her hand. 'At first I've got to say everything took me by surprise. *Things* happened so fast and just wasn't sure how I was going to deal with the situation - I was totally unprepared.'

Noticing that Laura's expression held more than a hint of concern and confusion, her mood quickly lightened, her features softening as her lips turned into a warm smile. 'But now I'm here, I'm just so happy and contented, in a way that I had never been before.'

Not entirely comprehending everything what Becky was trying to tell her, Laura picked up the jug from the table, offering her some fruit juice which she poured into a glass.

'But don't you miss working at the salon? You both worked so hard to get where you wanted to be, putting in all the time and money to make it a success.'

Becky took a sip of her drink, savouring the taste of the fruit. 'Oh, don't get me wrong, I was really glad to get the opportunity to make a go of things. And everything was looking so promising until...' Her expression darkened for just a brief moment as she reflected. 'But the great thing is about hairdressing that it's a skill we can take anywhere with us wherever we go. Believe it or not, I always have more than enough clients around this village. I'm mobile and it's a great way to drop in and catch up on all the gossip!'

The news genuinely surprised Laura, but then again as she recalled, Becky was very good at what she did and had such an engaging personality. So really it was easy to understand that the villagers preferred to have their hair done locally at a cheaper price by a likeable stylist than going into town and pay the expensive salon prices.

After spending some time reflecting on a few memories of their younger days, Becky had a suggestion. 'Why don't the two of you take some time out while me and Jessica finish off that washing-up?'

Oscar stood up from the chair, looking pleased at the prospect. 'A good idea if you really don't mind, Becky!' He peered towards Laura. 'It'll be the perfect chance to take you for a walk around the village and show you the sites. If that's ok with the two of you.'

Both Jessica and Becky nodded their approval. 'Come on Jess,' Becky prompted giving her a small wink. Let's get those dishes cleaned and dried, then we'll see what else we can do with our girlie time together!'

As they left the cottage together hand in hand, Laura realised this was the first time she would get to really see anything of the village since her first dream brought her here late at night. Although the surroundings were exactly as she remembered from her previous stroll, on such a bright and sunny day, the community in daylight took on a much less sinister tone. As they wandered around the corner away from Rose Cottage, approached the village green overlooked by houses and other cottages, with the small convenience store she recalled from her previous dream.

'This is such an enchanting place,' she sighed. 'So peaceful and tranquil.' Another thought came to her. 'I can't ever remember seeing any traffic which is pretty amazing for these days when just about everybody has a car!' Suddenly feeling a little foolish she laughed. '*Oh*, what am I *saying*? Why would I expect to see any traffic or be surprised by anything that happens in a dream!'

Oscar gave a chuckle. 'I guess the best thing is just to enjoy the moment and not to overthink anything.'

As she peered over to the village green to her surprise, noticed for the first time in the distance, children playing happily together with not an adult in sight to watch over them. Oscar seemed to know what she was thinking. 'It's ok, my love. I can vouch there's nowhere safer for them to be - no child would ever come to any harm here. They're free to wander and play to their hearts content.

'It sounds perfect,' remarked Laura sincerely. 'So sad nowadays that youngsters have to be wrapped up in cotton wool and not be able to run free like we did as kids.'

As they ventured along the pathway for the first time, she noticed other people in their front gardens; an elderly lady who was sweeping her garden path greeted Oscar, watching Laura with a look of pleasant surprise. A few houses further down they came across a middle-aged man, possibly in his mid-fifties, standing outside of his house as he busily cleaned his windows. As they walked by he gave a friendly wave. 'That's Jeremy Turner,' Oscar informed her. 'Known affectionately by the locals as Jez - always likes to keep busy while he waits for his wife to come home.'

'Well it looks like she'll be coming home to a clean house!'

Laura grinned. She stopped walking for a moment, sighing contentedly. 'This is something I miss living in a town - we just don't get this same sense of community. Don't get me wrong, most of the people I have met are really nice, but most of us wouldn't have a clue about who we are living next door to, and that's very sad.'

Oscar gave a wry smile. 'You'll find around here that we do things very differently.' He kissed her gently on her hair. 'Come, I'll take you to see Jessica's school.'

As they walked further along the path, bearing left, Laura realised that the village was larger than she had first realised, though losing none of its picturesque character, with houses overlooking gardens planted with a variety of colourful blooms, filling the air with a pungent fragrance.

When Oscar mentioned Jessica's school this had left her quite unprepared for what she was about to see, expecting the usual multi storey building surrounded by a concrete playground. But as they stopped at the neck of the wide, open entrance her eyes widened with her mouth agape as she stared in disbelief at the one-storey building.

Set back in its own spacious wooded grounds, the school was built with what appeared to be grey Cotswold bricks, blending pleasingly with its rural settings. In the place of the usual iron railings designed for pupils' safety, white picket fencing bordered the area, seeming to be more for decoration than security. Laura peered inside the grounds seeing all the usual climbing frames, even swings one would expect in a school; but unlike a conventional playground of concrete, was instead carpeted with a lush green lawn, speckled with wild flowers such as buttercups, dandelions and daisies. With a large willow tree overlooking a pond, and a variety oak and cherry trees, reminded Laura more of a park than the playing area of school. Without a doubt, this was unlike any educational establishment she had ever come across before.

Laura's attention focused back to Oscar who was smiling, clearly amused with the look of amazement written on her face. '*Never* have I seen a school so beautiful as this,' she admitted. 'So this is the place where Jessica will receive her education until she goes to the big school in town?'

Oscar shook his head. 'No, this is where Jessica and all the other children will receive their *entire* schooling, until she reaches twenty-one.'

'*Twenty-one?*' she repeated, certain she must have misheard.

He nodded. 'Yes, around here the children are educated to a later age, but not in the way we were during our school days.'

She blinked in astonishment. 'Wow, I couldn't wait to

leave school when I turned eighteen. But I guess if I'd been attending a school like this one, I wouldn't have been in such a hurry to leave!'

Taking her hand gently again, to her surprise, led her into the grounds of the school.

'Won't the teachers mind?'

Giving a shake of his head, chuckled, his amused expression suggesting she wasn't understanding what he was trying to tell her. 'How many times do I have to tell you we do things *differently* here? Come now, let me take you on a brief tour.'

Oscar led her towards the willow tree, that stood over the small pond, covered with small dark green lily leaves from one sat a small toad, its eyes firmly fixed on a blue dragon fly that hovered over the water before flying away out of reach into the distance.

She gave a start as she heard the slam of a door, looking in the direction of the school, seeing a small group of children, young boys and girls of around Jessica's age, leave the building. The boys wore a uniform of pale blue tee shirts and shorts, with the girls in light pink dresses similar to the one she had first seen Jessica wearing. Not far behind followed a man and a woman.

Instead of being met with hostility by the two adults,

both looked their way, smiling in recognition towards Oscar. The man who appeared slightly older than Oscar came over, firmly shaking his hand, followed by a brief hug. The woman slightly younger than Laura also hugged him, placing a friendly peck on his cheek.

They gazed over towards Laura with curious smiles. 'Let me introduce you,' suggested Oscar. 'This is Laura. Laura this is Richard Tucker, Jessica's music teacher and Selina Carter, her amazingly talented art teacher.'

To her surprise, both regarded her with undisguised pleasure as they gently embraced her in turn. Selina in particular looked very pleased. 'Oh Laura, it's *so* lovely to finally meet you. Oscar has told us so much about you – it's such a pleasure to finally meet you!'

By the heat radiating from her face, knew that she was blushing like crazy, which was ridiculous when this was all a dream.

'Jessica's so talented,' remarked Selina with enthusiasm. 'She's so keen to learn as much as she possibly can and has such a natural flare for colour. What I love about her work is her originality and how she thinks outside of the box and gets it down on paper!'

Michael nodded in agreement. 'Yes, she's such a happy,

bubbly child and wherever she goes, leaves a big trail of happy vibes!'

Oscar smiled proudly and for some reason that made Laura feel proud too.

Selina looked deeply into her eyes. 'I appreciate you're just visiting at the moment, but we really look forward to the time when you finally come to stay - I know how much that will mean to Oscar. And to Jessica too.' She glanced briefly towards Michael. 'We have to go now, but *please* feel free to come inside of the school whenever you like - I think you'll see just what a wonderful place this is!'

Laura watched on, feeling more than a little disturbed as the teachers disappeared into the distance. 'What exactly did she mean about *when* I finally come to stay? How *can* I live in a place that only exists in my dream?'

Oscar sighed, placing his arms around her, before gently cupping her chin to face him. 'Sweetheart, try not to think too deeply into any of this - Selina was just a little excited to see you as I've told her so much about you and she just got a bit carried away. To tell you the truth, just about everybody in the village knows about you and they feel such a love for you.'

Laura blinked rapidly, feeling slightly disturbed by his remark.

He could see the anxious look clouding her face. 'Look,

don't mind Selina, she's just an excitable character and always so full of enthusiasm. It's just her way.' He changed the subject. 'Would you like to take a look inside the school? Everyone is free to come and go as they please and that includes the pupils!'

She declined his invitation. 'I think I'll have to pass on that one today - there's just so much to take in.'

Oscar nodded in sympathy. 'It's ok, I do realise this must be all a little over-whelming for you.' He thought for a moment. 'Actually, there is something I think you might like to see when you're next here. Jessica belongs to the school choir and there will be a concert in a few days' time.' Seeing the look of reluctance marking her face, added with an appealing smile. 'I know it would mean the world if you could come to watch her.'

Laura couldn't hide her amusement at his optimism that she'd returning soon. 'Well, I've got to say that one's a little out of my hands, because that rather does depend on where my dreams will take me!'

'Something tells me you'll be back in time to see Jessica perform.'

'Well, when you put it that way with those puppy dog eyes and if fate dictates, I would love that too!'

He kissed her lightly on the lips. 'Well, I guess that's a date. Fancy dropping in at our local pub for a quick drink before we make our way back home?'

They strolled along hand in hand to the Silver Lion, the small country pub, with its white walls adorned with a number of large hanging baskets filled with an abundance of crimson geraniums and bright yellow marigolds all in full bloom, the large bay windows all made for a far more welcoming sight in the light of day in sharp comparison to her first visit at night where the darkness added an almost sinister shadow of mystery.

Inside, she was immediately enchanted by the décor of the quaint pub, with its tables, seats placed around the room, with the walls and almost everything furnished in a soft mint green, apart from the shining wooden floorboards stained in a warm caramel brown. The lounge was almost empty apart from a couple of elderly gentlemen sitting in the far corner quietly, each chatting away over a pint of stout.

They walked up to the small bar where a barmaid was busily wiping the counter. She smiled in greeting to Oscar, clearly suggesting to Laura they were well acquainted. As he introduced her to Maggie, the young woman's smile appeared to fade as she studied her. At a glance, she would have guessed her to be in her early thirties, her long fine hair in an unnatural shade of burgundy, matching the colour of her top. Laura was drawn to the pallor of her bared shoulders with one decorated with a small tattoo of a rose. At the sight of Laura her long slim face already quite pale seemed to go a shade paler with the small gem stud pierced at the end of her long slightly hooked nose, sparkled as it reflected the ceiling light.

Laura felt a small shiver ripple down her spine as Maggie served their drinks, her stare seeming to penetrate through her with those cold blue eyes, making her feel she was holding her accountable for some unforgivable crime.

'That woman just doesn't seem to like me!' she protested as they sat at a small table close to one of the windows.'

Oscar gave a small chuckle as he took a sip of his beer. 'Oh, don't mind Maggie, that's just her way with everybody she meets for the first time. She comes across as deep and moody, but once you get to know her then you'll find her to be quite warm and friendly.'

'Not an ex of yours?' she suggested with a smile, trying her best not to feel jealous.

He gazed at her through narrow eyes, before laughing as if she'd said the craziest thing. 'No, Maggie's not an ex, more of an acquaintance than a friend to be truthful.'

He picked up one of the small place mats, tapping it gently in thought on the table.

'She's actually quite new to the village, moved here a few months ago after leaving her boyfriend behind. Apparently before coming her she'd been poorly, but she's now made a full recovery.'

Laura raised her eyebrow as she took a gentle sip of her white wine. 'Wow this village seems to have a way of attracting people parted from their loved ones!'

For a moment he appeared to be lost in thought as he stared at the froth in his pint of beer. 'Yep, I guess you're not wrong there.'

Laura couldn't say she was too sorry when it was time to leave. Although Maggie kept her distance, felt distinctly ill at ease, feeling she was constantly being watched and scrutinised as she seemed to be forever peering over at her from over the bar.

Relived as they finally made their way out of the door, the relative silence was punctuated by the sound of glass breaking as it crashed on the floor. Both startled and alarmed, Laura quickly ran back inside, watching as Maggie bent over with a dustpan and brush, quickly sweeping up the broken fragments of a beer glass that she'd dropped. As Laura offered to help, the woman declined, vigorously shaking her head insisting she could see to the mess. But before she had a chance to make her exit, Maggie's final words chilled her to the bones, '*Please* don't hurt him whatever you do - he's a good person, you know.'

As she joined him outside her puzzled expression wasn't

lost on Oscar.

'Hey, is everything ok? Did Maggie hurt herself?'

She gave a shake of her head, feeling very confused and more than a little disturbed by the woman's parting words, wondering why she would think her capable of hurting Oscar. Her intuition dictated that she should allow the subject to drop as was unlikely to get any further knowing the truth, gave a small smile to reaffirm this.

'Good. Well, let's head back home and see if Jessica and Becky managed to finish clearing away those dishes!'

Laura gratefully held his hand that he offered to her, as they slowly made their way back to Rose Cottage.

Not only had they finished clearing away the dishes, Becky had just put the final touches to styling Jessica's hair into a long French Plait, intertwined with daisies and buttercups and really looked quite beautiful.

Jessica showed Laura proudly, giving a twirl.

'My, you do look pretty,' she remarked. 'Just like a flower princess! I can see Becky is amazing as ever with her hairstyles.'

Becky poured herself some orange juice. 'Hope you enjoyed your walk around the village. Did you manage to get to see the school?'

She sat down on one of the patio chairs. 'Yes, I did - well at least from the outside. Wow, that's some school where pupils can go to lessons when they please!'

Becky placed herself down on the seat opposite while Oscar went to the garden with Jessica who wanted to show him a hedgehog that had somehow made its way inside near the begonias.

'Yes, it's really an amazing place to learn. Although me and Chris never had kids, we do go quite often to see the concerts.' Her lips curled into a soft smile as she reflected on her visits to the school. 'There's something really great and heart-warming about listening to the kids singing their hearts out and playing their musical instruments.'

Laura sipped at her orange juice thoughtfully. 'You know, there's still chance for you and Chris to have children of your own - I remember you always saying that one day you would like to have a couple of kids - a boy and a girl.'

The faraway look in Becky's eyes wasn't unlost on Laura as she sighed deeply. 'Well, it does seem that some things are just not meant to be.'

Noticing the look of pity of Laura's face quickly added, 'But really, I can't complain - life is great here and there's more than enough kids around here to keep us happy. Especially the ones that head this way, feeling lost and confused.'

Laura frowned, not quite understanding what her friend

was telling her. 'You mean that you work at a children's home?'

She thought for a moment before shrugging her shoulders. 'Of a kind, I guess. Let's just say it's not just the adults, that come this way feeling more than a little lost. There are quite a few children of all ages too, many not younger than Jessica, needing a little help in finding their direction. Would you believe that as well as the usual run of teenagers, some are no more than babies?'

Laura was astounded. 'Wow, for a quiet village, there's certainly a lot going on here dealing with broken families that I've yet to see. It must keep you very busy with your hairdressing as well.'

Becky laughed lightly, with her blue eyes sparkling happily. 'Yes, I'm certainly kept busy. But it's also a labour of love and great to have the opportunity to help children come to terms with their situation and helping them adjust to making them a part of this lovely community.'

'You make it sound like it's a lot of fun,' Laura remarked.

Her friend looked on thoughtfully. 'Perhaps *fun* isn't the best way to describe what I do, but it's very rewarding helping to guide others into adapting to life in the village.'

Laura described her encounter with the teachers she'd been introduced to on her visit to the school and Selina's strange remark about her returning to the village on a more permanent basis.

Her friend smiled brightly, clearly not sharing her concerns. 'Oh, try not to worry, Laura - I know none of this is really making sense and you're very likely feeling very confused, maybe even a little frightened. We're all very aware of the tough times you've been through over the past few years - it hasn't been easy. So just take one day at a time and enjoy your visits here as they come.'

Jessica returned, her excitement spent at seeing the hedgehog, was clutching a bouquet of poppies that she had just picked after wandering in the nearby meadow, offering them to Laura who smiled ruefully. 'I *wish* I could take those back with me so I could put them in a vase and cherish them.'

'I have an even better idea,' piped up Becky. 'Let's make a lovely flower chain to go around Laura's head. Those red flowers will look beautiful against her long dark brown hair, don't you think?'

Within a few minutes Becky, with the help of her young assistant had made a beautiful flower chain of poppies that Jessica finally placed around her head like a crown.'

Oscar came back into the house, watching Laura with unconcealed admiration. 'My, you *do* look incredibly beautiful, my flower angel,' he remarked, the emotion thick in his voice. As he slowly made his way towards her with Becky and Jessica watching on, both smiling, he held her in her arms, gazing into her green eyes intently. As he gently brushed his lips against hers, she closed her eyes, savouring the sensation, feeling as if she was floating through the air like a white cloud of cotton candy, drifting slowly through the sky. Never before had she experienced this feeling of complete euphoria in such a long time.

As she finally opened her eyes, with no sign of Oscar, let alone Becky or Jessica, much to her bitter disappointment, realised she was lying down in her own bed. Gazing above towards the ceiling of the darkened room with just a shaft of light from outside coming through the opening in the curtain to afford some brightness, was immediately swept away by a huge wave of loneliness. Although her dear friends were just a dream away, they might as well have existed at the far side of the universe.

CHAPTER ELEVEN

'**W**ell it's pretty fair to say that Edwina's not in a particularly good mood,' Karen remarked with her eyebrows raised in exasperation as they exited the conference room after the morning meeting. 'I know sometimes in her position she's got to make some tough decisions, but boy, I've never seen her quite this stern before!'

Laura had to agree. 'I've got to admit all her ranting was a bit out of character. But I guess despite the fact she's leaving soon, is still be the one that gets it in the neck until it's time to go - never a good sign when there's been a sharp spike in the volume of complaints over the last three months,' she added nervously biting her bottom lip. 'The reports don't make for great reading when so far in the current period we've had four breaches, two of which were considered quite serious.' She took a sharp intake of breath, shaking her head in despair. 'Even more when one of those breaches just happens to be within our own team - and we all know what happens when we get too many of those.'

'Yep, the Financial Conduct Authority come down on us like a ton of bricks!' Karen confirmed, finishing off the sentence. She helped herself to a drink from the nearby water cooler, shaking her head in despair. 'I just don't know what's got into Chloe, attaching a statement to another policy holder's correspondence. We all make mistakes, - but just so unlike her to be making all the silly ones she's made lately.

'A good thing when the lady that called in was very nice and understanding about it,' Laura let out a deep sigh. 'But just really bad luck she did the same for Lance Oliver who just happens to be the financial adviser from hell.'

'Hmm, yes of all the people, it just had to be the very person that will kick off if we so much as sneeze in the wrong way. Definitely not somebody we can afford to upset when he brings a lot of business our way.'

'Exactly! As much as I detest the man, it would be a bad day for us all if he was to pull the plug and go elsewhere. I bet Edwina will be glad to see the back of all this when she goes.'

Karen knew there was more to come as her friend beckoned her over to a nearby corner, looking grim. 'I might as well tell you because I know you'll keep this in the strictest of confidence.' Seeing she had her friend's undivided attention, paused for moment, making sure she wouldn't be heard by a few of the remaining managers leaving the meeting room.

'Chloe, mentioned to me a few weeks back that she thought she might be pregnant.'

Clearly taken by surprise at the news, Karen almost choked on her water. 'You're kidding me! She's only seventeen, for heaven's sake, just a year or so younger than my Emma!'

'I'm afraid there's more to come,' she revealed solemnly. 'Just as she broke the news to her boyfriend, he announced that he'd been about to finish with her - turns out the ratbag had been seeing someone else behind her back.'

'Ouch, poor Chloe, no wonder her head's all over the place. I guess it's just going to make it that much harder having that conversation about the breach.'

Laura's gaze followed Edwina who walked by seemingly lost in her own thoughts. 'I know, but she does need to be told. Thankfully the news isn't all bad - she's mentioned since she took a couple of tests just to be sure and found out she isn't actually pregnant after all. Turned out to be a false alarm.'

'Phew! Well looks like it turned out to be a blessing in disguise, after the way that creep has treated her!'

'I won't argue there. 'I'll book in a meeting with her after lunch and have a catch up to see how she is.' Laura looked briefly at her watch. 'Well, better press on with those KPI's - would hate to make Edwina's mood any worse!'

Returning to her desk Karen winced as she took a sip of her coffee now cold, wishing she'd taken it with her to the longer than scheduled meeting. 'So, as you mentioned earlier, Dan got in touch this morning and asked you for a date?'

Trying hard not to look like the cat that got all the cream, gave a nod. 'He sent me a text this morning, not long after I got out of the shower.'

'Well, it sounds like you were in his thoughts during the night. So, where's he taking you?'

'We're going to the new Green Garden Chinese restaurant that opened last week.'

Karen stifled a yawn. 'Well, let me know what it's like, me and Andrew have been talking about giving it a try - the reviews online have been pretty good.'

As she logged back onto her PC, Laura thought back to the events of last night's dream, probably happening at the very time her future date was thinking about her. She was feeling more than a little ashamed in wishing she could have been going on a real-life date with Oscar; her mind regressing to her previous dream of the amazing picnic, remembering vividly the taste of the food and the heady feeling she knew wasn't entirely down to the wine. Most importantly, she recalled her heart racing wildly as they shared their first proper kiss. Suddenly aware that Karen had been trying to gain her attention and was watching her with a grin, stirred from her thoughts feeling more than a little embarrassed.

'Hmm, I can see for a moment you were lost in your own little world - no doubt thinking about your big date this evening.'

Laura waved her hand dismissively. 'Oh, don't mind me, I was just thinking how I'm going to manage to get those reports done by lunch - the lovely Edwina can be such a hard taskmaster.'

Noticing the blush colouring her friend's cheeks along with her very lame excuse, decided to swiftly change the subject. 'Getting back to boring work stuff, have you got the extension number for Larry at head office?'

Before getting down to the vast work ahead of her, she promptly sent the calendar invite to Chloe who accepted immediately peering her way, clearly feeling very nervous at the prospect of receiving a dressing down by her manager.

Although she succeeded in getting her reports completed, had been at one point, touch and go. It took some effort on her part to get these finalised and emailed to Edwina, and much to her dismay, her boss announced she also needed a detailed report about the future of the Investments Solutions team as seen from her own perspective. She apologised for the very short notice, but due to the urgency, asked Laura if she could send this before leaving for the day. Feeling she had little choice in the circumstances, complied with her request. Without a doubt, this wasn't really coming from Edwina directly, she mused; Laura was certain that since the older woman had handed in her notice, the future of Global Life understandably was no longer her top priority. For some time, the tired, worn expression of fatigue displayed by her boss hadn't gone unnoticed, and knew this was coming from a much higher level.

Earlier in the day after her meeting with Chloe to discuss the breach, and the remaining time making sure she was ok on a personal level, had all taken longer than anticipated. As far as Laura was concerned, the entire welfare of her team members was always top priority. Thankfully on this occasion she felt more optimistic when her young team member assured her she wouldn't make the mistake of getting back with her two-timing ex-boyfriend, feeling more hopeful that the lack of serious mistakes would also extend to her work.

As well as finishing work later than her normal time, to add to her day from hell, the journey home was delayed by a traffic hold-up due to an accident along the motorway, causing the surrounding minor roads in town which Laura normally commuted, to become congested with much heavier than normal traffic.

Now at a complete standstill, she sat helplessly in her car, watching the police cars and ambulances speeding by with their flashing blue lights and loud sirens, diverting her attention from the Ed Sheeran album she'd been listening to on her iPod.

Then suddenly like a bolt of lightning, her mind flashed back to an event that had until now, been locked safely in the deepest vault of her mind; to another time, another place when she had been driving home with fire engines, police cars and ambulances speeding past her frantically to get to the route of an emergency, blissfully unaware of their destination.

Had she checked herself in the rear-view mirror, would have become immediately aware of how the blood that had drained from her face, making her appear a deathly white. Her hands gripped the steering wheel tightly, her knuckles turning equally as pale, before she began to tremble as a tidal wave of nausea swept over her.

Just as she was on the brink of losing complete control of her mind, a sudden sharp toot of the horn from the vehicle behind immediately brought her back to her senses, now aware the traffic ahead was finally moving along. Putting a hand to her forehead coated with a cold sheen of perspiration, quickly composed herself, before continuing on with her journey home.

Feeling badly shaken by the ordeal had been on the point of calling Dan to postpone their date. But by the time she finally arrived home, after listening to the soothing Castle on The Hill from her playlist, had recovered sufficiently from her *moment* with enough just time to get ready. She was glad for being organised the previous evening, putting aside the purple dress and accessories that she would be wearing on her date.

Within just over an hour, both showered and changed, left the flat, with Dan having just pulled up at the kerb in his black Mercedes-Benz. He climbed out his vehicle, full of compliments, remarking how stunning she looked and how the colour of her dress complemented her hair. She smiled in appreciation as he opened the car door for her like the perfect gentleman.

Despite an awkward beginning as, far as dates went, Laura felt the evening had been a great success, especially in comparison to the unpleasant experience she'd had not so long ago with Julian. The food was good at the Green Garden. Having admitted her own knowledge of Chinese cuisine was somewhat limited and undecided on what to choose, Dan made some well recommended suggestions from the menu.

Much to her dismay seeing her date use his chopsticks as if he was a native to China, felt more than a little foolish at having difficulty with her feeble attempts at picking up her food with her own. Failing miserably with her efforts to get to grips with them and on the brink of starving after her long day, finally relented apologetically by resorting to her trusty knife and fork as Dan kindly reassured her most that people found more traditional cutlery by far the easiest.

Over the meal, they discussed their work as he filled her in, in some detail about the builders' merchants he'd worked for since leaving school. He explained although his job had its ups and downs, on the whole, loved what he did and couldn't imagine working for another firm. Laura enlightened him about the three years she'd spent at Global Life working her way up to team manager, but never offered to go into any detail about what happened before moving to Minsden.

His face clouded with sadness as he told her about the breakup of his marriage when his wife left him for somebody else. They were very happy to begin with he explained, but Madelyn had always been very career orientated and worked long hours. She became attached to her boss, Dominic who she had become good friends with, and on a few occasions, they went for meals or to the theatre with Dominic and his partner Martha, and at the time never struck him as particularly odd about the situation.

So, he informed her, it came as quite a bombshell when she came home one evening and admitted they'd been having an affair. Madelyn explained to him as she broke down in tears, that she'd fallen in love with Dominic who apparently felt the same way about her. It wasn't his fault she insisted, he hadn't done nothing wrong, just that with *him* she felt such a huge connection that she'd truly never experienced with Dan. Through her tears, came the announcement that she was leaving him, and Dominic had made the decision to part from Martha. Looking back with hindsight, Dan sensed things hadn't been quite right between them for some time and could see how they were slowly drifting apart.

At the beginning, the transition had proven to be a very upsetting time for his sons Craig and Lewis, he informed her solemnly, with the separation unsurprisingly making them feel that their whole world had been torn apart. But in the circumstances both him and Madelyn agreed reluctantly it was probably in the boys' best interests for them to stay with their mum and where would he would have them most weekends and during school holidays.

His face brightened as he came back to the present, explaining that despite all the odds stacked against him with juggling his career with family commitments, the bond with his sons continued to strengthen and were able to enjoy some good quality time together. Quite often he would take the boys to see their favourite football team play both home and away, or sometimes go on a weekend break. Despite the difficult breakup, was glad of the good relationship they had developed with Dominic who was now married to their mum and felt rest assured that all parties had the children's best interests at heart.

Between their courses of Satay Chicken and Sweet and Sour Prawn, he went on to tell her about Margaret. After three years of being single and some dates he would prefer to forget about, they fell in love. He already knew from the outset she was in remission with leukaemia, and seemed fit and well having gone for regular check-ups at the hospital. But after a year of the tell-tale signs of tiredness reappearing, it was discovered the disease had returned and was far more aggressive than previously. Within about six months of the diagnosis, had moved into a hospice where she eventually passed away peacefully.

Laura felt saddened at the hurt he was clearly still feeling. She did wonder if six months was perhaps a little too soon for him to start dating again, but kept those thoughts to herself.

Trying to find out a little about her own previous relationships, Dan could see by her alarmed expression wasn't keen to discuss. It was much to her relief when he agreed that whatever happed before should stay firmly in the past as it was the present and the future that was most important.

After their date, Dan drove Laura directly outside of her flat, informing her he'd enjoyed their time together and maybe they could meet up again soon, if she would like that too. She agreed it would be nice. Without making any firm plans he opened the door of the car for her, gently placing a kiss on her cheek before she went inside the entrance to the building. She was grateful that he didn't seem in the least put out when she didn't invite him for a coffee, making it clear she had an early start with work the following morning.

Laura gazed in the mirror as she took off her make-up, removing all traces that reminded her of the date. It was very early days she was aware, but Dan *did* come across as a genuinely nice guy and at least she knew from Karen that there were no secret wives and to the best of her knowledge, no other girlfriends on the scene.

She studied the reflection of her face only moments before so carefully concealed by her cosmetics, now completely bare and natural, noticing the tell-tale dark shadows under her eyes through lack of sufficient sleep. Placing her hand to the cheek he'd gently placed a kiss at the end of their date, realised with sadness she'd never experienced that same euphoric feeling of her heart skipping a beat and the butterflies flying around inside her stomach in the way they had done with Oscar.

She roused from her bleak thoughts with a start as a loud text alert come through on her phone from the bedroom nearby. Unsurprisingly it was from Dan, confirming that he'd had the most amazing time and thoroughly enjoyed her company, finishing off by saying he looked forward to seeing her again soon.

As she climbed into bed, giving a weary yawn, promptly switched off her phone, deciding she would reply tomorrow after literally sleeping on the matter.

Slowly opening her eyes, Laura felt the sensation of the warm rays from the sun kissing her skin, along with the realisation that she was no longer in her bed, but laying on a lounger in the back garden of Rose Cottage. Duke who'd been lying at her side on the grass, wagged his tail excitedly at seeing her waken, quickly lapping up the attention as she gently patted his furry white head. Much to her surprise, realising she wasn't alone, quickly sat up, peering towards a man standing on a stepladder looking her way clearly in the process of trimming the hedge.

Noticing her look of apprehension and perhaps fear clouding her pretty face, broke into a friendly smile, lighting up his plump, ruddy complexion. 'I'm very sorry my dear, I didn't mean to give you a fright.'

As she studied him with a troubled frown marking her brow, came the realisation he was the man who she saw on her walk around the village with Oscar just a few days ago.

He slowly climbed down from his ladder, wiping his hand on his navy denim jeans before giving her a firm handshake. 'Jez Turner's my name,' he said. 'And you must be *Laura*. Young Oscar's always telling us about you!'

'Nice to meet you, Jez,' she replied and meaning it, instantly warming to his round, friendly face with piercing blue eyes that seemed to look burn through to the core of her soul. For a fleeting moment there seemed to be something strikingly familiar about him, as if she had been acquainted with him in the distant past, but knew that couldn't possibly be the case.

'And I bet you're wondering where your Oscar is,' he drawled in his west country accent with a knowing smile, as if reading her thoughts. 'He's just taking young Jessica to the school, ready for her concert.'

'Yes, he did mention about that, and invited me to come along.' She was overcome with an overwhelming feeling of disappointment, realising she had just missed out on the opportunity to attend.'

He looked at her with sympathy. 'And now you're thinking that he's gone without you. Well, you've no need to worry young lady, because he knew you'd be coming back today and he'll be returning to bring you along!'

Laura let out a sigh of relief. 'I've got to admit I was a bit worried due to circumstances beyond my control that I might not be able to make it.'

'Well, it looks like you were wrong,' he remarked kindly.

She glanced over to the hedge he'd been clipping and could still see he had some more work to do before finishing the job. 'You must be thirsty - would you like something to drink?'

'I definitely wouldn't say no to that!' he returned with a wink and a chuckled. 'I have it on good authority that Oscar just might have one or two beers put away, but of course I'll be more than happy to settle for a nice glass of water.'

Within less than a couple of minutes she was serving him a chilled glass of beer and was lucky to have quickly found the bottle opener in one of the drawers.

Quickly downing half the contents of the glass sighed appreciatively. 'Beautiful, just beautiful! Very thirsty work trimming those hedges, I must say.' He wiped away a light coating of froth from his lips. 'I usually do his hedges twice a year and for the other good people of the village too. It's hard work, but I enjoy it because it gets me out and about.' He winked again, tapping the end of his nose. 'It's also a good excuse to catch up with the neighbours and cadge the odd meal or two with a few drinks thrown in!'

Laura couldn't help but smile as she instantly warmed to Jez and his way of thinking. 'Have you lived around here for a long time?' she enquired. Within an instant she regretted her words, seeing the smile fade from his face as if she might have hit a raw nerve, realising she was coming across as much too inquisitive to a person she barely knew.

But much to her relief he didn't appear fazed by her direct question. 'Well, it must be coming up for four years now!' His eyes narrowed in concentration. 'It's got to be said that I came here in very unexpected circumstances and it meant me having to leave my Bella behind - that's my wife,' he explained.

'I'm very sorry. You must miss her very much.'

'Yes, I do *miss* her, and it does mean having to step back, allowing her to get on with her life and to be happy.' He rubbed his chin in thought.

'It'll be some time before she can come to join me, so in the meantime I wish her nothing but all the love and happiness she deserves.' Giving a small sigh, he knelt on the grass, treating Duke to a much-appreciated tummy rub.

'But I will say, I'm very happy and contented here. When I first came to the village, everybody made me so welcome and soon made me feel a part of the family. So, when it's finally time for my Bella to come and join me, I know she'll be very happy here too.'

Laura couldn't fully comprehend the reason for Jez's separation with the wife he clearly still loved, but felt it was best to allow the subject to drop. After all, it was up to him and Bella how they lived their lives.

The moment was broken as the back door of the cottage opened, with Oscar smiling in undisguised pleasure at seeing her, placing a gentle kiss on her lips as he held her in his arms. 'I hope this one's not been distracting you too much,' he remarked to Jez with a teasing wink.'

'Well, as much as your young lady is very pleasing to the eye, she did offer me an even more interesting diversion with a glass of your finest beer!'

Oscar gave a chuckle. 'I'm very glad to hear that.' He peered over to the neatly trimmed hedge approvingly, admiring Jez's great workmanship. 'Well, once you've done, there's some nice cold chicken and potato in the fridge - so please help yourself.' With a grin he added, 'You might also find another bottle or two of beer there to wash that all down with!'

Clutching his hedge cutters, Jez gave a hearty laugh. 'How can a man refuse such a generous offer? Well, I'd best get this finished before I can get to enjoy my feast!'

As the neighbour pressed on with his hedge cutting, Oscar's attention focused back to Laura, his smouldering dark eyes managing to make her heart do somersaults. 'Are you ready to come and see the concert?'

'I'm ready!'

Offering her his hand to hold, which she gratefully accepted, remarked, 'That's good to know, because Jessica's been so excited for days about you coming to see her.'

'Well, I did have my concerns that I might not be able to come.'

He gently rubbed her hand with his own. 'Well, I *knew* you would be able to make it and I guarantee you're in for an amazing time!'

Before departing, both waved goodbye to Jez as they set off on their way to the concert.

Much to Laura's delight the school was every bit as unique inside as it was from the outside. As they stepped inside the entrance, saw other people she assumed must have been parents of the pupils, busily chatting amongst themselves. To her surprise, Mrs Lock came along with a tray of drinks, offering a choice of Bucks Fizz or as an alternative just plain orange juice. Considering this to be a special occasion, both of them went for the alcoholic option.

'It's very nice to see you again,' greeted the elderly lady

excitedly as she peered over her spectacles. 'Jessica's been taking her rehearsals very seriously and getting in as much practice a she could possibly squeeze in,' she informed Laura with a warm smile. 'She's been very much looking forward to you coming to see her perform – you're definitely in for a treat!' Glancing over towards the entrance appeared a little harassed, noticing some more parents arriving. 'Well, I must press on, these refreshments most certainly won't get served by themselves!'

As she sipped her drink while Oscar chatted to a middle-aged man she assumed to be one of the teachers, peered around the room, gazing at all the paintings displayed on the walls contributed by the pupils. At a guess, she would have said that the age of the artists' work ranged anything from infant to young adult.

Oscar returned back to her side, much to her own embarrassment and could see from the way he studied her with that knowing smile that she'd been caught out lost in her own small world of thought.

'I was just thinking how incredibly different this is from any school evening I've known from my childhood,' she quickly explained. 'Even when we lived in a much less politically correct era, I could have never imagined booze being served at a parent evening or any school function come to that!'

He gave a shrug of his shoulders as he peered into his glass. 'The same went for me back in the day when your choice was either coffee or tea. But hey, we're all responsible adults here, so what harm can possibly be done?'

Feeling a light tap on her shoulder, she turned around letting out a whelp of delight when standing behind her was Becky, with Chris at her side.

The two women hugged each other warmly followed by Becky's husband giving her an affectionate peck on the cheek.

'No offence intended, but I didn't expect you two to be here tonight!'

Becky held up her own drink, giving a wry smile. 'None taken! I see you went for the alcoholic alternative like we did!' She flicked back her hair with her hand. 'Remember I mentioned on your last visit, we never got to have kids of our own? Well, the thing is ever since we've been here, we're just crazy about these little ones and they've become a really huge part of our world!'

While Chris chatted away with Oscar, Becky introduced Laura to a few of the parents. Some were relatively young she could see, in their early twenties, but others could have sworn looked long past their child-bearing years. A few were clearly of more mature years, and surely must have been grandparents.

After a few minutes, Mrs Lock gained everybody's attention as she ushered them along to the assembly hall with another helper of similar years leading Laura, Oscar and her friends along a small stairway. As they passed through the open entrance to a balcony, Laura was immediately taken aback by what she encountered. With the plush seating in colours of red and gold velvet arranged in a semi-circle over-looking the assembly area on the ground below, would have been forgiven for thinking she had stepped into a theatre in the heart of London's West End instead of an assembly hall of a village school.

Her attention gravitated towards the floor below where parents chatted away as they took their places on equally comfortable looking seats in front of the large centre stage draped by red velvet curtains.

Placing herself down next to Oscar with Becky to her right, studied the oil paintings adorning the magnolia walls. Some were images of flower-filled landscapes with others bearing portraits of people she didn't recognise but assumed were clearly of some significance within the community, possibly of much-loved individuals. With a frown creasing her forehead in thought, Laura couldn't help wondering if this was some private school as couldn't imagine any of this kind of luxury in a non-fee-paying establishment.

Feeling increasingly curious noticing as others in the audience peered under their seats, with Becky prompting her to do the same. Much to her surprise, she found a small tray laden with a plate of sandwiches, a small cheesecake and a glass with some kind of beverage which she presumed to be lemonade.

'My goodness!' she exclaimed in wide-eyed astonishment. 'We're certainly being very well catered for!' Looking over to Oscar with concern said, 'I guess to have the best seats in the house couldn't have come cheaply to you. If it wasn't for the fact that this is all a dream, I would insist on chipping in.'

Clearly amused, Oscar let out a peel of laugher before gently placing a kiss on her cheek. 'Darling, that's really very sweet of you, but I can assure you that none of this is at a cost to any of us at all - the school have taken care of all this. Even if there had been some expense, that's something I would insist on seeing to. So just sit back and enjoy the concert!'

The audience was lulled into silence as the lights dimmed with the red velvet curtains slowly opening, revealing the large stage now lit by spotlights directed towards the young choir. At a guess, Laura would have said in total, there had to be at least fifty pupils in the group; towards the back stood young men and women with the junior members at the front. The females of the congregation wore long dresses in dusky pink, with the opposite sex in all wearing white shirts with trousers in a shade of blue-grey. At the very centre of the front row Laura immediately sighted Jessica looking very pretty and radiant with her long dark hair hanging loosely around her shoulders.

Suddenly the silence was filled by the sweet melodious sounds of a harp being played by a woman sitting a short distance away from the choir. Until moments ago, before the stage was lit, could see now the performer was Selina the teacher she had met just days before. Wearing a long satin dress in a shade of ivory, made a striking contrast to her short bright auburn hair, the glow of the lighting making her appear almost luminous and ethereal as she plucked expertly at the strings of the large instrument.

As the almost magical sounds filled the assembly room to the best of Laura's knowledge without the aid of microphones, the pupils began to sing along to what could only be described as a hymn, but one she had never come across before. With its clear simplistic lyrics, Laura could say in all honesty this was one of the most beautiful songs she'd heard in a very long time. Jessica peered their way towards the balcony, beaming excitedly clearly very happy that Laura had managed to make it to the event.

Enjoying the choir's performance of a variety of lively songs, Laura followed the example of the others by tucking into their food, as Mrs Lock and a few other ladies coming around to refill their glasses with the delicious thirst-quenching lemonade.

As the medley of hymns finally came to an end, everybody gave a huge burst of applause. Once the clapping finally came to an end, Richard Tucker announced that the final song of the evening was to be sung by Jessica Devereux. The room filled with silence in eager anticipation as the spotlight focused on Oscar's daughter, as she began to sing a rendition of *Greensleeves*, with Selina playing the harp to perfection.

Alas my love you do me wrong
To cast me off discourteously;
And I have loved you oh so long
Delighting in your company.

Greensleeves was my delight,
Greensleeves my heart of gold
Greensleeves was my heart of joy
And who but my lady Greensleeves.

I have been ready at your hand
To grant whatever thou would'st crave;
I have waged both life and land
Your love and goodwill for to have.

Greensleeves was my delight,

Greensleeves my heart of gold
Greensleeves was my heart of joy
And who but my lady Greensleeves.

Thy petticoat of slender white
With gold embroidered gorgeously;
Thy petticoat of silk and white
And these I bought gladly.

Greensleeves was my delight,
Greensleeves my heart of gold
Greensleeves was my heart of joy
And who but my lady Greensleeves.

Laura sat, mesmerised as she listened to the beautifully haunting melody of the timeless song. As the young girl finished her performance, there were a few seconds of hushed silence before the audience suddenly broke out into a rapturous applause as they got to their feet in a standing ovation.

Overcome with an emotion that took her completely by surprise, Laura wiped a tear that gently trickled down her cheek.

Oscar placed his arm around her, pulling her gently closer to him as he placed a kiss lightly on her head with Becky looking on with a smile.

'That was absolutely amazing!' said Oscar proudly. 'What a

talented daughter we have!'

Laura grimaced, feeling more than just a stab of jealously for the woman that should have attended, and couldn't help thinking unkindly to herself that if Jessica's mother had just a shred of love for her daughter then would be right there watching her with pride.

After the performance, the parents joined their children in the dining area where more food and drinks were on offer.

Jessica came over hugging her dad who was feeling immensely proud. Laura looked on with a watery smile, with emotions bubbling away which she couldn't understand and much to her surprise felt the need to give the child a hug too, but held back.

'That was just beautiful, Jessica,' she praised sincerely.

'Thank you!' she beamed. 'I'm so glad you could make it - I've been practising every day.'

'Well it certainly paid off. You have the voice of an angel!'

Enjoying the compliment, the young girl smiled brightly as she rushed in the direction of a boy of a similar age.

'That's Simon,' Oscar explained. 'They've become firm friends since we came here. They have a lot in common - like Jessie he's brilliant at art and he's actually the one that' sparked her interested in joining the choir. She never had any particular aspirations for singing until she came here.'

As he became engrossed in a conversation with Chris and one of the parents, Becky came along, offering her a cocktail.

Laura couldn't help but chuckle as she took a sip of her drink. 'I never knew a school evening could be such good fun - this is much more like a party. I'm just having such an amazing time.' Her face became solemn as she contemplated her words. 'I wish this didn't have to be all just a dream.'

Becky's look of sympathy wasn't lost on her. 'I know this is a lot for you to get your head around hon, but just try not to overthink any of this.' Her lips pursed into a small pout of concentration. 'All I can say is that one day this will all make some kind of sense.'

Shrugging her shoulders, she nodded, tried hard to mask the fact that she was unable to stretch her imagination to make any kind of sense of all this: A dream that would take her to a beautiful village, a place she would return to if she was lucky. To a place where she'd met a man who she'd fallen head over heels in love with, but didn't really exist outside of that world. A man with the sweetest of daughters who was apparently abandoned by her mum. Here in this world, she had known Becky her entire life and as much as she loved Karen, felt more engaged with her non-existent friend and their supposed shared history of long friendship filled with happy memories.

Throughout the evening, with Oscar, Becky and Chris, mingled with parents, finding this a great way of becoming better acquainted with the people of what until now had been a mysterious village community. At intervals Jessica would come along excitedly to introduce her to Simon and a few of her other school friends.

Laura gave a long yawn, realising for the first time just how tired she had become, unsure if it was down to the alcohol, even if only consumed within in a dream, or perhaps the excitement of the occasion. Whatever the reason, the night had certainly taken its toll.

'Are you feeling sleepy?' enquired a small voice. She looked down and saw Jessica gazing at her with her large green eyes, open wide with concern. She glanced briefly to Oscar, Becky and Chris who were busily engrossed in conversation with teachers Richard and Selina.

Laura gave a nod. 'I must admit I am a little, Jessica - it's been an amazing evening and was simply awesome to listen to you sing so beautifully. But I've got to say all this excitement has taken it out of me a little!

The child took hold of her hand as if she was the adult. 'You must have a rest!' Leading her to a wooden chair sat in the corner of the room where the crowds were less dense, Laura placed herself on the comfy padded seat, giving a deep sigh of contentment.

'I'll let Daddy know where you are!' Jessica called out as she rushed back into the thick of the crowd.

She relaxed back on the comfy red cushion on the chair, not realising just *how* tired she was until she sat down. Her eyes feeling increasingly heavy, gave a long yawn, before falling into a deep sleep.

Although aware she had been asleep, Laura had little idea as to how much time had passed, as she opened her eyes to find herself back in her own bed with the covers thrown back.

Giving a shiver with her skin feeling cold, she pulled up the covers tucked firmly under her chin.

CHAPTER TWELVE

After reading the best part of a chapter from the latest read on her Kindle, Laura managed to get back to sleep, but this time there were no dreams of returning to Jessica's school. Instead, to her dismay, woke up to the tell-tale signs of another migraine throbbing relentlessly over the right-hand side of her temple. Reaching for the ready supply of paracetamols tucked away in her bedside drawer, swallowed a couple quickly, hoping desperately that she had managed to avert a full-blown attack.

Her mind wandered back to the events of the night before, finding it almost impossible to believe the amazing concert and the after-party with the parents had all taken place in a dream. Placing her fingertips to the side of her head gave a wry smile, almost believing that the headache could be put down to all the glasses of wine that had been on offer. Slowly her fingers slid towards her mouth where not so long ago, Oscar had tenderly kissed, hoping desperately to detect the tell-tale bruising where their lips had caressed or at the very least to capture the fragrance of his aftershave on her skin. But unsurprisingly, there were no tell-tale signs.

Immediately she was stirred from her thoughts as a text alert came through loudly from her phone, causing her to splatter some water from her glass, onto the bedsheets.

As expected, the sender was Dan and remembered much to her shame she hadn't bothered returning his message from last night, promising herself she would leave that until the morning. His latest text mentioned again he'd had an amazing time and hoped she would have a great day at work. This was followed by three kisses.

She let out a deep sigh knowing there was little chance of having a great day at work if this migraine kicked into full swing. With her face set firmly into a grimace she quickly tapped away on the keyboard, confirming she'd enjoyed the evening and hoped he would have a fab day. Biting her bottom lip in concentration studied her text, hoping he wouldn't read too much into the three kisses she'd included. Deciding he wouldn't as everybody used kisses and all kinds of meaningless emoji's these days, quickly pressed the send key before having the chance to change her mind.

Apart from her head feeling as if it had been run over by a steamroller, the morning went fairly smoothly at work. Chloe seemed much happier after yesterday's meeting, undoubtedly relieved that she wouldn't be facing a disciplinary. Unable to apologise enough for causing those breaches, feeling she had badly let the team down, was keen to assure Laura that Tom now her ex, was history and would forget all about relationships for the time being and focus on her job.

Although Laura had no doubts of Chloe's sincerity and had the best of intentions, was also well aware she was considered very attractive by her male contemporaries. With a combination of her striking looks and engaging personality, felt it was just a matter of time before someone else would come along on the scene to win her attention. Which was fine, just so long as the next one didn't turn out to be the type to treat her badly. Or worse still, Tom didn't manage to worm his way back into her affections.

Returning to the office from her morning catch-up with Edwina, was feeling increasingly unwell from the migraine which the tablets had failed to take away.

Karen peered over her spectacles with concern noticing how pale her friend's face appeared as she sat back at her desk. 'I take it things didn't go too well?'

She waved her hand dismissively. 'Oh, everything went better than expected. Apart the incident with Chloe and her breaches, on the whole Edwina's reasonably satisfied with how our team is performing.'

'Well, that's good to know. Compared to both Drawdown and New Business we get very little in the way of complaints.'

Laura logged back onto her PC to check the ten emails that came through while she was away from her desk. 'Yes, that's true - we're a brilliant little team and it's just great we all get on so well! But there's always room for improvement!'

Always proud of the great rapport she shared with Edwina, could tell her manager was keen to make a friend of her, especially since her big announcement to step down to take early retirement. Her mind regressed back to the time when she came for the interview at Global Life just over three years ago, when her soon to be boss learned just about everything what had happened to her, quickly taking her under her wing to give her a second chance.

For that Laura would always be forever grateful. No amount of words could ever express the gratitude she felt for all her kindness and compassion given at her greatest time of need. But as to being her friend, she felt that certain boundaries should never be crossed, even if she just happened to be leaving the company soon. Most of all she didn't need to be constantly reminded about her past and what had happened.

She raised her eyebrows in question as she felt Karen's

gaze almost burning through her in accusation.

'You're having another one of those migraines again, aren't you?'

'Look I'll be ok, I took some tablets as soon as I noticed the signs. I've got to know the drill - it'll be gone in next to no time.'

Judging by the redness colouring her cheeks, Karen was unconvinced and clearly more than a little cross. 'Really, you seriously need to think about booking in to see the doctor. You just *can't* carry on this way!'

'Oh, stop worrying about me, I'll be fine! I keep telling you there's not much that can be done for migraines, and the last thing I need is some drug that'll give me a whole host of side effects.'

Taking a sharp intake of breath as she removed her spectacles, Karen gently placed them on the desk, peering at her thoughtfully. 'Look, I don't mean to scare you, but has it ever occurred to you that you might not be dealing with a migraine? It could be the sign of something else.'

'Such as?'

She shrugged her shoulders. '*Oh*, I've no idea, I'm not a doctor! I'm sure it's a migraine like you say, but unless you get it properly diagnosed, you can't be one hundred percent sure! Besides, taking all those paracetamols can't be doing your liver any good.'

Laura gave a sigh. 'Ok, I'll give it some thought. If they carry on, I'll make an appointment, even if it's just to stop you nagging and have me down as having a brain tumour!'

'You promise?'

'I promise, *Mum*,' she said with a wink. She glanced towards her PC monitor. 'Well, these reports are not going to get done by themselves. I'd best get cracking, otherwise Edwina will take back all the good things she's said about us!' With a smile she added curtly, 'And if you decide to stop nagging me, I just *might* tell you about my date with Dan last night.'

Karen sat back in the crowded coffee shop in town at lunchtime, listening with interest as Laura updated her on her evening out. She blew on the froth of her coffee thoughtfully.

'Well from what you've told me, it sounds like the Green Garden restaurant came up to your expectations - after your rave review about the meal and great service I'll definitely be giving it a try with Andrew.' She gazed at her friend thoughtfully through narrowed eyes. 'Well, it sounds like the food certainly wowed you, but what about *Dan*?'

Wiping the crumbs away off the table from her chocolate muffin, Laura placed the uneaten contents onto her plate.

'Well, what *can* I say about Dan? It's still very early days, but so far, I guess he ticks all the right boxes when it comes to being the perfect date. He told me quite a bit about his ex and poor Margaret. It's so sad that after everything, he finally got to find some happiness and just seems so cruel to have lost her in that way.'

Karen nodded grimly. 'Tell me about it! Seems like all the good people just get all the hard luck, no matter what they do.' She took a sip of her coffee. 'So, do you think *you* might be the one to turn his life around?'

Taken aback for a few seconds, she suddenly burst out laughing, causing a few of the people on the nearby table to look over in her direction. 'Hey, no pressure then!' Her expression became more serious. 'He does come across as a nice person from what I've learned about him so far...'

'But...."

'But it's much too soon to be looking so far ahead - only time will tell.' For a moment Laura appeared distracted as she screwed up her paper napkin into a ball, tossing it onto her plate. 'I wasn't sure whether or not to tell you, but I'm still getting those dreams.'

Karen was unable to mask her curiosity. 'You mean those ones about Oscar?'

Nodding reluctantly, she made her confession. 'Practically every night. After I'd seen Dan and got to sleep, I returned to the village, on the day of this school concert to see

Jessica perform. Oscar already invited me to it a few days in the previous dream,' she explained. 'And well, for very obvious reasons I wasn't sure whether or not I would be able to make it.' With a wry smile, continued. 'Well it turns out that I *did* make it and had a lovely time.'

Seeing she clearly had gained her friend's undivided attention, went on to describe the events of the evening in detail, about Jessica's performance, the food, her friend Becky and how she even become acquainted with some of the other parents.

After she finished describing the evening, glanced back to Karen who remained ominously silent, the look of pity written on her face was unmistakable. 'Hey, it's ok, you don't have to say it - I know you think I've gone completely crazy.'

Her friend shrugged. 'To tell you the truth, I really don't know what to think about all this. I know we all have strange dreams from time to time, but to keep visiting the same place and the same people in a dream is very unusual to say the least. I won't lie Laura, but I'm worried about you.'

Laura gave a weary sigh, immediately questioning her own decision to share these details with her, realising she must be coming across as completely insane.

'You've got no reason to worry about me - I promise you I'm fine. I guess the trouble with me is I've just got an overactive imagination. I go to sleep and from there it takes over. That's all there is to it.'

Karen's face softened. 'I'm sure it's something like that. But could it simply be that you're feeling a little lonely?' She gently placed her cup onto the saucer. 'What really concerns me is the way you describe your meetings with Oscar and the school concert like it's some real-life event. But as harsh as this might sound sweetheart, all this just exists inside of your head. I know I haven't always been hanging out with you as much outside work since Andrew moved in, but I just wish you had a few more friends to spend time with.'

Laura smiled, trying to put her friend's mind at rest. 'I promise you have no reason to feel bad about having a life where you've been lucky enough to have found your soulmate. Andrew's such a lovely guy and I'm very happy for you both. I certainly don't expect you to be there for me 24 /7 when you've got your own life to live.'

She gazed at her indignantly. 'As for the record, Karen Bright, I'll have you know I'm not lonely! As much as I love your company, I also happen to enjoy having my own space. You know more than anybody that I've never been much of a social butterfly - that's the reason I no longer bother with stuff like *Facebook*, *X* formally known as *Twitter* or heaven forbid, *Instagram*!'

'Ok...ok, I get what you're staying. But these dreams only started occurring recently, didn't they?' She bit her bottom lip in concentration. 'More to the point they began occurring when you started getting those headaches more frequently. Maybe there's a connection there somewhere?'

Laura gave a snort. 'Now look who's the one with the over-active imagination!'

Her friend shrugged her shoulders. 'It's possible. How's your head, by the way?'

'Better than it was earlier.'

From the way her eyes shifted to the unfinished muffin sitting on her plate, next to the screwed-up paper napkin, knew Karen remained sceptical. 'Good. Because I'm your friend and it's within my job description to be worried about you! And I would feel most hurt if you found it difficult to be honest with me. I know it's still early days with Dan, but I'm glad things are going well so far - you both deserve a piece of happiness. He's been through some very difficult times and I would hate to see him get hurt again.'

'I would never deliberately hurt him!' interjected Laura.

'That's good to know. Because how can anybody possibly compete with some gorgeous, *Prince Charming* that only exists inside of your imagination? For goodness sake, give the poor guy a chance. Give *yourself* a chance. With a bit of time you might well find he really grows on you and once that happens, those dreams will very likely come to a stop!'

Laura forced a broad smile at Karen's logic, but a smile that didn't quite reach up to her eyes. Maybe Karen was right, she mused. Although with Dan she had never

experienced those same ripples of excitement as she had with Oscar, had only met him twice. For heaven's sake, she was a grown woman well into her forties! Those feelings of butterflies fluttering inside your stomach were only experienced by the females in those cheap romantic paperback novels, or by teenagers having their first big crush. This was real life. And *true* love was something that only grew with time.

On her return home later after what had proven to be a busy day, finally ate dinner and cleaned the dishes, before making a start on another art project that had been running through her mind during the day. In the tranquillity of the spare room, she sat down at her easel and began to frantically sketch.

After an hour of pure concentration, with some trial and error, looked on with a smile of satisfaction as her latest piece of art began to take form.

She gave a start as her mobile rang loudly, breaking harshly through the silence from the small table holding her collection of paints. Seeing from the screen it was Dan, reluctantly took the call.

He enquired about her day and politely she replied that it had been busy but ok. His day also went quite well, he explained after what had been a shaky start which had almost resulted in a complaint from a major client that had thankfully been resolved. During the conversation, they made small talk about the weather and the fact there wasn't anything decent to watch on TV at the moment, with programmes not being as good as what they had been a few years ago.

He paused for a few seconds before asking if she was doing anything special on Saturday evening. It wasn't that he was being presumptuous he stressed a little nervously, but wondered if she would be interested in going to a charity dinner and dance being organised by his work. There were mostly couples going, he revealed solemnly and was almost on the verge of thinking of an excuse not to go; but with the proceeds of the evening to be donated to the hospice that cared for Margaret so well in her final days, felt this was something he couldn't miss.

After enlightening her about this piece of news and his reasons, how could she possibly refuse? He clearly wanted to have a night out and to remember the woman he loved in the nicest possible way. It was true on Saturday she'd already made arrangements to go out clothes shopping with Karen to look for a dress for the Global Life awards ceremony; but they'd made no plans for the evening as she was already going out with Andrew to some West End show that he'd got tickets to.

Yes, she said, she would love to go, wondering how Dan would introduce her to his friends and work colleagues. At this point in time she was not exactly in the throes of a relationship with him.

After hanging up, already began to regret her decision. She wasn't sure how she felt about meeting the people he worked with who knew him so much better, or worse still, the kind of reception she might receive. They were bound to be protective of their colleague and would undoubtedly be surprised that he had moved on so quickly from his recent loss and might also question her own motives. She gazed solemnly at the mobile still clutched firmly in her hand, thinking on a more positive note that she was long overdue a night out and there was a nice lacy black dress sitting in her wardrobe that would be just prefect for the occasion.

She glanced over to her painting from which she'd been interrupted only moments earlier, and nodded in approval as she studied the image she managed to capture, the moment when Jessica wearing her beautiful pink dress looked with delight towards both of them sitting in the audience as she sang to the timeless lyrics of *Greensleeves.* The love and happiness that shone in those beautiful green eyes was unmistakable. Picking up her paintbrush Laura continued from where she had left off, even though she was feeling tired despite of her unforgiving headache.

After a couple of times in which she was sick, her headache began to slowly ease. Despite all her best efforts over the following days, was unable to join Oscar and Jessica in the beautiful village that she was slowly growing to love. Her latest dreams had been very ordinary in comparison, with most of them having been forgotten by morning. As much as she valued her friendship with Karen, for some reason felt a deeper bond with Becky and their many years of friendship, even though the fact remained those pleasant memories only existed inside of her imagination.

Much to her own surprise Laura received a phone call from her mum asking if she would like to speak on Skype over the weekend. They were all missing her, Mum explained a little nervously and was sure that young Toby was almost beginning to forget about his Aunty Laura. Apart from photographs that she received through the post, and the occasional phone call, there had been little contact on her own part. The guilt was still raw after that surprise visit when

Mum and Lou had literally appeared on her doorstep. But to her greatest shame had taken the cowards option by quickly retreating into town on the bus without being seen. The guilt that they had drove all that way on a wasted journey and had been too spineless by ignoring their calls and texts asking her to get in touch.

After a few seconds of silence as an overwhelming feeling of panic swept over her, Laura tried to make her excuses, explaining she was going out shopping with Karen at the weekend and the following evening, which strictly speaking was true; but this time Mum wasn't to be deterred, insisting they could speak the night before. She was on the brink of saying that the camera wasn't working on her laptop, but knew Mum would see this for the ridiculously lame excuse this was, so she finally relented.

Her next few days at work were relatively uneventful, that was apart from a complaint made by an angry financial adviser that she needed to deal with, but that was all a part of the glamour in the job description for Team Manager. Karen as always very perceptive when it came to her friend knew there was something playing on her mind.

'Come on, what is it?' her friend demanded, her face stern as they sat at their PC's working on a *PowerPoint* presentation.

'I hope you're not still mad at me about speaking my mind over your dream man?'

She shook her head. 'Oh, of course I'm not. Besides, I love your honesty, even if it's not always what I want to hear.' Clicking the Save button, she let out a sigh. 'Mum wants to speak to me on Skype with Louise tonight.'

'And I take it from your apparent lack of enthusiasm that you're not so keen on the idea?'

Laura bit her bottom lip nervously. 'Now you put it like that, it does sound pretty awful that I don't want to chat to my own family, doesn't it?'

Karen's expression softened. 'Look, I do realise that you've not been particularly close to your family, at least since you moved to Minsden - but it really looks like they want to make things up with you.

'I know, but...'

'But yes, I understand it must be difficult and even without knowing the reasons for this rift, family is very important. Well, at least I think so.'

Giving a deep sigh, Laura knew her friend deserved the truth. 'Actually, there was no big row...no fallout, but I had to leave Dorset for my own good. To begin a new chapter of my life was what I needed to do.'

Her friend regarded her with sympathy. 'I guess I've got

no right to surmise without knowing all the facts why you made the decision to move away and start again - but what I do know is that you're clearly missing your family as much as they miss you. You never know, you just might *enjoy* the experience of speaking to them on Skype and it'll be a good chance for you all to clear the air.'

'I guess you're right,' she agreed reluctantly. 'I've got to admit I do miss them all. Like Mum said, Toby has probably forgotten all about the aunty he never sees.'

That evening Laura had little appetite for the lasagne that she'd heated up in the microwave, along with the fresh carrots and broccoli heaped on her plate. It was crazy to feel so nervous about the idea of speaking to her own mother and sister, she told herself; so *why* was her heart racing like crazy at the very thought? Guiltily, she emptied the contents into the food caddy, trying hard not to think of all the hungry people of the world.

As the time fast approached 8 o'clock, the time they agreed to Skype, her hands shaking, she nervously pressed the button on her laptop that sat perched on the coffee table.

While the machine loaded up, she went to the kitchen to pour herself a glass of white wine that had been chilling in the fridge. She took a long drink before leaving her glass in the kitchen. The last thing she needed was Mum and Louise being left with the impression she had turned into an alcoholic. That would *really* give them something to worry about!

Laura nervously placed herself on the edge of the sofa, with the laptop across her knees. It had been a long time since she'd logged onto Skype but was sure she still remembered her password. She typed it in slowly, but to her alarm was incorrect. Re-typing it again came with the same message. With a feeling of panic, her heart raced with the realisation if she got it wrong a third time, she would be locked out her account and would probably have to get her password reset.

With a twinge of guilt, a part of her felt relieved as this would give her a genuine reason not to speak to the family. But she quickly put those thoughts aside, as appreciated just how much Mum had been looking forward to this evening. Throughout the week she had texted her daughter several times to emphasise the fact, followed by some messages from Louise who was equally excited to be in contact with her older sister. Both clearly wanted to make sure she wouldn't change her mind and felt she owed it to them not to let them down.

Her attention turned back to her laptop as she suddenly remembered that some of the letters should have been in capitals. This time she typed them in slowly and breathed a sigh of relief as she managed to successfully log in. Much later once her mind cleared, realised that Louise would have been easily able to contact her through FaceTime had her attempts at logging in had failed completely.

She peered at her contacts list to all the friends and acquaintances that she hadn't spoken to in years, then saw that Louise was online, clearly waiting for her to get in touch.

Suddenly without warning, a call came through, displaying a photo of Louise with Toby on her lap, and husband Mike at her side.

Her heart racing wildly, she quickly smoothed her trembling hands over her hair before answering the call with more than a little feeling of apprehension.

On the screen of her laptop came images of Mum and Louise sitting there clearly looking every bit as nervous as she was feeling. The picture was surprisingly sharp thanks to the good broadband connection in Minsden.

By their animated smiles of delight, it was clear both could see their much-loved long-lost member of the family.

'Oh Laura!' Her mother cried out as she eagerly studied her daughter, overcome with emotion, before bursting into tears, causing Laura to do the same. It was plain to see her mum had aged considerably over the last three years. Her once smooth, radiant skin appeared tired and pale, with lines etched around her mouth more pronounced than she remembered and her eyes displayed a more sunken appearance. The dark shoulder length hair she once had was now sprinkled liberally with grey. As for Louise, her hair was longer than she remembered and appeared to be a few shades lighter.

For a few moments, they gazed in shocked silence towards Laura, unable to believe their luck at finally seeing her after all this time even if it was just through Skype. Without her realising, the tears were rolling down Laura's own face too, watching as Louise offered her mum a tissue before they dabbed their faces.

'Oh Mum! Louise!' She cried. 'I'm so sorry for letting you both down!'

'No, my darling,' interjected her mother. 'It's me that should be apologising. I'm the one that let you down. You should never have felt any reason to leave us!' With that she wept uncontrollably with Louise joining in as she huddled closer to her mum.

'No!' Laura cried out. 'Neither of you did anything wrong! After...after things as you know, I was in deep shock. You both knew what kind of place I was in for a long time - but you both got me through it. Without you, God only knows where I would have been.'

'It's so sweet of you to say,' replied her mother trying to compose herself. 'But if you'd managed to come to terms with... things, then you wouldn't have felt the need to go away and write us out of your life. Can you imagine how that makes us feel? There isn't a day goes by that I felt I could have done things better. Something to make you feel you didn't have to *escape.*'

Laura shook her head. 'No, Mum, no! There was nothing more you could have done any better - you were all amazing, even when I was being a right difficult cow. You both stuck by me and helped me get through things - heaven knows how you managed to put up with me.'

She wished she had that glass of wine close by to steady her nerves as her hands were shaking like crazy. Seeing that they were clearly heartbroken, she looked at them sternly. 'I'm the one that should be apologising. All you both did was to love me and to support me through those dark times. But I repaid you by leaving home and making a new life for myself. Selfish I realise now, but felt it was the only way I could forget everything...as if it had never really happened. A new job, a place of my own and new friends. I was being thoughtless and self-centred for not realising I was hurting all those that love me.'

'Oh sweetheart!' cried her mother. 'You're not being selfish and self-centred! You had to go through things that nobody should ever have to go through. For you, your only way was by making this fresh start.'

Laura decided to change the subject and to put the past firmly behind for everybody's sakes. 'How's everybody? And Toby? How's my favourite nephew? I bet he must have really grown these past three years!'

They both assured her they were all fine, but Laura could tell they were anything but fine. Mum was keeping busy she explained and was often out and about with the neighbours she'd known for many years. Louise was also getting on with life and had returned to work part-time as a receptionist at the car showroom where she had worked for many years; Mum was more than happy to take care of Toby in between. Mike was unable to join them on Skype Lou explained as was out on a stag night of a close friend.

Louise disappeared for a few brief moments announcing that she had a surprise. Within a couple of minutes, she was back with Toby sitting on her lap. His fair hair so much like his dad's but with those same pale blue eyes so similar to Louise's. She could see he was restless as Louise beckoned him to look at the computer screen.

'Look Toby, look who's here - it's Aunty Laura!' He reluctantly turned his attention turned towards the screen, suddenly looking very shy. When she'd left, he was barely two years old, she thought with sadness and was little wonder he was unable to remember her.

She peered at her young nephew with tears in her eyes, trying her best to give a friendly smile. 'Hello Toby! I'm your Aunty Laura. How are you, sweetheart? Mummy tells me you're doing very well at school and top of the class at reading!'

He listened, studying her intently and for a moment it looked as if he was about to smile. Maybe, just maybe there was a part of him that remembered her, she thought hopefully. But that thought was soon quashed as he suddenly wriggled out of his mum's arms and went off, probably to watch something on TV.

'Don't mind him,' Louise explained. 'He's watching *Topsy and Tim!*'

With absolutely no idea about who *Topsy and Tim* might be, they continued to catch up by exchanging news and both mum and sister were delighted that she had become a finalist for *Most Loved Manager* at Global Life.

'That doesn't surprise me one bit,' revealed her mother proudly. 'You always had a way with people and I'm sure you'll win. Is there any chance of us coming to see you?'

'It's for staff only, Mum,' Laura explained truthfully. 'Besides, I wouldn't get your hopes up too much because it's unlikely I'll get anywhere. Would you know I'm up against three very strong contenders? So, the competition is pretty stiff - but be sure to expect plenty of photos of the big night!'

'Are you still dating?' enquired her sister quickly changing the subject. Clearly Mum had shared her latest news.

Laura shrugged, as she thought back to the devious Julian. 'I'm afraid the one you're referring to didn't work out, but I'm kind of seeing somebody else, though it's still early days.'

Judging by the beaming smiles on their faces, they were delighted at the news.

'That's wonderful!' her mother gushed excitedly. 'It's great that you're dating again. Perhaps he might not turn out to be The One, but it's lovely to see you're moving on and having some fun!' Louise nodded approvingly.

They spoke for the best part of an hour about family and work when Laura announced she had to be up early to go shopping with Karen to look for a dress for the awards ceremony.

Her mother said that it would be nice for them to get together soon, either that she could come to them for the weekend or they could drive over to Minsden. She agreed it would be a nice idea, but not sure how she would feel about actually meeting them after all this time.

By the time she got to bed, her head was aching. Perhaps it was down to her migraine, or as she suspected, more likely down to all the turmoil of her first real conversation with her family since moving away.

As Laura climbed into her bed, tiredness suddenly swept over her, leaving her both physically and emotionally drained, not even having the energy to pick up her Kindle for a read. Despite her unforgiving migraine, within a few minutes of her head touching the pillow, fell into a deep sleep. After what might have been an hour, or perhaps two, she woke for no apparent reason. As she turned her head to the side, slowly opened her eyes, looking into the darkness of her bedroom; her heart missed a beat as she discovered Oscar watching over her.

With a combination of surprise and confusion, she quickly sat up, putting on her bedside light and it soon became evident she was still inside her own bedroom and not the cosy retreat of Rose Cottage.

His face registered with what appeared to be pity, Oscar knelt down bedside her gently placing a kiss on her lips. 'I'm sorry sweetheart, I didn't mean to frighten you, but you just looked so beautiful and peaceful while you slept.'

Laura smiled at this unexpected surprise. How could she possibly be frightened to see this lovely man who made her feel so happy...so alive? 'Hey, this is a lovely surprise! But I guess this is another dream, though I don't really care, because as far as I'm concerned this feels more real than anything in my life at the moment.'

He gently took hold of her hand, taking comfort from the warmth of his touch. 'It must have been quite an experience speaking to Angela and Louise on Skype tonight!'

She didn't question how he knew, as nothing surprised her about the whole situation. 'It was *quite* an experience,' she admitted.

'Do you feel it helped?' he asked gently.

Laura nodded. 'I felt after three years it was about time we had a real conversation apart from the occasional telephone call - I feel so bad for causing them so much hurt by finding any excuse not to see them,' She gazed at him intently, her green eyes sparkling with passion. 'This evening made me realise just how much I've missed the family - time has slipped by and now my own nephew doesn't even know who I am.'

Oscar watched her thoughtfully. 'I know it would mean a great deal to Angela and Louise if you were able to get together, even if it's just for the day.'

She felt anxious 'I don't know...'

His expression turned grim as he desperately tried to make her understand. 'Life is short, Laura, and we've got to make the best of every moment.'

He sat down on the bed beside her. 'Sweetheart, *please* arrange to meet them - I know you're not keen on going back home because of all the memories of what happened, but I'm sure you realise they're worried out of their minds over you. Maybe you could meet them half way, perhaps go somewhere for the day and spend some quality time together.'

She nodded wearily. 'You're right. It's crazy to keep behaving in this selfish way - they are my family for heaven's sake and they need me!'

'You need them too,' he reminded her softly, stroking his finger gently across the palm of her hand. 'Get together with them and enjoy - even if it's for just one last time, because family is *everything*'

Yes, she would call her mum and arrange to meet up, and despite what Oscar was telling her, it definitely wouldn't be for the last time. This would be the first of *many* times they would spend together.'

She stifled a yawn before he gently placed a kiss on her lips. 'Now go back to sleep,' he told her sternly but with a mischievous twinkle in his eyes. 'You've an early start with Karen tomorrow looking for something nice to wear for your big awards event. I strongly suggest to go for emerald green - that will match your beautiful eyes perfectly. Remember you have just the *perfect* jewels to match those to!'

Smiling blissfully, feeling completely at peace with herself after their frank and thought-provoking conversation,

Laura switched off her bedside light, as she placed her head back on the pillow. After giving a long yawn as she relaxed herself, glanced over to the side of the bed where Oscar had been only seconds ago and found he was gone.

CHAPTER THIRTEEN

I t was an early start for Laura, having to get up at 7.30 on a Saturday morning when normally she would have enjoyed a lie-in. But once showered, she soon felt more awake and her migraine a little less intense. Her mind regressed back to last night's emotional conversation with Mum and Louise with mixed feelings. As much as she was glad to have spent time with her family albeit over Skype, the whole ordeal had left her feeling emotionally drained, bringing to the surface some memories she would rather have left buried. As she towelled herself down, she thought back to the moment Oscar appeared in her bedroom. Although she accepted it was just another dream, clearly recalled the sound of his steady breathing as he watched over her; the feel of the freshly laundered bedsheets so cool against her skin. Most of all she remembered the touch of his fingers gently caressing her skin.

She managed to eat some breakfast before Karen arrived at 9 o'clock on the dot, calling her from her mobile, waiting outside the flat to pick her up. Taking a final swallow of her mug of coffee and emptying the remainder down the sink, left to join her friend who was waiting patiently in her Volvo parked alongside the kerb. After a quick debate, they decided to go to one of the neighbouring towns with a large shopping centre hosting a greater variety of shops. On the way, Laura updated her friend about the difficult and emotional conversation she'd had with her mum and Louise, not daring to mention about her surprise visit from Oscar.

'Oh, that's fantastic!' Karen gushed excitedly, turning to her briefly before negotiating the road ahead. 'You *needed* to have that conversation, it's so important to keep those family ties alive.' Her face became solemn. 'There are just so many times I've wished I could have said all the things I wanted to say to my dad - so many things I could have done better. He died so suddenly and I never got that chance. Make the most of *every* moment.'

'From now on I will,' Laura promised sympathetically. 'Mum and Louise want us to get together soon to spend some time together.'

'I hope you said yes!'

She hesitated for a moment. 'I will. I've got to admit I don't feel ready to go back home, so I might arrange somewhere we can meet.'

'Why not invite them to *yours*?' Karen suggested. 'You have a nice flat in a good part of town - definitely nothing to be ashamed of!'

Although still quite early in the morning, the town was already getting busy, with the bright weather attracting shoppers intending to take full advantage of all the sales taking place.

After going to a few boutiques, with neither of them having found quite what they were looking for, finally decided to try their luck at Debenhams. Karen found a nice electric blue dress and another in pink at half price ready to try on. After some searching amongst the eveningwear Laura found a beautiful, long evening dress in the very emerald green Oscar suggested.

'That looks lovely,' remarked Karen looking admiringly at the dress. 'I wouldn't get away with a colour or a style like that, but it'd definitely suit you.'

After going to the changing room, she tried it on, gazing at her reflection in the long mirror, knowing within an instant this would definitely earn a big thumbs-up from Oscar. The long, strapless green satin creation fitted perfectly to her body, accentuating her narrow waist, as the glossy material flared down to her ankles. She twirled, studying her mirror image, seeing how the strapless top displayed her shoulders, with the small embroidered beaded pearls adding some sparkle around the bustline.

As she left the changing room to seek a second opinion from her friend, Karen blinked with astonishment, never having seen her friend looking quite this beautiful before.

'Oh, wow, you look absolutely stunning! That's definitely your colour and the style really does suit you. I don't want to make you big-headed,' she added with a grin, 'but you'd definitely give one of those Hollywood A-listers a run for their money.'

Feeling somewhat taken aback, Laura laughed. 'Well, I'm not quite so sure about being A-lister standard, but after a compliment like that, I guess I'll have no choice but to buy it!'

Noting Laura's less than enthusiastic response to her chosen outfit, Karen gazed at her own reflection in the long mirror with unmasked disappointment. 'It's not me, is it?' she remarked. 'Come on, be truthful, because it's written all over your face.'

It was true, the light pink shade did little to flatter her pale skin tone, Laura mused and fitted just a little too snugly over her generous hips.

'Try the other dress,' she suggested diplomatically deciding honesty was the best policy. 'I think blue is more the colour for you.'

After a few minutes, Karen came out of the changing room wearing her second choice. The long evening dress with its looser fitting far more flattering to her curvier figure, the vibrant blue making her fair hair appear an even brighter shade of blonde. The silver sequins around the neckline added just the right amount of razzmatazz for an awards ceremony.

'You look sensational,' Laura said truthfully. 'You'll definitely be the belle of the ball!'

Karen grinned. 'Oh, what are we like handing out all these compliments to each other.' With a wink she added, 'But you're right. We *are* sensational and we'll really knock them out at the awards!'

'Absolutely. No doubt, we're simply the best - and we ought to be at the prices they charge here!'

'Hmm, you're not wrong there. But who cares when it's for such a special occasion - to see my best friend, pick up the trophy for the *Most Loved Manager* award!'

Laura rolled her eyes towards the ceiling with a grin. 'Well, looks like I've certainly got a lot to live up to, so no pressure!' Hey, shall we go for a coffee? Don't know about you, but I feel I could do with a caffeine shot after such an early start - my treat. Then maybe we can go and look for some shoes to complete our Hollywood look!'

When they finally arrived back to Minsden a little later

than anticipated after getting stuck in heavy traffic, Karen popped into the flat to collect a novel Laura had read and recommended for bedtime reading. Unlike her friend who was more into e-books these days, Karen preferred the feel and smell of a good old paperback or hardback copy.

Whilst Laura dropped her carrier bags onto the sofa announcing she had to pop to the toilet, Karen made her way to the spare room knowing where her friend kept all her favourite reads.

She quickly found the book lying on top of a pile of sketchpads placed on a stool. Giving a smile as she picked up the well-worn paperback, with turned-up corners of the pages, knowing Laura who could never resist a bargain had probably been bought at one of the second-hand bookstalls in town. Karen would often tease her good naturedly about being too thrifty by not going to *Waterstones*, but her argument had always been that it was the quality of the story that mattered, not the book itself. Maybe Laura was right she thought giving a shrug, and was probably the reason she now opted for a Kindle to read her books these days. Knowing her to be a minimalistic kind of person would see this as doing away with the clutter.

Her attention was caught for the first time by the easel set back in the far corner of the room. With a frown marking her forehead, studied the painting Laura had been working on laboriously, with the image of the handsome man, knew this had to be the non-existent Oscar looking boldly at her from the canvas. As she gazed into those brown twinkling eyes, with the dark hair slightly ruffled and the heart-melting roguish smile, Karen began to understand why Dan hadn't managed to completely capture her friend's heart so far. For some reason there was something strikingly familiar about him she mused, but was sure he couldn't have been a man she'd crossed paths with before. As she gently touched the painting with her fingertips, realised there was another painting hidden underneath. She gently turned the paper and her eyes immediately fixed firmly to the image of a young girl with long, dark hair. As she looked into the wide, innocent green eyes of the child, Karen's face turned as white as a sheet.

She flinched guiltily as Laura entered the room, watching her with a frown, 'Did you manage to find the book?'

'Yes...I did. I'm sorry I didn't mean to pry, I was just...'

Her face softening, waved her hand dismissively. 'Hey, it's ok - just some paintings I did, a little something to do in the evenings...you know.' She couldn't help noticing her friend was looking as if she had seen a ghost. 'Is everything ok?' she enquired with a teasing smile. 'Don't you think much to my artwork?'

Karen tried to compose herself. 'I do. Actually, I think

they're really lovely. I guess the first one doesn't need any introductions - your Oscar looks seriously hot.' She nervously bit her bottom lip gazing back to the portrait of the beautiful young girl. 'Is...is this *the* Jessica you mentioned to me? The daughter of Oscar? It's a gorgeous painting...she...she's very pretty.' Reluctantly turning her attention away from the painting stared at Laura intently.

'Are you sure you're ok?' Laura asked, beginning to feel more than a little concerned about her friend, whose face had turned pale and appeared more than a little troubled.

'I'm fine,' she reassured her, forcing a smile. 'I guess the shopping trip and that crazy traffic took it out of me a bit.' She glanced at her watch. 'Well, I'd best get moving - I need to get ready fast before me and Andrew get the train into London. Thanks for the book - I've been meaning to read this one for ages!'

'You'll love it,' Laura promised. 'It's a real page-turner. Have a great time this evening.'

She walked into her bedroom and opened the door to her wardrobe, lifting out the painting of Rose Cottage with its surrounding garden in full bloom. Now mounted in a silver frame by the arts and craft shop in town, made a promise to herself to make time later to hang on the wall directly opposite her bed. What could possibly be any better than waking up each morning than to feast her eyes on this perfect setting? But first she needed to call her mum to arrange a weekend when they could all meet.

The following week at Global Life went along fairly smoothly, apart from when Charlotte, her apprentice turned up late for work on Tuesday morning, her normally rosy complexion looking distinctly pale and was unusually quiet. It was within less than an hour of slowly getting through the morning's post when she rushed to the toilet and was violently sick. On returning to the office claimed she had woken up feeling unwell with a stomach upset, but Laura heard whispers from a few of her least loyal colleagues that she'd been out partying and had over-done on the drinking.

Seeing that the girl was in no fit state to work, decided to send her home. Because this was so out of character with her normal behaviour, chose to go along with her story about having picked up a sickness bug.

Karen was looking more than a little bemused as she logged back on to her computer. 'I know it's your call, but are you sure you should've let her off so lightly?'

'Yes,' she replied without hesitation. 'And to tell you the truth I don't think she's got off with anything lightly - I can see she's got the hangover from hell and she'll be paying the price for the rest of the day and maybe beyond.'

'You're not wrong there because she did look pretty rough.'

Laura glanced at the many incoming emails she would need to see to within the next hour. 'She's learned a harsh life lesson about over-doing the booze, and I'll let her off just this once having been there myself at her age.'

'Me and you both,' said Karen with a grin. 'Each time I swore I would *never* touch alcohol again. That lasted all of two days! Mind you I find as I get older I've become much more of a lightweight.' She saw her friend was distracted by a message on her mobile.

'It's from Mum,' Laura explained. 'We've made arrangements to meet at my place this weekend then spend the day at the zoo. The weather's meant to be good so thought it would be something nice for Toby to see all the animals.'

'That sounds great. Feeling a bit nervous?'

'Yes,' she admitted, clutching onto her smartphone in thought. 'It's going to feel pretty surreal and for sure it's going to be very emotional. But I've got to say, it'll be so good to meet them after all this time.'

Karen looked at her with sympathy. 'I'm sure you'll all have an amazing time. Just focus on enjoying spending time with them and the day ahead of you.'

That was sound advice she thought, and drew some

comfort from what Mum had also mentioned in her text. When she stressed there was no need to discuss the past if that was her wish.

'Have you heard any more from Dan?' Karen enquired, taking a sip of her coffee.

'Yes, he gave me a call last night and always sends me little texts in between.'

'That's sweet. So, are you all set for his works do this Friday?'

'As ready as I'll ever be! No doubt his colleagues will be curious about me.'

'Oh, *let* them be curious! I'm sure they'll be pleased he's met someone who's put a smile back on his face.'

Laura was cynical. 'Too early days to come to that conclusion!'

Her friend looked stern. 'Laura Winters, just for once, take your mind off your imaginary man and his daughter and just enjoy a fun night out with a guy that really does exist and is very much into you!'

The next few days seemed to fly by without any major events or dreams of returning to Rose Cottage. As far as she could remember, her sleep had been without any dreams at all. There had been times in between, she'd been on the verge of making her excuses not to go on her date. It was true she faced an early start the following day as Mum and Louise were hoping to be in Minsden for 10 o'clock, but she had no desire to explain herself by going into details with Dan about the special reunion with her family. Having an upset stomach or a cold sounded too cliché and knowing her luck would come down with either or worst still, both! Besides the evening was his way of remembering Margaret and didn't have the heart to spoil this for him.

Laura put on the silver heart-shaped necklace that matched the earrings she would be wearing for the evening, looking long and hard at her reflection in the long mirror of her wardrobe. The little black dress was always unbeatable for any occasion, she mused, especially a works dinner and dance. Not that she was likely to dance, she thought as she thought with smile. Somehow, Dan didn't strike her as the kind to be the life and soul of any party, so little doubt she would be spending the evening watching other couples dance as he discussed work, or perhaps Margaret or even his ex-wife.

After a spray or two of her favourite perfume, the intercom buzzed as her date for the evening arrived. She picked up her jacket and handbag, taking one last glance of herself in the mirror before finally leaving.

Dan as always being the perfect date, paid compliments

on her dress and how beautiful she looked. For the evening he was dressed smartly in a dark suit with a deep red tie, and from the strong heady aroma hanging inside the car, had been very liberal with his aftershave. Although Laura wouldn't have described him as particularly handsome, felt he'd made a great deal of effort with his appearance.

Along the brief journey to Minsden Community Centre where the function was being held, he briefed Laura about what to expect of the evening. He went into detail about the local band that would be playing, with a chance to win some great prizes on a raffle. He mentioned some of colleagues he was particularly close to and how all the proceeds for the evening would be donated to the hospice that had cared so well for Margaret.

When they pulled up in the car park, Laura began to feel quite nervous as she processed everything he'd told her and worried she would be judged by his work buddies. When they entered the building he gently took hold of her hand and was sure he must have felt her palms getting sweaty with anxiety.

As they entered the hall with Locked Out of Heaven by Bruno Mars playing in the background, Dan was immediately greeted by some of his colleagues, shaking hands, clearly eager to be introduced to Laura who they regarded with undisguised curiosity. The first was the area manager, John Sterling and his wife Fiona, followed by his other workmates, husband and wife, Steve and Claire who Dan both worked closely with.

At the bar where more than a few people took a sneaky glimpse or two her way, Dan bought her a Bacardi and coke which she quickly took a gulp of to steady her nerves. Steve's wife, Claire tried to stifle a giggle as she watched on with amusement, suggesting kindly to space out her drinks as she wouldn't be steady on her feet when it was time to get onto the dancefloor with her later!

Laura smiled apologetically, realising by Claire's empathetic nature that she could see she was clearly terrified and nodded in agreement as she peered with embarrassment at her half full glass. The woman was right, she thought; the last thing she wanted to do was to get completely wasted and make Dan look a complete fool, by giving a false impression to those he had to see on a daily basis that he was dating some alcoholic. As far as she was concerned she was here this evening to help Dan remember Margaret and despite Claire's presumptions, there was no way she would even contemplate strutting her stuff on the dancefloor, especially not with anybody she barely knew.

As everybody made their way to the tables with places specially designated with name cards, Dan sat directly opposite her, with John Sterling sitting to her left and Claire to her right. The music came to a stop abruptly, with the chatting coming to an end as a tall portly man in a charcoal grey suit stepped onto the stage. Claire whispered excitedly in her ear that this was Alex Chapman, the CEO for the chain of warehouses, with Minsden being just one of ten other branches across the country.

Chapman made his opening speech by wishing everybody a fabulous evening. He ran his audience through the itinerary for the evening, which he announced would begin with the up and coming local band called *Blue Jump*, followed by a delicious three-course dinner being served. Later, he informed his audience, there would be a raffle with the chance to win some wonderful prizes and how it was dearly hoped as much would be raised as possible for the Heart of Minsden Hospice, in memory, he stated solemnly, of Margaret Mealing, the loved one of one of their own loyal members of staff who'd been cared for so well in her final weeks.

Laura's heart melted when she watched Dan bow his sadly with others looking his way in sympathy as Claire whispered in her ear dabbing her eyes with a tissue, how heart-breaking it all was.

On a lighter note, the CEO ran through all the great achievements made by the company so far in the past year and proudly mentioned some of the prestigious awards won by the company. Chapman watched his audience with pride as he informed them this was a reflection on all the amazing people that worked for the company and that each and every one of them should be proud of what had they had contributed to make this all possible.

With a wry smile and a knowing wink, he remarked he was sure they would all be pleased to know he'd now finished his piece and would allow them to enjoy the rest of the evening before asking them to give it up for *Blue Jump*. The audience gave a tremendous round of applause, with some loud whistles thrown in as he walked off the stage.

Everybody clapped and cheered as the band began to play, setting the scene with their rendition of *Outkast*'s *Hey Ya!* Claire informed Laura with enthusiasm that she'd been to a few of the band's gigs where they would often play at local clubs and colleges and were knockout. Within next to no time the starter was being served for the three-course meal that had been pre-ordered some days before. Laura nodded her approval as she tasted her carrot and coriander soup, with Dan looking over to her as he dutifully filled her glass with Pino Grigio Blush. Claire who coincidentally had chosen the same soup as Laura complained it didn't have enough seasoning for her liking, sprinkling it liberally with a ton of salt.

Laura found the fillet of sea bass that followed later was

delicious, but felt let down by the over-cooked vegetables. She rolled her eyes in despair as Dan left his carrots, protesting he hated most vegetables with the exception of broccoli.

Once the waitresses came around to clear up their plates after dessert, Claire grabbed Laura enthusiastically by the arm as she led her to the dance floor, with Dan waving his hand dismissively to let her know that was ok with him.

Over the loud music, they somehow managed to exchange snatches of conversation as Claire briefed her on Dan's turbulent marriage with Madelyn and how it affected their two sons for some time. She admitted that although his relationship had been fairly brief with Margaret, it was soon clear to see that they were really into one another and so sad that it all had to come to an end in the way it did. Mistaking the troubled look on Laura's face for sadness, Claire added brightly how it was great to see that Dan had finally found someone that could make him happy again, as hadn't seen him smile as much as he did of late.

There was one thing she could say about Claire, thought Laura and that was for a forty-something like herself, had plenty of energy as she danced relentlessly. Maybe it was mainly thanks to all the alcohol, but despite her earlier promise to herself not to get up and dance, Laura felt completely energised and found herself moving along in a way that she hadn't done since her clubbing days; but after a while even her energy began to flag, unlike Claire who gave many of the younger people a run for their money with many taking a breather by making their way to the bar or to chat with friends and colleagues.

After almost an hour of nonstop boogying, much to Laura's relief, the music came to a stop to make way for the raffle draw. Earlier she'd bought four tickets, with Claire clutching excitedly to six strips of her own. Discovering one of her numbers came up, her newly found buddy gave a loud shriek of delight, learning she'd won a weekend for two at a health spa. Much to her own surprise, Laura won a bottle of red wine, with Dan clapping proudly as she went to claim her prize. As she gingerly made her way to the stage could feel all eyes fixed firmly on her, watching her with unmasked curiosity as they cheerfully applauded.

Laura returned to her chair, with a heavy feeling in her heart, and her face solemn as she clutched onto her bottle of Shiraz. It was at that moment she knew that she couldn't do this to Dan. After tonight was over and done with, she would make her excuses not to see him again. There was absolutely no chemistry on her part as far as she was concerned, especially when much to her own shame gladly allowed herself to spend the best part of the evening with the chatty and lively

Claire, leaving poor Dan to his own devices. With her mind taken over by thoughts of Oscar, knew without a doubt she loved him deeply, even though the fact remained there was zero chance of taking things further. Why did life have to be so unfair, she thought with sadness. They might only exist inside of head along with the village and Rose Cottage, but Oscar and Jessica felt every bit as real as anybody she knew in her real life; not to mention her special bond with Becky.

Blue Jump returned to the stage with the music settting to a slower pace with a rendition of *Unchained Melody*. It came as an unexpected surprise when Dan invited her for a dance; not sure what to say, glanced over to Claire who was already up and ready to dance with her Steve. Maybe it was down to all the wine she'd drank, but felt she couldn't refuse his offer without drawing attention from his colleagues. Together they took to the dance floor and allowed herself to be enfolded into his arms for the very first time. The feeling wasn't as unpleasant as she had first anticipated, as he slowly led her around the room. He asked softly in her ear if she had enjoyed the evening which she replied truthfully, she had but felt it would have been cruel to add that was mainly thanks to the bubbly Claire. As he held her closer still, he informed her he was sure a lot of money had been raised tonight for The Heart of Minsden Hospice and the grand total would very likely be announced at work on Monday or Tuesday; but he would keep her posted, he promised.

Dan informed her with his voice thick with emotion that Margaret would have been so chuffed about this evening's event and what had been raised, thrilled how this would go a long way in helping others in the final stages of their lives. That was one thing Laura couldn't disagree with and for some reason felt an overwhelming feeling of sadness. The song finished and continued with Lionel Richie's *Hello* as he held her closer still no doubt thinking back to all the happy times with his lost love. As the song came to an end, he glanced at his watch, his face stern as he suggested it was probably time to head for home, if she didn't mind. No, she assured him with a sense of relief, glad that she would soon be home and tucked up in her bed. With the anticipation of her early start tomorrow for her long-awaited family reunion was keen to make sure she felt at her best after a good night's sleep.

The slow songs played on with Claire snugly in her husband's arms, almost sleepily peering over her shoulder as she spotted Laura leaving the dance floor with Dan. Realising the couple were about to leave, gave a wave and called out to Laura how lovely it was to meet her, before giving a knowing wink and a thumbs-up sign. She waved back with a forced smile, knowing with certainty there was absolutely no chance of anything happening in the way she was suggesting.

As they slipped out into the night, gave a shudder as the cold evening air made contact against her skin. Maybe it was down to the drink or more likely once away from the party atmosphere, when Laura was swept over by a huge tide of sadness as her own bitter memories floated to the surface; memories she would much rather forget about forever. When he politely suggested they pop back to his place for a coffee, as the boys were at their mum's, she immediately took him up on his offer. As if for the very first time suddenly became all too aware that all she had to look forward to was going home to an empty flat; so really just going back for a quick coffee and nothing else was absolutely fine.

They pulled up on the short driveway to his semi-detached house in the cul-de-sac where he lived, and climbed out of his car. Judging by most of the houses shrouded in darkness, most of the neighbours had long retired for the evening.

Inside, felt warm and welcoming as he led her into the living room. While he prepared the coffee in the kitchen, she took in her surroundings. The burgundy leather sofa with black décor furniture adding a distinct masculine feel to the surroundings. On the mantelpiece over the electric fireplace complete with artificial flames, sat a couple of framed photographs with Dan and his two teenaged sons at each side of him smiling brightly towards the camera.

He brought in the coffee on a tray, complete with sugar bowl and a small jug of milk. They had only seen each other a few times so had no idea that now she took her coffee. He chuckled seeing her wince as she watched him scoop three heaped teaspoons of sugar into his own cup, admitting with a sheepish grin he knew it wasn't good for him but he'd always had a sweet tooth.

He took a sip of his coffee before sinking back on the leather sofa letting out a deep sigh, admitting that the evening as wonderful as it was had really taken it out of him emotionally. She looked thoughtfully into her own coffee, taking comfort from the warmth of the cup she held with both hands, feeling an overwhelming feeling of sadness as a tear trickled slowly down her cheek.

As Laura wiped away the tears with a tissue she found in her handbag, watched on with curiosity as Dan took the cup from her hands placing this alongside his own on the tray. Gently, he turned her face towards his as he kissed her lightly on her lips. Much to her own surprise, she responded by kissing him fiercely as he held her closely in his arms, running his fingers frantically through her hair.

He stopped for a moment watching her intently, his

enlarged pupils making his normally pale eyes seem dark and mysterious, both of them breathless as they contemplated what had just happened. Without thinking they both stood up, as he led her by the hand, climbing the stairs to his bedroom.

Laura woke, peering over towards Dan at her side, still soundly asleep, listening to the sound of his gentle snores. For a moment, she'd hoped it was all just a bad dream, but as she placed a finger to her lips still sore from his urgent kisses, inhaled the pungent aroma of his aftershave lingering on her skin, with harsh reality washing over her, as her mind slowly processed all that had happened. Gently, she eased herself from his arm that was placed around her firmly, grateful that he was a heavy sleeper before quickly getting herself dressed. Not an easy feat when the room was shrouded in darkness and was glad of the slight gap in the closed curtains, allowing her to make full use of the street lighting outside. While he was still asleep she decided she would call for a taxi and be gone before he woke up.

As her mind wondered back to earlier events, she felt herself being gripped by an overwhelming feeling of panic at what had happened. What on earth made her jump into bed with him in the way she had? It wasn't as if she felt anything for him and-

Her thoughts were suddenly interrupted as Dan switched on his bedside light, the dazzling light flooding the room in brightness that blinded her for a moment. He watched her, his expression grim as she finished putting on her dress.

Feeling foolish at being caught in the act of walking out on him, explained she hadn't wanted to wake him, but reluctantly admitted what happened had been a huge mistake on her part. Seeing the hurt look etched on his face at her news, quickly assured him this was no reflection on him, but was the first time she had done anything of this kind in a very long time. It was soon becoming apparent there had also been regrets on his part when he admitted this was the first time he'd slept with anyone since Margaret, before holding his hands to his face in despair. No longer feeling nervous and embarrassed, instead began to feel pity for him, sitting on the edge of the bed letting out a deep sigh as she looked towards the ceiling becoming lost in her own thoughts, as her mind wandered back to happier times. Times, she never thought would come to an end.

He gazed at her apologetically, his face looking drawn making him appear older, offering to give her a lift if she wasn't in a mind to stay over. He wouldn't have her going home in a taxi at this time of the morning, he insisted and wanted to

make sure she got home safely.

She went downstairs while he got dressed, not wanting to witness seeing his naked body a moment longer even though just a short time ago neither of them had left anything to each other's imagination.

He re-joined her in the living room where she sat perched uncomfortably on the leather sofa, peering across to the photos sitting on the mantelpiece with the clock on the wall seeming to tick louder than what it had done before.

They both drove back in silence with neither of them having anything left to say. He dropped her off outside of her flat, this time with not so much as a peck on the cheek or the promise of any future dates to meet. Laura knew in her heart that this would be the last time they would ever see each other again. After last night it became crystal clear neither of them was anywhere near ready to embark on another relationship. He smiled sadly as she left the car and being the perfect gentleman, waited until she was safely in the flat before driving off, never to return.

Laura breathed a sigh of relief as she switched on the light to the living room. It was at that the moment as she gazed at the empty sofa, listening to the sound of silence, realised just how incredibly lonely her life was and broke down in huge sobs of tears that shook her body.

After there were no further tears inside her to shed, took a hot shower, scrubbing away any last traces of Dan from her body, leaving her skin red and raw. The time was 3.30 in the morning with just a few hours remaining before Mum and Louise would be appearing at her door. How she wished she hadn't arranged for this weekend to meet them, she thought grimly; but knew had she that put them off for another week would only cause more upset and disappointment all round, especially for her mum and couldn't bear the thought of causing anymore heartbreak.

Quickly climbing into her own bed where she felt safe and comfortable after all the turmoil of the evening, didn't expect to fall asleep so quickly. She opened her eyes to find herself standing in the garden of Rose Cottage on the middle of the front garden; through narrowed eyes she glimpsed the tangerine sun in the sky beginning to set in the west. Her attention then turned towards the cottage noticing Oscar waiting for her expectantly outside the front door, his expression as if unsure what to expect from her. Unable to wait a second further, she rushed down the pathway into his arms, where she felt safe and warm.

As he held her firmly close to him, she immediately broke down in a flood of tears. 'I'm *sorry!*' she gasped through heavy sobs, I'm so, so *sorry!*'

He kissed her lightly on her hair as she leaned her head on his shoulder. 'Hush my sweetheart, you have nothing at all to apologise for. I promise.' Taking comfort from his loving embrace, she relaxed until her weeping finally came to an end. He took her by the hand as she wiped away her tears. 'Come, step inside and have a nice hot cup of coffee - Jessica's very eager to show you her latest painting!'

She managed a weak smile, feeling after what had proven to be a very difficult day, that she had finally arrived home.

CHAPTER FOURTEEN

L aura woke early the next morning, at best having only had four hours' sleep. Through blurred vision she gazed at the luminous display on the bedside clock, with a deep sigh, guiltily wishing she wasn't having this long-awaited reunion with her family today of all days.

She picked up her mobile kept on silent and saw apart from a couple of the usual emails from Amazon and Superdrug, there hadn't been messages any from Dan. Feeling a combination of disappointment and annoyance, her mouth set firmly into a grimace. Although she realised now without a doubt that she had no desire to embark on a relationship with him, a small part of her expected to at least receive a text to see how she was; after all last night had been quite a big deal. Well, at least it had been for *her*. But really, *why* should he? What was there left to say? After last night he'd made it perfectly clear that he wasn't ready to move on from Margaret and rightly or wrongly, knew she would never be able to fully give her heart to any other man apart from Oscar.

An inner peace came over her as her mind regressed back to last night's return to Rose Cottage and her pleasant evening spent with Oscar and Jessica, where they took Duke for a walk around the village. Along the way they would chat to people, some she had already become acquainted with at Jessica's school concert, a few others for the very first time. Much to her trepidation they crossed paths with Maggie walking towards the Silver Lion pub about to begin her shift. For a barmaid she was very much lacking in people skills, Laura mused, with that same solemn expression as she had glared at them within her previous dream. So, it came as quite a pleasant surprise when she suddenly gave the warmest of smiles, immediately adding a natural beauty to her pale face. As they passed her by, Laura took one final glance over her shoulder as Maggie continued to watch her in what could only be described as pity.

On their return to the cottage, Jez Turner dropped by, bringing along a bag of homegrown tomatoes and carrots. Over a much-appreciated glass of beer he made some pleasant conversation, where much to her surprise Laura discovered the kindly man had moved to the village at pretty much the same time as Oscar and Jessica. Despite their protests at his flying visit, he wouldn't stay too long he stressed, as didn't want to outstay his welcome and encroach on their special time together.

She studied herself in the bathroom mirror gazing back at her reflection; the face that looked back at her was pale, with the skin appearing to have an almost grey tinge, with sunken eyes circled with dark shadows from months of broken sleep. What on earth would Mum and Louise think of her looking like some sleep-deprived zombie?

She immersed herself in the warm shower, trying to scrub any further traces that might have remained from their regretted night of passion, even though she'd already showered thoroughly before retiring to bed.

It was just as she'd finished getting herself ready and microwaved some porridge, when she received a call from Mum. Already feeling bad at hoping they wouldn't be able to make it after all, reluctantly took the call.

'Nothing to worry about, sweetheart,' her mum announced reassuringly. 'We're just stuck in traffic - the tailback seems to be going on forever! It looks like there's been some accident further along the motorway, hopefully nothing too serious. We seem to moving on a little faster so hopefully we shouldn't be *too* long!'

Laura tried to keep her mind occupied by catching up on some dusting that had been neglected over the past week. She was eager to prove to her mum and sister that she was managing ok.

Her mum was as good as her word when the intercom buzzed loudly at about 10 am, startling her while she sat nervously on the sofa brushing some imaginary dust from her trousers. Nervously as her heart began to race, pressed the button to allow her family to come up to her flat.

Unsurprisingly the reunion was a very emotional scene where apart from Toby, there were more than a few tears being shed.

Her mum held her tightly as if she would never let her go, gazing at her through tears that smudged her mascara. '*My little girl*! Oh, it's so good to see you, darling. I've missed you *so* much!' She looked at her mother while she dabbed her own eyes with a tissue, noticing she somehow appeared smaller than she remembered and could see just how much she'd seemed to have aged in the past three years.

Louise looked at her sister with tears slipping down her own cheeks as she held Laura firmly in her arms. There were times in the past when the siblings hadn't always seen eye to eye, but whatever differences they might have shared, their love for one another had always remained strong.

At first glance Louise appeared as beautiful as ever with her long fair hair lighter than she remembered before leaving town, but on closer scrutiny looked slimmer and more fatigued as if she hadn't slept well in a long time. She only hoped that was down to bringing up a young child and that she wasn't sole the cause of her stress.

Laura peered down to Toby, studying the adults with a puzzled expression as he sucked on his thumb. She knelt down, giving him a kiss on the cheek which he quickly rubbed away with his hand, before hiding shyly behind his mum as he continued to watch her.

Louise smiled lovingly at her son. 'Hey, that's your Aunty Laura who I'm always telling you about. I guess you don't remember, but she always spoiled you rotten with loads of toys and clothes when you were just a baby.' She gave her sister a teasing wink. 'But I guess she's entitled to do that seeing that she also happens to be your godmother too!'

Laura glanced guiltily at her nephew. 'Not that I've been much of a godmother to him these past few years.'

'*Stop thinking that way!*' her mum chided gently. 'That was down to circumstances at the time. What matters now is that we're all here together as it should be. That's what's important.'

Laura made some tea for her mum and sister who'd travelled some distance to come and see her, giving a glass of lemonade to Toby, along with some paper and crayons bought especially for the occasion to keep him occupied.

Her mum took a sip of her tea, sighing contentedly. 'I really needed this after that journey - just typical to get stuck in a hold-up today of all days. She looked around the room, taking in her surroundings. 'Well, I must say you have furnished your flat beautifully. I know it's very different to where you lived before...but it's very nice all the same.'

Louise watched her sister with concern as she blinked rapidly for a moment, before gazing vacantly into her teacup as she reflected on the reasons that had brought her all the way to Minsden. 'Hey, it's ok, sis,' she said softly as if reading her thoughts. 'All that matters now is the present - we can see you're very happy here. So, all you need to do is focus on now and the future. Ok?'

She smiled at her Louise apologetically. 'Oh, don't mind me Lou, I'm fine. Really. I just didn't sleep all that great last night.'

Louise peered down at Toby sitting on the floor busily colouring away on a figure he'd drawn and coloured bright green. 'I think that's meant to be Aunty Laura,' she remarked with a grin.

'That's very nice, Toby,' she said brightly, praising her young nephew.

He looked at his aunt shyly, before handing her his work of art.

'Oh, thank you, sweetheart! I'll hang this up on the fridge later - I *love* it!' Just maybe there was a small part of him that remembered her even though he was very young before she went away.'

Just before they were about to head to the zoo, her mum wanted to pop to the bathroom and mistakenly tried to open the study which was locked firmly. Giving a puzzled frown, she wondered just exactly what it was that her daughter had to hide.

Within less than an hour they arrived at Whipsnade Zoo, in Louise's Range Rover, deciding to use the car park rather than take the vehicle into the grounds. Because of the particularly fine weather, meant there was more visitors than usual and had to queue for a good while before being able to get their entry tickets.

They all had an amazing time as they took full advantage of their programme guide, watching *Birds of The World* where exotic macaws, hawks and owls would swoop over the audience. To begin with Toby was a little scared, worrying he might be their next meal, but once he realised he would come to no harm, thoroughly enjoyed the whole experience.

Plenty of photos were taken of the elephants, giraffes and tigers and Laura's young nephew enjoyed interacting with the Lemurs. Most of all he loved the children's zoo and the penguins. The day seemed to go by much too fast but to her delight, Laura found the bond with her nephew becoming stronger, with Louise capturing those tender moments on camera, taking as many pictures as possible of the two of them together.

When they had their dinner in the zoo restaurant, an expensive alternative to a picnic, but more convenient not to mention this was a special occasion, one of the waitresses kindly offered to take a photo of the four of them together. Laura knew she would treasure that picture until the day she died.

She could say hand on heart, that today was one of the happiest days she had experienced in a very long time. In the past, there had been some amazing moments to look back on with fondness, but to reunite with her family was definitely amongst the very best. She watched Toby happily tucking away into his ice cream, with some of the contents smeared around his face, which Louise quickly wiped away with a wet wipe. She thought back to her own memories as a child when Nanna Eve would come along with them to outings at the zoo. Coming back to the present, her face grim, couldn't help feeling she had robbed herself of some of the most important years of seeing Toby growing up and spending time with her family.

When they stopped off at a country pub on the drive home, sat out in the grounds at a table, making the most of the glorious sunshine, keeping an eye on Toby close by as he sat on a swing in the children's play area. Louise had taken out her iPad from the Range Rover and treated Laura to some photos of the family. She explained her husband Mike was doing well in his work as a self-employed plumber, promising that next time he would join them, feeling that today was especially for them to spend their time together.

In some small way, Laura felt browsing over the images helped her to bridge the gap in those lost years. She could see Mike had put on a small amount of weight around his waist and his fair hair now streaked with grey, was also beginning to recede around his temples. Her mum never made any secret she wasn't happy about their relationship to begin with as he had bit of a reputation with the ladies; and at one time, before him and Louise had started dating, had his sights set on Laura. But it soon became clear that once Mike hooked up with her younger sister, had fallen deeply in love with her and to the best of her knowledge had never played around since.

Laura took hold of the iPad from her sister, flicking through the various images of Toby back to when he was newly born right up to the present. She tapped on to another album called *Family Photos Part Three* and saw Louise's worried expression as she bit nervously on to her bottom lip, explaining they were just pretty much of what she'd seen earlier. But as Laura was one of those people who genuinely never tired of catching up with anything where family was concerned, insisted on taking a look. To her delight, she glimpsed pictures of Toby around the time she remembered him before she went away. Oblivious of the worried glances exchanged by Mum and Lou, a warm smile spread across her face, seeing her nephew cradled lovingly in his mum's arms with Mike looking fondly towards him as if he was the luckiest man alive. The next image was of Mum looking delighted as she held her grandson, pressing him closely to her as if he was the most precious gift in the world. She swiftly swiped to the next photo, where her smile quickly vanished as the colour drained from her face, making her look deathly pale.

Her eyes fixed intently on the young woman holding Toby on her lap; a woman she once knew well, her glossy dark hair worn in a longer style to the one she had of late, hanging lankily with neglect over her shoulders. Her face told a thousand tales as she peered into the camera lens, her complexion both pale and gaunt, making her green eyes appear large; eyes that had seen so much heartbreak, smudged with dark shadows from months of broken sleep. She gazed at her photo image with an overwhelming feeling of sadness, appalled how at how thin she became during those dark times where each day she relived all the terrible events that had taken place to completely tear up the happy life she had once taken for granted, into shreds.

Her mum gently took the iPad from her hands, looking at her with deep concern, asking if she was ok.

Laura nodded at her forcing a smile which turned out to be more of a grimace, feeling annoyed at herself for ignoring Louise's warning not to look at the photos in that album. Heaven knows what else she would have discovered had she dared to venture further!

As Louise saw to Toby, pushing him on his swing, Mum tactfully changed the subject, asking about the young man she'd been seeing. As Laura informed her that things hadn't worked out, the disappointment written on her face was clear to see. But she put on a smile, saying there was plenty more fish in the sea and it was just a matter of time before someone special would come along.

After a bittersweet day that Laura knew she would never forget, they pulled up outside her flat, her mum declaring they would head straight home as Toby was fast asleep in the back seat. They said their goodbyes, hugging and kissing with more than a few tears being shed. Holding her mum firmly in her arms, Laura promised this would be the first of many times they would meet. As she waved them off until they disappeared around the corner of the close, firmly believed just maybe with time she would find the courage to return home.

As she entered her flat, switching on the light, took her mobile out of her handbag, noticing a missed call on the screen followed by a voicemail alert. Frowning, she listened to the message from Dan.

Sounding somewhat nervous, wanted to apologise for what happened last night but was keen to let her know he hadn't set out to try to take advantage of her. She was the loveliest of ladies he'd ever met with a heart of gold, he wanted her to know, but realised he wasn't ready to move on to another relationship and was so sorry for any hurt he'd caused her.

She rubbed her eyes wearily as she heard the emotion so raw in his voice and could empathise with the way he was feeling. Dan paused for a moment as he added that although he knew so little about her that it was clear to see she also had a lot of unfinished business from her own past that needed to be dealt with before she was also able to move on, and wished her well, hoping she would find someone who was worthy of all the love she had to give.

She hung up, rubbing the right side of her temple that was beginning to throb with the first signs of the all too familiar headache which seemed to have become a permanent fixture in her life. No, she wasn't really angry with him; angrier with herself for being allowed to be talked into another date by the well-meaning Karen. Yes, it was great her friend had found her soulmate with Andrew, but she knew now without a doubt there would never be another living soul who would ever come close to the way she felt about Oscar. Giving a deep yawn, decided after her emotionally charged day, she needed an early night.

Laura opened her eyes, realising she must have fallen asleep quickly. But instead of looking up at her bedroom ceiling, saw in front of her a blue and almost cloudless sky, enjoying the warmth of the sun caressing her skin. With a feeling that somebody was watching her, peered over to her left and saw Jessica standing there, watching her expectantly holding a glass of orange juice in her hands.

Realising she was laying on the sun lounger in the garden of Rose Cottage, sat up as she handed the drink to her.

'Thank you,' she smiled appreciatively, before Jessica sat on the grass beside her, picking up her sketch pad and pencil, lying comfortably across the lawn before continuing with a drawing she'd begun earlier.

'Daddy said you'd be back soon,' she informed Laura,

studying her as she took a sip of her drink.

Laura peered at the young girl who was looking particularly pretty in a yellow dress that complemented her long brown hair hanging loosely over her shoulders. 'Well, it looks like your Daddy was right, though I never know for sure when that's about to happen!'

Jessica green eyes widened excitedly as if she was eager to share some good news with her. 'Daddy told me that soon you'll be staying with us *forever*!'

Taken aback, her forehead knotted in a frown as she placed the glass onto the lawn beside her. 'That's a really lovely thought Jessica, but I really don't see how that's going to happen.'

The child glanced over to her thoughtfully, shrugging her shoulders as she continued with her sketching. 'Well, that's what Daddy told me - said you'd be living with us and that finally we would all be together again and that nothing would ever part us again.'

Feeling curious, Laura had to ask, 'How would you feel if I *could* be here forever?'

Jessica smiled. 'That would be awesome. My friend Teagan doesn't have her parents here and she's being looked after by Mrs Lock until they come. My other friend Simon, he's living with his Nana Styles until his mummy and daddy can come to the village.

Laura shook her head in disbelief. 'Well, it seems so many people around here that are not with their loved ones and that's very sad. I guess that's the way of the world these days. We all lead busy lives with work and sometimes it's not always possible for us to connect to be that one big happy family.' She peered over the child's shoulder, looking at her incredibly realistic drawing of Duke who was sleeping in the corner of the garden. 'Don't you sometimes miss your mummy?' As soon as the words left her lips, she regretted asking such a personal question to somebody so young.

But Jessica didn't seem at all concerned. 'I have missed having Mummy with us, but I've always known that's she's around and that she loves me.'

Laura's heart was filled with by an over-whelming feeling of sadness for the child who hadn't seen her mother since heaven knows when and yet she never doubted the love that her she had for her. How could anybody leave such a kind and loving man and his child, she wondered; because she knew without a shred of doubt that there wasn't a bad bone in Oscar's body. It couldn't be easy for him having to raise a child on his own.

Jessica studied Laura, her young face looking so serious. 'Daddy said you've been feeling very sad because you haven't been well and you've been having a difficult time.'

Laura watched her as she busily sketched, wishing Oscar never made such promises to a child that he knew could never be kept. How she would love to spend her life in this beautiful village, such a contrast from the urban jungle in which she lived; a world from where she travelled each day to work, to an office doing her job, living an ok but fairly mundane existence. Now here she was in her dream escape, which felt more real in many ways than her own world, living this parallel life, a life she could never truly be a part of, because as much as she loved Oscar, Jessica and her amazing friend Becky, the only place they lived was inside of her imagination. Even if she could smell the fragrance of the grass brought to life by an earlier rain shower and the sound of the birds singing in the trees. Being free of those monster headaches and the heartbreak of meeting men who could never fill that void in her heart. How she bitterly regretted allowing herself to sleep with Dan!

'Hello, sleepyhead,' came a familiar voice behind her, taking her away from her dark thoughts. She looked up to see Oscar grinning at her, his hair slightly ruffled as he bent down to kiss her lightly on the lips. 'I hope Madam here didn't wake you up. You looked so peaceful sleeping on that lounger that I didn't have the heart to disturb you.'

She sat up giving a long yawn, watching as the child ran

into the house. 'Not at all - she's been as good as gold.' She gazed at him through narrowed eyes. 'Though she says you told her I was coming to live with you both *forever*.'

The smile slipped from his face. 'How would you feel if it was possible?'

Laura looked at him in disbelief as if he was crazy. 'But you and I know as much as I love the idea, that's never going to happen.'

'But just *suppose* it was possible...would you like to?'

'You *know* I would love nothing more, but as much as I love you both, I can't wish for something that can never happen.' Her face turned grim as she thought back to Friday night. 'I just wish I'd never slept with Dan. I know this is all a dream, but I can't help that feeling that I've let both you and Jessica down.'

He held her closely in his arms. 'Hey, I told you to forget about that - you've been in a confused place and it's all history. I know where your heart belongs and most importantly so does Jessica.'

She allowed herself to be bathed in his love as he held her closely to him, enjoying the warmth of his body, enjoying the oasis of calm and peace of Rose Cottage, a place she knew without a doubt where she belonged.

Oscar led the way into the cottage, gently taking hold of

her hand as he led her to the small kitchen. To her surprise and delight, he'd been busily cooking dinner, the smell of roast beef and vegetables ready to serve whetting her appetite. Insisting he needed no assistance with serving, reluctantly sat down at the table with Jessica while he busily placed down plates in front of them, each loaded with a generous serving of food.

'Well, this is rather nice,' she remarked to Jessica with a grin. 'It makes a pleasant change to be waited on, instead of all the usual cooking I normally have to do after a busy day at the office.'

Oscar kissed her lightly on the head as he took his place at the table next to her. 'Well, I hope you enjoy - you deserve to be taken care of, doesn't she, Jessica?'

'Yes, and Daddy's a great cook too,' the young girl revealed excitedly, as she picked up her fork and dug this into one of her potatoes.

Taking in the aroma of the freshly cooked beef and vegetables, as they sat closely together around the table a sudden feeling of familiarity embraced her, stirring memories of times long ago that had been safely tucked at the back of her mind.

She cut into her beef, placing the slice in her mouth, savouring the hot, tender meat that seemed to melt on her tongue, her eyes widening in astonishment as a flashback came to her like a bolt of lightning, to a time when she'd last tasted food cooked to such perfection. To bygone days when she would cook the Sunday dinner for those particularly special in her life. A time when she believed herself to be invincible where nothing could possibly go wrong with her happy life. Yes, *he* knew she wasn't the greatest cook in the world, she thought with a bittersweet feeling in her heart; but despite her lack of culinary skills, *he* loved her unconditionally. *He* would sit at the dinner table, eating her over-cooked potatoes and vegetables, with Yorkshire puddings that somehow seemed to turn out flat and always manged to burn despite her best efforts. But all the same, *he* would eat whatever she put on the table without any complaint and with relish, as if *he* was sampling the world's finest cuisine.

Tearing herself away from her memories of moments gone forever, she discussed her big family reunion and the amazing day they'd spent together.

'It was *so* good to see everybody,' Laura admitted, with her face tinged with regret. 'I just wished that I'd taken the plunge to meet them sooner - I can't help feeling I've missed out on a huge chunk of my life. Mum has visibly aged and I'm sure most of that's down to me taking the selfish way out by moving to Minsden.'

Oscar put down his cutlery, placing his hand gently over

her own. 'Sweetheart, you shouldn't be so hard on yourself. I know more than anyone that you went through some very difficult times - stuff that nobody should ever have to experience. Believe me, your mum and Louise understand far more than you realise.'

She dug her fork into a carrot slice, stirring it into a small pool of gravy on her plate. 'I think what really brought it home to me was seeing how much Toby had grown in those past three years. At first, he was so shy when he saw me - he had no memories of his Aunty Laura.'

Oscar smiled as he gently rubbed her hand within his own. 'I wouldn't be so sure of that - he loved sitting next to you on that steam engine and feeding the animals in the children's zoo. You had a lot of photos taken together too. That'll definitely be something for Angela and the rest of the family to treasure for years to come. Toby will look back and cherish that special day he'd spent with his Aunty Laura.'

'Definitely something for me to treasure too,' interjected Laura. 'I'll have to make the time later to download them from the camera. Louise took some pictures too, so no doubt we'll be swapping those through iCloud.' She gave a wry smile. 'Just a pity I have no way of sending any here for you to see.'

Oscar gave a chuckle. 'My darling, believe me when I say I have no need to look at any photos to see how the family are doing. I know that Angela's getting on with her life.' He took a moment before delivering his news. 'She never mentioned this to you yesterday, but I guess now's the time for you to know this - remember Bob Herbert that lives a few doors away? You might recall he got divorced some years ago when Grace left him for someone else. Well, it seems his friendship with your mum has developed into something more serious.'

Laura was stunned. 'Well, she kept that one quiet from me.' She gave a deep sigh. 'Not that I blame her when I've gone out of my way to not be a part of everybody's lives. Actually, Bob's a really nice chap - Mum's been on her own for far too long since Dad walked out on us as kids and had a really tough time bringing us up as a single parent. He's never shown any interest in us since he moved to Canada with his other woman - so it's about time she had some happiness of her own.'

Oscar took a sip of his glass of water. 'I think Angela just didn't want that news to overshadow your big reunion as she felt that the day should be all about the family. I'm sure she would have told you in good time.'

Laura's brow knitted into a puzzled frown. '*Would have*? We have made plans to meet up again soon. Not sure when, but today wasn't a one-off as far as I'm concerned, so I guess she'll tell me all about it when the time is right.'

Oscar gently placed his drinking glass back on the table.

'Today was one of the happiest days that your mum and sister have experienced in a very long time. I know you don't want to think about the past because at the moment you've closed your mind to it.' His face softened. 'It's not been easy for any of you over these past few years, seeing the family practically torn apart. I do know your health hasn't been good of late either with those headaches - life's been difficult all round.'

Laura was feeling confused. 'I'm not sure what you're trying to say - you keep speaking as if I'm never going to see my family again. But believe me, I've finally come to my senses and I don't have any intention of letting go of them again. As for Mum, I'm really pleased she's hooked up with Bob.'

Oscar nodded in agreement. 'Yes, it's great she's finally found some happiness.' He paused, looking particularly solemn. 'I guess in life, although we can experience some pretty amazing moments that we'll cherish for the rest of our lives, sometimes along the way, we may also have more than our fair share of darker episodes to contend with. It's good to know Angela will have Bob to care for her - I feel he's the kind of person who'll always be around for her at her time of need.' He pierced a small potato on the end of this fork. 'While Louise has her own small family unit with Mike and Toby for support, I'm sure she'll draw some comfort knowing her mum has someone special to help guide her through those difficult times.'

Laura felt a shiver ripple down her spine. 'Now you're *really* beginning to scare me. What do you *feel* could go wrong? Surely nothing could possibly be any worse than what happened before?' She smiled apologetically, not wanting to alarm Jessica who was listening intently to their conversation. '*Oh*, don't mind me, I'm just over-thinking as usual. After all the stuff that's happened over the past few days I guess I'm still feeling a bit touchy. But I think you're right about Bob as he does strike me as the loyal type.

Before Oscar had a chance to reply, saw Laura's attention was focused on Becky who was standing in the doorway to the kitchen. 'I'm sorry if I'm interrupting anything,' her friend remarked apologetically. 'I can always come back later.'

'You're ok, Becks,' Oscar assured her with a smile, ushering her into the small living room to join them. 'You know you're always welcome here anytime.' He gave a knowing wink. 'Besides, we were *expecting* you!'

Laura's moment of panic was replaced by an overwhelming feeling of joy at seeing the friend that she loved almost as much as her own sister; even though the fact remained she didn't exist outside of this dream world.

Becky was looking particularly happy, with a smile almost as radiant as the long yellow dress she was wearing. As she helped herself to some water, filling her glass from the jug that sat on the table, peered over to Oscar sheepishly.

He shook his head, with that smile that never failed to make Laura's heart melt. 'No, I haven't got around to telling her yet.'

'Telling me what?'

The three of them looked over to her before Oscar finally spoke up.

'We're having a party on Saturday and you're the guest of honour.'

Laura's eyes widened. 'A party where *I'm* the guest of honour? Well if it happens to be this coming Saturday, then I'm afraid I won't be able to make it - it's the night of the awards.'

Jessica gave a quizzical frown, watching her dad and Becky before turning her attention to Laura. 'But that doesn't matter because-'

'It's ok, sweetheart,' Oscar said, gently stroking his daughter's head. 'Laura will be attending her works event because that's very important to her. But once she's enjoyed her special moment, then she'll be coming to join us.'

Laura laughed, feeling slightly puzzled. 'Well, if there's any way I can attend then I will gladly be here. But as you well know, that one's really beyond my control.'

'You'll be here,' Becky insisted with a mischievous smile. 'And I *just can't wait*! We have so much to catch up on! Oh, by the way, Jez sends his regards and said he'll be coming with his legendary homemade elderberry wine!'

Laura laughed. 'Jez's famous Elderberry wine? I've heard so much said about it, but I've not had the pleasure of trying it!

'Well, once you've tried Jez's signature wine you'll realise what you've been missing out on all your life!'

'Even better than all those spritzers you used to drink in our clubbing days?' Laura teased.

'*Even better*!' she grinned as she reminisced back to those days. 'Ha! Wasn't I just the minx? As you well know until Chris came along there'd been a few guys on the scene I was glad to see the back of - not to mention a few banging hangovers along the way!' She looked at her friend with affection. 'I always teased you for being a Miss Goody-Two-Shoes because you were so completely the opposite to me, but that's one of the many things I love about you - you always brought me back down to earth with a bang.'

Laura placed her knife and fork back on her plate after managing to eat every bit of the generous portion of food that Oscar served her. 'Well, I'm afraid I can't claim to take all the credit for that one, because once Chris came along you really settled down.'

Her friend looked so contented her face happy and positively glowing with radiance. 'Oh, I know this all sounds so cliché, but as soon as we met I knew immediately he was The One. She watched Laura intently, her light blue eyes unblinking as if she was looking deeply into the very core of her soul. 'When somebody special walks into our lives, within an instant it makes us realise just *why* things never worked out with the others. Don't you agree?'

Laura felt a shiver run involuntarily down her spine as a distant memory leaped to the surface of her mind, shrouded by a thick, grey mist that she was unable to penetrate. From deep within her came the stirring of times, distant times when she had felt blissfully happy, when she loved so deeply, knowing without a shadow of a doubt that this love was reciprocated unconditionally. Her face became eclipsed with a deep sadness shadowing her face as she thought back to all those happy times; the best times of her life when she was blissfully unaware that she was about to have her heart shattered into a million pieces, with her life being completely torn to shreds.

Becky looked on with concern at her friend's far away expression. 'Laura, all you need to know for now is that everything's going to be ok. All isn't lost you know - before you know it, you'll find yourself to be blissfully happy again. I bet you're finding that hard to believe - but I promise that's how it's going to be.'

Laura peered over to that clock on the wall with the hand permanently stuck at five o'clock, before turning her attention back towards Oscar, Becky and young Jessica who were all studying her intently. Suddenly conscious she was firmly gripping hold of the white napkin in her hand, quickly placed it back on the table beside her empty plate.

Oscar kissed her lightly on her head. 'Sweetheart, you're looking a little tired. You've had a lot to think about on this visit - maybe you ought to take a little rest on the sofa.'

Unsure whether her tiredness was down to the emotional reunion with her family or her latest visit to Rose Cottage with all the seemingly cryptic remarks from Oscar and Becky, realised she was feeling quite drained. She had to admit that both had proven to be very emotional experiences, causing her mind to regress back to times she would much rather permanently forget.

Since her very first dream escape to Rose Cottage she was always welcomed, made to feel she should consider this her second home, to come and go as she pleased. A warm glow enraptured her as he her led to the living-room, towards the sofa, moving some cushions aside to make way for her to lie down. Jessica not far behind, held a crocheted patchwork blanket which she carefully covered over her. She watched Laura her face serious before gently placing a kiss on her cheek. Feeling moved by the unexpected gesture, came the stirrings of distant memories of being hugged by a child during happier times, unaware as a tear trickled down her cheek.

Jessica moved aside to make way for Becky who came over to her. 'Hey, it's ok hon - everything's going to turn out well, I promise.' She gently wiped the tear from her friend's cheek with a tissue. 'Enjoy your awards ceremony and do a few dances and have a few drinks on my behalf!' She smiled brightly. 'We'll be here waiting for you when your other do comes to an end.' A look of excitement spread across her face. 'I'm *so* looking forward to finally being back with my bestie.'

Finally, it was Oscar's turn to come over to her while Becky and Jessica watched over in the background.

Seeing her face looking so troubled and pale, gently held her in his embrace as he placed a lingering kiss on her lips that made her heart feel it was about to melt with happiness. She nestled in his arms feeling safe and comfortable, knowing without a doubt there would never be any other man that could ever take his place in her heart.

'Well, I do hope I can make it to my party,' she remarked with a longing sigh.

'You'll be there darling,' he assured her. 'You have my word.'

She allowed herself to smile. 'Well, if it's in my power then nothing will keep me away.'

He looked deeply into those green eyes that seemed to sparkle like emeralds in the darkened room. 'Darling, we know more than anyone about all you've been through - but Saturday is going to be your special day. You're going to nail it at the Global Life awards and win that trophy for *Best Loved Manager* - there's no doubt you'll be the star of the show.'

Laura laughed. 'I just wish I could have your confidence that I'm going to win - I'm up against some pretty stiff competition.'

He lightly stroked her cheek; his expression more thoughtful and intense with his eyes seeming to probe deeply into her soul 'From now on there is nothing left to fear.' He paused for a moment as if allowing her to digest what he was saying. 'Should you get one of those headaches, please don't worry, because it'll soon disappear. Nothing's going to stop you from enjoying your special day - you'll be spoken about with love and affection for years to come. And once you have accepted your award, you'll be returning to the village for the most amazing party ever!'

Laura grinned. 'Now that sounds like an offer I can't

possibly refuse!' To tell the truth I'm unable to share your confidence about me winning that award - that remains to be seen. But to be attending two parties in a row, even if one happens to be within this dream, sounds like a whole lot of fun.'

Oscar gave a wink as he stroked her hair tenderly, 'It's possible you might not be back for a few days until the big day, but once you get here you'll be in for a very happy time and that's a promise.' He tucked the blanket around her to make sure she was feeling warm. 'Now off to sleep you go. If you don't always feel at your best in between then, take it easy. Enjoy your special day because you'll look absolutely stunning in that emerald dress. And don't forget about those beautiful gems!'

Finally feeling relaxed and at peace, she closed her eyes and what seemed like seconds later, opened them, peering at the clock next to her on the bedside cabinet, seeing the time was ten o'clock. Much to her surprise she had slept solidly for at least two hours.

CHAPTER FIFTEEN

'**I**'m *so* sorry,' Karen commiserated as they sat at their desks, her face written with sympathy as she discreetly passed her the bottle of wine, inside a carrier bag, along with the earrings both left behind in haste at Dan's on Saturday night. 'He brought these over after our telephone conversation, she explained. 'I think he just felt after everything you wouldn't want him coming over to your flat.'

With reluctance she looked inside the M&S carrier bag, taking out the large silver earrings, thinking she would never be able to wear them again without thinking about that night. As for the wine, she'd never been one for red. White or Rose had always been more her thing.

'Are you ok?' her friend asked, clearly concerned about the situation.

During Sunday evening, not long after she'd woken from her dream, Karen called her to see how everything went with her reunion with Mum and Louise as well as all the gossip about the date from the night before.

At the very mention of the date, Laura had broken down in tears as she admitted to sleeping with Dan shortly after going back to his place. 'I can't even put it all down to the drink,' she explained to her shame. 'Yes, I'd had a few glasses and was a bit merry, but I really felt I was in control of the situation. After leaving the community centre he suggested going back to his place for a coffee.' She could tell by Karen's silence what must have been running through her mind. 'Yes, yes, I know, the oldest line in the book about going back for a *coffee*. Maybe I was being naive but I really believed in this case it was just for coffee. Maybe for him that was the original plan too - I truly never felt he had some ulterior motive in mind.'

She sighed as she thought back. 'Well, he did get to make one, but before we knew it we were all over each other like-like...it's not as if we'd even kissed before that night. But I know like me he was feeling sad over things.' She broke down again sobbing uncontrollably. 'He must think I'm a right slapper.'

'Don't be so hard on yourself,' Karen chided. 'It takes *two* to tango. I could certainly tell you a story or two of my own from the past that I regret. For what it's worth from what I do know of Dan is that he wasn't deliberately out to hurt you. I know for a fact since Margaret there hasn't been anyone else and he's certainly not a player. I would like to believe he's a good enough judge of character to realise you're definitely not the type that sleeps around.'

Her friend had offered to come around to console her, but it was late and they both needed to be up bright and early for work.

Karen decided to change the subject. 'Did everything go well with your mum and sister?'

Blowing her nose in a crumpled-up tissue, Laura's mood lightened. 'It was *amazing*,' she admitted. 'I just wished I'd bitten the bullet and done it sooner. It was almost as if we'd never been apart. Just that Toby has grown so much and forgotten all about me. Mum has hooked up with Bob her next-door neighbour.' But she didn't go into the details about Oscar being the bearer of this news.

'Wow! So, you're going to keep in touch?'

Laura smiled. 'From now on, *nothing* is going to stop me. One thing this has all brought home to me is that for me family is *everything*. As far as I'm concerned, nothing's going to tear us apart.'

She came back to the present, finding herself clutching on to the carrier bag. Dan clearly had no intention of trying to get back with her and there was certainly no wish on her part to rekindle something that had never really began. As far as she was concerned this was an episode of her life she would much rather put firmly behind her and move on.

'Keep the wine,' Laura offered, handing the bottle to her friend. 'I don't like red, but I know you do. *Please.*'

With a shrug of her shoulders Karen reluctantly took it from her. 'So, any dates in the offing when you're meeting up with the family again?'

'Nothing definite arranged yet, but I'll keep you posted on that one.'

They both gave a start as Karen's internal phone buzzed into life. The display showed it was Edwina Charlton. 'Wonder what she wants,' she remarked giving a puzzled frown. 'Not often she calls.'

'One way to find out,' Laura grinned.

'Hi Edwina,' Karen greeted, hoping she sounded more confident than she felt. Glancing briefly to Laura, her expression turned grave. 'Yes, yes of course. I'll be right over.'

Afterwards, she gently placed down the receiver, looking more than a little concerned. 'Edwina wants to see me right away,' she announced. 'Sounds a bit ominous.'

'Did she say *why?*'

'Not a word. She doesn't sound angry or anything like that, though that doesn't necessarily mean anything. I hope there's nothing wrong, something I should or shouldn't have done - maybe there's been some complaint.'

Laura gave a wry smile. 'I'm sure it's nothing like that. If there'd been some kind of issue, I'm sure Edwina would have come to me first.'

'Let's hope you're right,' Karen sighed as she got up from her chair, equipped with notepad and pen.

At lunchtime, the town centre was unusually busy with shoppers, taking advantage of the particularly fine weather. Fortunately, they found one free table in the corner of a coffee shop. After each of them ordering some Mississippi mud pie and a café latte, made themselves comfortable as they possibly could on the straight wooden chairs.

Karen dug her fork into her slice of chocolate indulgence before taking a bite. 'I've got to say the whole episode took me completely by surprise - I had no idea Claire Rolfe was thinking of leaving the company.'

'I've got to admit I didn't see that one coming. Claire's been with the company for ten years. She's practically been part of the future.' Laura stirred her coffee in thought. 'Well, it's not often that you get offered a team manager role for the Annuities Policies Team. Congratulations, very well deserved.'

Her friend appeared mortified. 'I haven't confirmed yet

whether I'm going to accept the offer!'

Laura watched her sternly. 'But you *must*! I'm very well aware of the fact that you wanted team manager position for the Investments Solutions team at the time we both applied and not once did you show any resentment towards me when I was offered the job. You've more than earned this promotion - you'd be fantastic and with a decent rise in your salary to boot!'

Karen peered at her sadly. 'But I would so miss working with you. You're such a great boss and friend - that's why we all love you here.'

Laura rolled her eyes towards the ceiling. 'For goodness sake, you'll only be sitting at the other end of the office, well within walking distance! Besides, whenever you're not doing anything with Andrew we'll still hang out together as usual.'

Taking a gulp of her coffee, Karen reluctantly shrugged her shoulders, with a grin spreading across her face. 'Ok, I can take a hint when I'm not wanted. With Claire leaving, looks like I've got some pretty big shoes to step into - but if it's just to get some peace from you, I guess I'll have to formally accept the offer!'

'That's more like it!'

Putting on her reading glasses, Karen rummaged through her handbag for the sheet of paper Edwina handed to her during their chat, giving details of the job role description. 'Well Claire's working three months' notice so she'll be going through everything to ease me into the job.' She peered over her spectacles. 'I've got to say I'm quite disappointed Edwina didn't have the decency to let you know what she was planning to do - she should've at least discussed it with you first.'

Laura waved her hand dismissively. 'Oh, it's ok, she did send me an email when you were on your way and she'll be discussing with me later as we'll soon need to look for another team deputy.'

Seeing Karen was so clearly chuffed with her new job offer, didn't have the heart to admit Edwina had messaged her earlier that morning to say she wanted to see her to discuss this very matter, but for some reason the meeting had completely left her head. With everything that had gone on lately in her personal life, found she was having increasing difficulty in remembering short term stuff. It didn't help when she was getting almost constant headaches and double vision with those migraines which appeared to be happening all too frequently of late. When meeting up with her boss later she would make a point of apologising to her.

After arriving home from what had proven to be a particularly demanding day, gave a long yawn as she sat down on the stool, ready to eat at the kitchen bar. With no inclination to cook anything from scratch, peered at the pasta meal in front of her still piping hot from the microwave. Oh, she knew she was taking the lazy option, but after all had only herself to please, and by her own admission with her lack of culinary skills, could hardly claim to be a contender for *The British Bake Off*. But by adding some freshly boiled broccoli and carrots felt she had redeemed herself slightly by transforming her ready-meal into something healthier.

With not just her day to day work to contend with, also had to squeeze in some time to take part in a video shoot along with the other finalists in preparation of the Global Life awards ceremony. Filmed by the very talented Jermaine, not just a much-loved colleague who worked in their IT department, but also happened to a very keen amateur filmmaker. With his lilting Trinidadian accent and winning smile, soon put everyone at their ease as they danced and mimed to a rendition of Queen's *We Are the Champions*.

She thought back to her earlier meeting with Edwina who as was as friendly as always while at the same time remaining very professional. Although her boss was always very approachable with an open-door policy, felt more than a little uneasy when she was being summoned to a meeting room. Edwina welcomed her with a smile, inviting her to take a seat in the room booked especially for the occasion. That in itself felt a little ominous as meetings of a more informal nature were usually conducted in the canteen, or if weather permitting, in the scenic works grounds.

Her boss was looking particularly elegant in a blue shift dress with silver matching necklace and earrings making the 56-year-old woman appear both youthful and chic. The senior manager made small talk about the warmth and sunshine with not a cloud to be seen in the sky, but Laura knew she wasn't there to discuss the latest weather forecast.

Her boss cut to the chase, explaining that she wanted to apologise for offering Karen the position of team manager for Annuities Policies without having first discussed the matter with her. She informed her that based on her outstanding hard work and previous discussions about her deputy's interest and aspirations to progress within the company, made her the perfect candidate for the position. However, she stressed, couldn't help expressing her concern about the fact that Laura hadn't responded to her Skype message to discuss Karen's suitability for the role before making the formal offer.

Feeling bitterly disappointed with herself, Laura felt she needed to twist the truth slightly by apologising to Edwina for not having seen the message to meet with her. She explained whilst going through her many incoming emails had somehow overlooked the flashing sign of her manager's instant message.

With that Edwina became remorseful and seemed slightly ashamed, adding with hindsight perhaps she should have just simply called her. She admitted to being waylaid in a large amount of work of her own and looking back could have perhaps handled the situation better herself.

The manager studied Laura, her expression one of concern. She couldn't help noticing her team manager was looking a little peaky lately and wanted to know if everything was ok.

Laura admitted she was experiencing some personal problems but nothing she couldn't deal with and wanted to assure her boss that she would ensure in future she wouldn't allow these matters to overlap with her work.

Edwina smiled, advising reassuringly despite the open office plan that her *door* would always be open if there was anything she needed to discuss. Her face softened stressing she realised Laura had been through some very traumatic experiences, appreciating these were sometimes difficult to overcome without a little support. She asked if she'd considered re-continuing with her counselling sessions. Laura shook her head, informing her this would only succeed in raking over all the bad memories and was now time for her to move on with her life as normally as possible.

They made some small talk spending a few minutes discussing the Global Life awards ceremony where Edwina admitted at looking forward with mixed feelings to what was to be her last social event with the company; making it very clear that Laura's nomination and reaching the finals for *Most Loved Manager* was a credit to her excellent managerial and people skills.

Laura left the meeting feeling happier than she had anticipated, with Edwina reminding her to let her know should she re-consider some more counselling then to call her at any time if there was anything further she wished to discuss.

As she began eating her meal, Mum called on the landline.

'You're sounding a little down,' Angela remarked, her voice sounding very concerned.

'Just tired,' sighed Laura, wearily rubbing her eyes that were beginning to feel heavy, and her vision beginning to blur.

'It sounds like they're working you too hard,' her mum grumbled. 'Seems to be the same everywhere, these workplaces will stop at nothing to get their pound of flesh from you.'

'It's ok - really. It was just a busy day.'

Her mum paused for a moment and was clear she sensed there was more to this situation. 'Ok, but you know you've got to stick up for yourself if they're over-working you.'

'Don't worry about me,' Laura reassured her. 'I'm more than capable of looking after myself.' She decided to swiftly change the subject. 'So, how's everything going with Bob?'

Her mum went silent for a few seconds clearly surprised that Laura knew about her relationship before giving a chuckle. 'Now *who* told you about Bob? *Need* I ask? Lou was never one for being able to keep a secret! Sweetheart, actually I was on the brink of telling you. Well, you know Bob, he never changes. Hmm, I tell a lie because since Grace left him he's really brushed up on his cooking skills and did a perfect Sunday roast yesterday with all the trimmings.'

'That's amazing,' Laura gushed as she stirred the heated pasta on the plate that she very little appetite for. 'It sounds like he's really spoiling you. I'm very happy for you both.'

'Thank you, dear. Yes, he's a darling, though he's the first to admit when Grace was around he was never into the domestic thing. But to be fair he was always really busy with his carpentry work and as you'll remember she was a part-time school secretary with more time on her hands.' She was silent for a moment and just before Laura was beginning to think the call had terminated, her mum cleared her throat before continuing with the conversation. 'Bob has suggested about us going on holiday to Portugal. He's been there a few times before and says there's some nice, quiet resorts.'

Laura knew by the silence that her mum was seeking her approval. 'Oh Mum, that would be fantastic. You've *got* to go!'

'I just wanted to make sure you were ok with that.'

Laura smiled. 'Mum, you know you don't need to seek my approval! For what it's worth, I think Bob's a great chap and you deserve to be happy. Dad's been off the scene getting on with his own life in Canada and I'm sure Lou and Mike are delighted about the two of you getting it together. Enjoy!'

'Oh, thank you, sweetheart that really means a lot. Lou was ok with it but it's important to me what *both* of my girls think. We're looking at going in a few weeks, hoping to get a last-minute deal.' There was a moment's silence before she continued. 'Actually, we were wondering if you fancied coming down next weekend? I know Bob would like to catch up with you - he's always asking about you and Mike will be around too. Thought it would be a nice way for us all to spend some more time together. We could do something nice like go and see some ice show, then perhaps follow it up with a meal.'

Laura bit nervously on her bottom lip, not knowing what to say. Was she ready to go back home and face all her ghosts?

Angela immediately sensed her daughter's reluctance.

'Of course, that's if you feel ready to come home. It's entirely up to you, and if you felt the drive was a bit too much, you could always come by train. But we'll understand if...'

'I'll come,' Laura cut in quickly before she had a chance to change her mind.

By the short moment of silence, Angela was clearly taken aback.

'You *can*? Oh darling, that's wonderful! I'll let Lou know - she'll be over the moon and I know can say the same for Mike and Bob!'

Laura swallowed nervously, her throat suddenly feeling very dry, wondering if she'd perhaps been a little hasty with her decision.

Angela was clearly elated. 'Do you know, Toby hasn't stopped talking about his Aunty Laura? He's done a lovely drawing of you which has taken pride of place on the kitchen wall. I can't lie and say he's got your talent, but it looks amazingly pretty, coloured in red and yellow!'

Laura smiled, as she peered fondly over towards Toby's drawing of her hanging proudly on the door of the fridge. Without a shadow of a doubt she'd made the right choice in going back home. There was no way she was going to miss out any more on seeing her young nephew growing up or being in danger of drifting further apart from the rest of the family.

Her sprits having lifted at the reacquaintance of her family ties, went online from her laptop to order her mum a large mixed bouquet of flowers in a variety of the orange and yellow shades which she favoured, along with a note thanking her for an unforgettable weekend. For Lou and Mike, she ordered a voucher for a weekend break to spend at a country cottage retreat of their choice.

Finally, remembering from her conversations with Lou how Toby had a fear of the dark when going to bed at night, ordered him a *PJ Masks* Boys GoGlow Buddy Night Light, hoping that going to sleep with one of his favourite TV characters would help to make his bedtimes more fun, arranging to have it presented gift-wrapped. This, she thought with a look of defiance, she wouldn't leave in the hands of a courier; oh no, when she arrived at her mum's she intended to give this in person to her favourite nephew to hopefully see the look of delight on his face. Bearing her long working hours in mind, she arranged for the order to to be delivered to the reception area at Global Life. As a rule, her workplace didn't encourage staff to use the company as a collection point for personal deliveries, but knew on this occasion Edwina would turn a blind eye.

She reflected with happiness at the newly rekindled

relationship with her nephew; the overwhelming feeling of love for this little boy was beyond any words. Who would have believed not so long ago that she could never envisage finding the strength to be able to continue with her own life? Although she knew this reunion would never completely fill the void for all the time she'd lost, it was a start and would go a long way in helping her to come to terms with her troubled past.

Just as Laura placed the order at the online toy store and received the confirmation email, an iCloud message popped up on both her iPhone and MacBook Pro, informing her that Louise's device wanted to share photos with her. Quickly she accepted the request, knowing these would the eagerly anticipated of their day out she'd been waiting for.

After making herself a mug of coffee and washing up the dishes from dinner, the photos had all fully downloaded in their original high-resolution format. Quickly saving these to the photo library on her laptop, her face lit up with a radiant smile as she thought back to her day at Whipsnade with the family. The recent memories soon came rushing back vividly as she studied the images of Toby at the children's zoo watching the goats excitedly, and much to Lou's annoyance trying to chase the turkeys that freely roamed around the grounds. Then her focus of attention switched to some photos taken with her mum and sister and finally to the one where the waitress took one of the four of them smiling into the camera just before they got stuck into their meals. Undoubtedly, Louise would be posting most of these on her Facebook to mark the occasion, Laura mused with a smile.

Once she'd browsed through all the pictures knowing these would be treasured forever, took the opportunity to download the images from her own camera. Once done she'd shared these with her sister's iCloud, quickly received a text back from her sister thanking her, promising that Mum would be over the moon.

In total, she now had over one hundred photos of their special day, just the first of many she reflected. On her visit home Laura knew she would definitely be taking her camera to capture more incredible moments as they created new memories along the way.

She peered at a photo of Toby standing outside the penguin enclosure, holding his *PJ Masks* Cat Boy soft toy close to him, as he looked into the camera, his expression wide-eyed and serious with all the innocence of a young child; unaware a tear slipped from her eye, leaving a watery trail in its path. Memories flickered through her mind of another child that she had loved more than life itself, never guessing for a second that a cruel twist of fate would take place to completely turn everything on its head.

Trying to take a grip of her feelings, quickly wiped the tear from her cheek with her hand. She made her way to the dressing table draw in the spare room, taking out an A4 sheet of photo paper, which she slipped into the printer perched on the occasional table in the corner of the room. Returning back to the living room, she pressed the print button which sprung into life, wirelessly communicating with the printer, spilling out a glossy photo image of her young nephew.

Giving a chance for the ink to dry on the photo paper, Laura got to work by setting up her easel and water colours to quickly getting down to work on her latest project.

It was some hours and a few mugs of tea later, that she stepped back to study her latest work of art. A smile spread across her face, as she took in what she saw before her. There on the paper, much to her satisfaction felt she had succeeded in capturing the likeness to Toby, clutching onto his cuddly toy, with Jessica's arm around him protectively, her face directed towards the artist as if she was looking directly into Laura's eyes; with her long dark hair cascading over her shoulders, and her yellow dress making a perfect contrast to her nephew's light fair hair and the blue tee-shirt and shorts he wore that day. On the floor beneath them laid Duke with a small red ball beside him, taking a well-deserved rest from recent game of *Fetch*.

Her day had been long and arduous for many reasons but all not in an entirely in a negative way. Entering the living room, she gazed at the painting of Rose Cottage that now hung over the electric fire; the silver frame, glistening as it reflected the setting sun from outside, all the vivid colours of the flowers in Oscar's country garden captured forever when for the first time in her dream she'd walked along the path which led her to the dwelling where lived the man she undoubtedly loved with her heart and soul with his beautiful daughter; both of whom were deeply in her affections.

The following day had proved to be particularly busy and demanding as she focused on her job and was thankful there been little signs of those recurring headaches returning. Karen had begun her training with Claire Rolfe and was pretty much with the Annuities Policies team for the best part of each day. Laura herself was now looking to replace her much loved deputy and was inviting candidates within the company to apply. She was very pleased to see her own team apprentice, Charlotte had applied and believed she had the passion and ability required to fulfil the role. Although she would go through the interview process in a fair and open-minded way, felt it was most likely she would offer the position to her as she undoubtedly displayed all the desired attributes to do justice to the role.

During the week, she kept in regular contact with the family, mostly with Mum who made it very clear how much she was looking forward to seeing her the following week. She would ask her about the Global Life Awards ceremony and made her promise to take plenty of photos of the occasion, looking forward to a few of her being awarded her trophy. As Laura completed the final touches to her painting of Toby and Jessica, couldn't help smiling at her mum's biased optimism that she would win the award for *Most Loved Manager*.

She was certain young Charlotte was in with more than a good chance of scooping up an award in the *Most Loved Employee* category as the girl had been a real life-saver when getting her out of tricky situations with IT issues and always doing her bit with overtime when a team member called in sick or was on holiday. Without complaint she always went above and beyond the call of duty.

Whilst Karen had been busy learning in greater detail about her new position, meant they were taking separate lunch breaks, so she took the opportunity to walk into the arts and crafts shop to buy frames for her recent paintings.

She gazed towards the portrait of Oscar in his blue shirt, now taking pride of place on her bedroom wall opposite her bed. Studying his slightly ruffled dark hair, and those warm, smouldering brown eyes, knew she could never tire of the roguish smile that never failed to set her heart on fire. Her attention wandered to the neighbouring portrait of the beautiful Jessica and Toby, their faces full of innocence with their lives as yet free of all the hardships of adulthood.

Although she had dreams over the previous nights, much to her disappointment none of them had taken her back to Rose Cottage. As much as she'd tried, couldn't help herself from missing the company of Oscar and Jessica with the aching in her heart becoming almost like a physical pain. But at least each morning she had the next best thing by waking up to see the images of the three most important people in her life.

After a busy few days, the big night of the Global Life Awards Ceremony quickly came around. Ensuring she would have a stress-free day as possible, Laura had already booked a day's holiday in advance, allowing plenty of time to relax and to get ready for the big night. Although Karen was still spending most of her time with the Annuities team was also over-seeing to the Investments Solutions team in her absence.

She woke up feeling refreshed after having had the best night's sleep in a long time and truly looked forward to the day ahead. Before stepping into the shower, Laura gazed into the mirror noticing for the first time she didn't look quite so dark under the eyes, noticing a healthy glow to her skin that had been missing for some time. It was true, she mused that there was more than just a grain of truth in the saying about having your beauty sleep.

After eating her microwaved apple and blueberry porridge, phoned her mum, now with a genuine feeling of excitement at the idea of coming down to see the family, with her train booking having been ordered online. Unsurprisingly her mum chided her for spending so much money on the flowers and the weekend trip for Lou and Mike but could hear by the quiver of emotion in her voice she was clearly moved. It looked as if she was in for a busy but enjoyable weekend, she thought with a smile. On her arrival, Mum informed her, there was to be a barbeque in the garden with the family and of course not forgetting Bob. Later they would all drive into Bournemouth and maybe go on a boat ride if the sea remained calm with the evening rounded off with a spectacular ice-dance show Lou had managed to get tickets for. As for Sunday, the plan was to drive into Poole to enjoy a Sunday lunch at one of the many pubs along the seafront.

The weather forecast was good with the promise of warm weather and sunshine over the following couple of days with not a rain shower to be seen.

For once, feeling really good about her life, she'd already packed a small suitcase ready for the weekend ahead, sitting in the corner of the bedroom, along with the gift-wrapped toy for Toby. The delivery had arrived in good time at work, left in the reception area; although she never opened the box, knew without a shadow of a doubt that her young nephew would be delighted with his surprise.

After changing into her jeans and a sweatshirt, drove into town where she'd earlier made an appointment at the hairdressers to get a cut and blow-dry for her big night. As she entered the busy salon, came that familiar stirring feeling of anxiety and fear, with her heart beating ten to the dozen and her throat feeling increasingly dry. She breathed in deeply and slowly exhaled as she stepped inside, desperately assuring herself that everything would be ok. Her stylist Tanya greeted her with her usual friendly smile, but was unable to mask her look of concern, noticing Laura was looking particularly pale with an expression suggesting the world was about to come to an end.

Tanya had noticed on just about every appointment her client appeared to be in a state of fear, peering at her from inside the salon watching in bewilderment as Laura summoned up all her courage to step inside. They say it took all sorts, she pondered, but maybe she was being a little unkind as could well be suffering from some kind of panic attack.

Laura assured her stylist she was fine and pretended she'd got stuck in traffic and was worried she wouldn't make it to her appointment on time.

With her hair washed and towel-dried, sat down to a Flat White coffee from the newly installed coffee machine at the salon. All drinks were free of charge of course, but undoubtedly the steep bill would more than compensate for all the fancy beverages.

As usual the two women caught up on all their gossip. As she expertly trimmed Laura's hair, Tanya updated her on her latest holiday in Egypt with her fiancée. Next year they were getting married she informed her and would be a lot of preparation ahead of them. Although Laura never went into details about her love life, or the lack of it in her case, had already mentioned about the Global Life awards ceremony and being a finalist. She also casually slipped in that she would be spending the weekend with her mum, sister and young Toby as if it was the most natural thing for her to do. Seeing how clearly excited her client appeared at the busy weekend ahead of her, Tanya promised to make her look a million dollars.

Within an hour, Laura left the hairdressers feeling very pleased with the results. During the past three years, Tanya had learned just exactly how Laura liked her fine hair not cut too shortly and with as much volume as possible. She looked up thankfully towards the sky, glad that there wasn't a rain cloud to be seen.

After arriving home, she vacuumed throughout the flat and dusted everything in sight before making herself a cheese sandwich and a mug of coffee. With not a single important thing left to do until later, relaxed on the sofa with her latest Adam Croft read on her Kindle, with a warm glowing feeling that life at the moment was pretty good. Just maybe she could finally move forward, laying the past finally to rest. Her eyes suddenly feeling heavy as tiredness washed over her. She was sure for a fleeting moment she saw Oscar and Jessica looking over towards her, both of them smiling as if waiting in anticipation for something wonderful to happen, before succumbing to a deep and dreamless sleep.

CHAPTER SIXTEEN

Karen came over to Laura's flat 5.00 pm on the dot, equipped with her dress for the evening, protected inside a zipped-up clothes bag on a hanger, and a holdall filled with make-up and a whole host of accessories, just perfect to glam up for a big night.

Placing herself down on the armchair, she leaned back letting out a deep sigh as she gratefully accepted the mug of tea Laura offered her.

'It might have been just a half-day holiday for me, but boy was it one heck of a day!' she gasped. 'Jodie and Mandy on the Claims team had had a full-scale showdown. Nothing work-related, but turns out Jodie has been seeing Mandy's fiancée behind her back.'

Laura shot her a stare with eyes wide open in shock. 'Jodie messing around with Mandy's other half? You've got to be kidding me!'

Her friend gave a curt nod. 'As true as I sit here. The entire office went into complete silence as Mandy screamed at her about screwing other women's men. Just at the point I thought there was going to be a punch-up, Edwina came along and marched them both into a meeting room. Over one-fifty people on our floor as you well know, but the silence was so intense that you could've heard a pin drop!'

Shaking her head in disbelief, Laura sat down on the sofa. '*Why* does all this action seem to kick off when I happen to take a day off? Sometimes that place sees more drama than *EastEnders*! I can imagine the shouting between those two, they're such a feisty pair at the best of times - but probably the reason until now they got along so well together.'

Karen gave a chuckle 'Well, it looks like one friendship that's now come to a sudden end!'

Laura's face became solemn. 'All joking aside, it sounds like things turned really ugly. I guess Edwina will have to give them some form of disciplinary action - that's if she doesn't fire them both.'

Her friend grimaced. 'Hmm, I've got to admit I've never seen Edwina look so mad. Her face turned so red I thought she was about to have a coronary or something!' She gazed into her mug. 'What I did hear on the grapevine is she's sent both of them home to cool off, making it clear that their personal lives are not to spill over into the workplace. Actually, if that's the case she's letting them off both lightly all things considered, because it looks like she might be planning on moving Jodie to another team. More than likely that's going to be with New Business because they're crying out for extra people at the moment.'

Laura gave a wry smile. 'Don't think Jodie's going to be too bowled over with that one. From what I've heard, in all the ten years she's been with the company, most of that time has been with the Claims team as she's the go-to person for dealing with pension-sharing orders on divorce cases - what she doesn't know about divorce and death cases on our policies isn't anything worth knowing.'

Karen agreed. 'Yes, it's a pity, but it just goes to show none of us are indispensable - but she should've thought twice before stealing someone else's fella. She's a good-looking girl and could get just about anybody she chooses - there's plenty of decent single guys out there. But I guess for her it was the thrill of the chase.' She gave a knowing wink. 'I'd bet a year's salary within a few weeks that particular relationship's going to end in tears.'

Laura let out a deep sigh as she cradled her mug of coffee. 'I'm sure you're right. But it sounds like Mandy would be a lot better off without that self-centred loser - thank goodness there's no kids involved or any weddings on the horizon.' She paused for a moment in thought. 'Just hope if he comes back to her licking his wounds she wouldn't be crazy enough to take him back. Maybe this episode will be the making of Jodie and a change of team and acquiring new knowledge will push her out of her comfort zone. It's about time she broadened her horizons in other areas of the pensions' world - never a good thing to be just a one-trick pony!'

'I guess you're right,' mused Karen, helping herself to a chocolate digestive from a pack on the coffee table. 'I always felt with Investments we've been pretty fortunate as most of the work is very diverse and interesting - but over the past few days with annuities, I've learned so much in a short space of time that I didn't know before. They're a great bunch of people in the new team, but I'm going to miss you guys *so much!*'

'*Enough, Miss Bright!*' chided Laura trying her best to look serious. 'As I've mentioned over and over until blue in the face, you're only just around the corner and our friendship extends outside of work. You deserve this lucky break and the pay rise that goes with it.' She put down her mug onto the coffee table. 'Anyway, enough about work for the moment, let's move on to more important matters and let me take a look at those gorgeous nails you just got done at *Oasis Sanctuary!*'

Karen proudly held out her hands, showing her the nail extensions she had done with the shocking pink and silver gel nail polish that would undoubtedly complement the electric blue dress she was to wear for the evening.

Laura studied them with undisguised envy. 'They're beautiful - you really put my nails to shame. I guess I don't make the effort because I have to pop in contact lenses - I've not got much choice but to keep them short so I don't end up poking my eyes out.' She gazed at her own nails regretfully. 'So, I'm afraid for me it was just a couple of coats of Pearliest Pink gloss.'

Karen held her hand out for inspection before giving her nod of approval, before quickly turning her head towards the holdall on the floor close to her feet. 'Well, while we're getting ourselves spruced up for the big occasion, I felt we could do with some light refreshment.' From the bag, she retrieved a bottle of Italian white wine. 'Just out of the fridge and still nice and chilled.'

'Nice, but do you think that's such a good idea?' Laura murmured. 'Not wanting to sound like your mum, is it wise to get wasted before attending a works event?'

Karen laughed. 'Now you're *really are* beginning to sound like my mum.' She shrugged before letting out a deep sigh. 'But I guess you're right. Let's just have *one* glass each for the road and maybe you can finish off what's left over, tonight when you get back or whenever?'

After Laura took a couple of glasses from the kitchen

cupboard, they set to work on getting glammed up.

As they changed into their dresses and put the final touches to their make-up, took selfies on their phones, pulling silly faces like a couple of unruly teenagers. Karen had already posted one onto her Facebook and within a short space of time received fifteen likes.

In less than two hours they were both ready. Karen studied her friend, looking clearly moved; the emerald green dress really suited her pale complexion, complementing her dark brown hair, styled sleekly in a fashionable bob. 'Gosh, you look absolutely stunning, Laura Winters!' she remarked. If only her friend wasn't so held back by the events from the past she would never reveal; there was little doubt she could easily hook up with any man she chose.'

As a final touch, Laura had completed her glamourous appearance with a necklace and matching earrings made up of emeralds and diamonds; their stones sparkled as they reflected the lighting coming from the ceiling above. Bringing out the greenness of her eyes, Karen couldn't ever recall her friend wearing this particular jewellery collection before. She was no expert when it came to gems, but even she could tell this was the real deal and not some bling bought at a bargain basement.

'Thank you!' Laura smiled, blushing at the compliment. 'I've got to say you're looking pretty sensational too! We're definitely going to knock them out this evening and give the younger ones a run for their money!'

Karen felt more than a little alarmed when all of a sudden, her friend stared vacantly ahead with wide eyes, making her appear astonished and her face beginning to drain of its colour. 'Hey, are you ok?'

She nodded, blinking her eyes rapidly as she placed a trembling hand to her cheek looking pale and clammy. 'Yes...I think so. It's just that my vision seems a little blurred.'

'Oh no, of all the evenings to be getting one of your famous migraines!'

Desperately wanting to reassure her friend who was looking more than a little concerned, forced a smile. 'Hey, stop worrying about me, I'll be fine - I'll just pop into the kitchen and take a couple of tablets and it'll be gone in next to no time.'

'Yes, try and nip it in the bud - you don't want your evening spoilt.' She peered out of the window as she heard the toot of a car horn. 'Looks like our taxi's just arrived!'

After paying the cab fare, they stepped out into the car park of the Westbrook hotel where the Global Life Awards was taking place. Despite being early evening, with the sun setting in the east into a red sky, with the promise of the good weather to come the following day, the air was still pleasantly mild.

Outside the entrance to the venue stood a gathering of

work colleagues, dressed glamorously for the occasion. With everyone feeling in the party mood, kisses on the cheeks were exchanged, even with those they weren't particularly familiar with. As they made their way inside the entrance, gazed at the long tables laid out with choices of champagne, buck's fizz or just plain orange juice.

Karen gave a mischievous grin as she opted for the champagne. 'Well, I don't know about you, but I didn't come here just to drink fruit juice.' Taking a sip, she studied her friend's face that was looking alarmingly pale despite the applied foundation and blusher. 'Hey, is your head improving?'

Laura gave a brief nod as she picked up a glass of Buck's fizz. 'Yes, I think those tablets have started to kick in.' But judging by the sceptical expression written on Karen's face, knew she wasn't convinced; and the truth was although her vision had improved slightly, still seemed a little blurred and was having difficulty in focusing on everything around her. But she was hopeful after a little more time, things would get back to normal.

The crowds seemed to thicken by the second as more people arrived, with the atmosphere getting loud and lively. They met up with the rest of the Investments Solutions team, with everybody dressed snazzy for the occasion. Charlotte looked sensational wearing a short lacy black dress that fitted snuggly over her youthfully slender figure with all her team mates rooting for her to win the Most *Loved Colleague* trophy.

'Look, there's Donald White,' remarked Karen excitedly giving her a gentle nudge of the arm. She gazed discreetly at the CEO of Global Life, standing almost regally alongside Edwina, looking very elegant in a pale lemon dress. Engrossed in some discussion with a small group of directors, Donald peered over towards Laura, his face immediately lighting up in recognition as he approached her, placing a gentle kiss on her cheek as if reuniting with a long-lost friend.

The gesture wasn't lost on a few of her colleagues who looked her way, wide-eyed with surprise, whispering amongst themselves about what they'd just witnessed.

By adding more fuel for gossip, Donald placed a hand gently over her shoulder as the other directors watched her with candid smiles. She took in the aroma of his expensive aftershave, glancing discreetly at his designer suit realising this was clearly no off-the-peg purchase

'I *must* say you're looking particularly beautiful this evening, Laura,' he beamed with that notoriously winning smile she'd seen spread across images on their intranet service and publicity videos. Undoubtedly, she mused with thanks to a little help from some expensive dental work, adding an appealing contrast to his deep brown hair, enhanced by *Just for Men* hair colour, ensuring there wasn't so much as a strand of grey left to be seen.

Much to her embarrassment she felt herself blush as he looked deeply into her eyes, his hand lingering across her shoulder just a few seconds longer than was appropriate. Although Donald, or *Don* as known by his inner circle was a great showman, charismatic with a reputation of being a lady's man, was also known as being a ruthless player in the business world. Had they dared to, the senior members of the executive team could have shared a few tales about him in the boardroom coming down like a ton of bricks on those seen not to be pulling their weight.

Donald ushered over one of the three photographers who'd been hired for the occasion, inviting Laura onto a small stage with the famous blue and yellow Global Life logo displayed in the background. Standing with her, smiling radiantly towards the camera, held out his glass of champagne in a salute as a succession of pictures were quickly taken. Other photos were snapped of the CEO with members of the executive team and the other finalists smiling proudly, knowing this would be a day to remember for years to come. Donald ensured Laura was included in many of these as possible, barely hiding his soft spot for the pretty Investments

Solutions team manager. Although she would never entertain the idea of anything more happening between herself and the very much married Donald, was nice to feel desired and appreciated. Perhaps she might not win the award for *Most Loved Manager* she mused, but knew without a shadow of a doubt she would treasure this special moment for a very long time.

With the atmosphere lively and buzzing with excitement, was soon time to enter the arena, with *Blurred Lines* by Robin Thicke playing loudly in the background. Much to the delight of the Investments team discovered their specially reserved table was placed close to the dance floor, offering one of the best views of the stage. Laura was pleased she'd been seated next to her friend; Karen might not share the same wild adventurous personality of her dream friend Becky she pondered, but had grown exceedingly fond of her since their first encounter at the *Maple Leaf Hotel*, valuing her years of loyal friendship. When arriving on that crazy spur of the moment decision to come to Minsden, she had been her saviour, arriving with a heavy heart and a feeling of complete helplessness, never believing there would be any light at the end of that dark tunnel. After all the devastation that had torn her life apart, Karen had been right there delivering hope, injecting back some of the happiness she'd once had, proving that life could be made at least bearable once again.

Because of the busy itinerary for the evening, meant timing was of the essence with the pre-ordered meals, and not unlike Dan's work do, the reason for the planned seating arrangement, so as not to cause any confusion when the food was served.

'Looks like there's a lot more attending this year,' Laura remarked as she looked around the large crowded room. 'I guess that's down to morale being generally higher with the company's promise to be more transparent with their decisions and better reward.

Karen looked more than a little cynical. 'I guess the offer of free booze had a lot to do with it too. Well, let's hope they keep to their promise with the better pay.'

Within less than ten minutes to get themselves settled, the food began to be served, with Laura's tomato and basil soup and Karen's breaded mushrooms for their starters looking very appetising. The rest of the team chatted on enthusiastically, as they took photos with their mobiles, no doubt with many being posted on *Facebook* and *Instagram*.

Just before most had a chance to begin their starters, Donald White came onto the stage and in true showman style, holding on to his microphone greeting everybody cheerfully, as he welcomed them to the Global Life employee awards.

After running them through the itinerary for the evening, smiled warmly, stating how this was a fitting way to celebrate all the amazing achievements that had been made throughout the year.

The CEO looked towards his captivated audience with sincerity, emphasising although the evening would be about awarding recognition to certain individuals who'd really helped to make a difference at Global Life throughout the year, as far as he was concerned, each and every one of them was a winner in his eyes.

Donald remarked at how encouraged and astounded both himself and the rest of the executive team were at the way in which everybody had pulled together through particularly challenging times, exceeding all their targets and how they should all feel extremely proud about the immense commitment they had all made. He paused for a moment, the room so silent it would have been possible to hear a pin drop as he regarded his audience, before concluding he was exceedingly proud to be a part of the Global life family and wanted to take this opportunity to thank them all from the bottom of his heart for all their dedication.

As he ended his speech, Laura joined the rest of the crowd in giving a huge round of applause along with a standing ovation to the popular CEO. Although many might have considered his words to be a little clichéd, it was good to know that all the hard work hadn't gone unnoticed and was nice to feel appreciated.

Just as they began tucking in to their food accompanied by the sound of the live band of the evening playing in the background, Charlotte politely asked for Laura and Karen to pose for a selfie. How could they possibly refuse her request when feeling so unashamedly proud to have made it as a finalist?

As the plates were being swiftly collected to make way for the main meal, a few brave people ventured onto the dancefloor.

'Fancy a dance?' suggested Karen.

'Oh, not yet, far too early,' Laura protested, feeling more than a little self-conscious, preferring to wait until a few more people had joined the crowd.

'*Too early* for what? There's a lot to be said for that saying about *no time like the present*.' Karen got up from her chair. 'Come on, what are we waiting for? We're here to enjoy ourselves regardless of whoever wins!'

Seeing the rest of the team were watching her encouragingly, realised perhaps there was more than just a grain of truth in what her friend was saying, and finally relented, not wanting to come across as a party-pooper.

As they danced to a rendition of *I Gotta Feeling* by The Black-Eyed Peas, Karen peered at her friend with a smile. 'Well it looks like our illustrious *Dynamic Don* has got a huge soft spot for you!'

Laura rolled her eyes to the ceiling in despair. 'Oh *please*! Don't even go there! There's no way I want to add *marriage-wrecker* to my ever-growing list of relationship disasters. After what happened with Julian and now Dan, I intend taking a break from all that stuff and just focus on getting back on track with my family.'

Karen's face softened, clearly moved by her friend's successful family reunion. 'I think it's fantastic you've finally mended those bridges with your mum and sister - I just can't begin to imagine how much you must be looking forward to finally returning home this weekend.'

Laura bit her bottom lip nervously. 'If I'm being truthful, I've got to admit I've mixed feelings about that one. Sure, I'm looking forward to spending time with Mum and Lou, and of course my lovely nephew...'

'But...'

'But I'm just so nervous about returning to my home, where...' Laura gave a deep sigh. 'Yes, I know it must be hard for you to understand what I'm feeling when I've never mentioned what brought me here to Minsden in the first place.'

She paused for a moment, lost in her thoughts. 'It's just that I'm terrified of facing what I left behind.' She swallowed, her throat beginning to feel uncomfortably dry. 'I think once I've managed to do that, as difficult as that might be, I think I'll finally be able to move on.'

'You're doing so well,' smiled Karen encouragingly. 'Just a few months ago you wouldn't have even entertained the idea of meeting up with them - just look how far you've come! As for meeting Mr Right, it's true we sometimes have to kiss a few frogs before finding our prince - well, believe me, I've certainly kissed more than a few frogs in my time!' Her expression became one of immediate concern. 'Hey, are you ok?'

Much to her worry, Laura's face quickly turned very pale, blinking her eyes rapidly as she suddenly stopped dancing.

It took few seconds before she responded. 'Yes, yes, I'm fine. Just had a bit of that blurred vision returning.'

'What a *time* for that blasted migraine to flare up tonight of all the nights! Maybe drinking that booze at your place before we left wasn't such a good idea after all.'

Although Laura felt she might have a point, didn't have the heart to make her feel any worse as all her actions had been done with good intentions. 'Oh, don't be silly, I would have got that migraine anyway.' She peered over towards the tables, noticing the waitresses coming along with plates of hot steaming food. 'I think it's time to get back to our places, looks like the next course is on its way.'

She gently rubbed her throbbing temples feeling the tell-tale signs of the headache coming on as she returned to the table to join the rest of her team.

'You've hardly touched your meal!' chided Karen, placing down her knife and fork onto her now empty plate.

Laura toyed with the salmon and rice which she'd barely touched, before finally giving up completely and putting down the cutlery on her plate, with a deep sigh. 'Sorry, but I've just not got the appetite for this.'

'Thought salmon was one of your favourites.'

She took a sip of her glass of water, not daring to tempt fate with any more alcohol. 'It is normally, but my head's not feeling all that great.'

The look of pity that Karen gave wasn't lost on her. 'I guess it's too soon to take anymore tablets?'

'Yes, I would need to give it up to four hours first.' Seeing the look of worry etched on her friend's face, quickly added 'Look, don't worry about me, I'm fine, I've had much worse - it'll soon disappear once the pills have kicked in.

It seemed she was proven right as after about ten minutes the headache began to subside with her appetite returning. Karen was more than slightly relieved when Laura picked up her knife and fork and managed to eat most of her remaining food before the waitresses came to clear away the plates.

Her friend was even more pleased when she quickly led her onto the dance floor as they moved along to the sound of Deee-Lite's *Groove Is In The Heart*. As the music played on, with more people getting up to join in, Laura couldn't clearly remember aside from recently reuniting with her family, the last time she'd last felt this happy. And to think tomorrow she would finally be returning home for the weekend. Even though at the beginning she'd had many reservations about facing up to her ghosts from the past, all the painful memories of what had taken place, leaving her with no choice but to move far away from all those that cared about her. Until she'd taken that next huge step, she would never be able to rest easy, even if it was for just one last time as Oscar had suggested in the dream.

Her attention briefly turned towards Donald White who was standing towards the edge of the dance floor seemingly oblivious to one of the other directors chatting to him, as he gazed at her intently. She could easily imagine when he was away from his work, he would have been the first one getting up to dance and having a good time. However, she was taken more than a little aback when he saluted her with his flute of champagne, before giving her a short wink and drinking back the remaining contents from his glass. Regardless of whether or not she was to be announced as *Most Loved Manager*, as far as she was concerned with all the great things that had happened in her life just lately, felt she was already a winner.

As the desserts arrived, everybody made their way back to their respective tables; Karen was unable to hide her pleasure at seeing her friend tucking in with enthusiasm to her chocolate brownie with ice cream and finishing every morsel.

When the plates were taken away and replaced by a large dish of sweets on each table, Karen patted her stomach that was feeling particularly bloated after eating a large slice of Black Forest Gateaux with cream. 'Phew! I don't know about you, but I think if I ate just so much as one sweet, I would explode!'

Laura nodded in agreement, peering over to Charlotte in disbelief as she helped herself to a handful sweets. 'I just don't know where that girl puts it all! Not only did she polish off a full three-course meal, she'd had some of Jade's leftovers and now the sweets.' She watched on as she popped a couple of toffees into her mouth. 'What's even more astounding is she's as thin as a rake! I would *love* to know her secret!'

Karen gazed at the young apprentice with undisguised envy. '*Youth*, that's her secret. I remember at her age I was pretty skinny and could eat just about anything without putting it on. But once I got into my thirties that's when I piled on the pounds.'

'You and me both!'

'What nonsense!' said Karen, looking scornful. 'You've got an amazing figure - you really put me to shame. I'm just glad Andrew happens to go for the curvier type of woman!'

Their conversation was immediately cut short as the lights in the arena suddenly dimmed. The silence so intense as everybody's attention focused expectantly towards the large screen mounted on the wall next to the stage, now bursting into life.

A huge round of applause erupted as the video shoot came on with Laura and all the other finalists who'd taken part in the filming over the last week. She watched on with fondness at the fun times she'd had in the grounds of Global Life, miming to *We Are the Champions by Queen*, with her fellow finalists joining in playing on their air guitars. Everybody on the Investments table gave a huge cheer and a few whistles as a close-up was shown of Laura, much to her own embarrassment holding a walking-stick that she improvised for a microphone in a style Freddie Mercury would have been proud of. She was grateful for the dim lighting where nobody could see just how red she must be looking at witnessing the cringeworthy moment. But despite feeling more than a little foolish, at the same time it felt so heart-warming to have all the undying support of her loyal team.

After the recording came to its end, the audience cheered and whistled loudly, truly getting into the spirit for what they'd all come to see, their eager anticipation about to be satisfied.

On the stage came Edwina's PA, Bernadette Fielding wearing a bright red lace dress that fitted snugly over her full figure, the colour clashing with her mahogany dyed hair piled high on her head with a few strands having come loose at the side, hanging over one of her large gold dangling earrings. In many ways, Bernadette reminded Laura of a red-haired version of Patsy in *Absolutely Fabulous*.

Although Edwina's assistant might not have been a healthy role model, always buying large portions of food from the works canteen and a heavy smoker to boot, was practically her boss's right-hand woman when it came to sorting out her diary and helping her to prioritise her heavy workload. Without her efficiency, Edwina would undoubtedly have been at a loss.

Holding her microphone, she smiled radiantly as she greeted her audience, hoping they were all having a super fun time, to which everybody cheered loudly in response. She announced at long last the waiting was finally over and that the Global Life Employee Awards winners were about to be announced by the lovely Edwina Charlton and the dynamic Donald White. With that everybody gave a huge round of applause as the two more senior people of the company joined her on the stage.

Donald greeted everybody cheerfully, remarking on the amazing quality of the video and how great to see everybody having had so much fun in participating, making a promise to show some of the outtakes towards the end of the ceremony.

Laura smiled to herself, certain amongst those would be the incident when a wasp landed on her nose, causing her to yelp in horror, as she dropped the walking-stick, running around in circles like a headless chicken, much to the delight of the others, as the crazed insect decided to chase her!

The CEO went on to explain what was particularly special about the Global Life awards was the fact that the winning candidates had been chosen by colleagues and not by a board of directors and was a fitting way to celebrate all the appreciation and hard work within the company. As with previous years, the award for the winning candidate would be the prestigious Global Life trophy and Amazon vouchers to the value of £200.00.

'Have you decided what you'll be spending your vouchers on?' Karen asked with a grin.

'As much as I feel touched by your confidence in me, I will never count my chickens,' Laura chuckled waving her hand dismissively. 'With all the stiff competition I'm up against, I know I'm pretty unlikely to get anywhere. They're all pretty good managers who are loved by their teams.'

'And the Investments team *don't love* their amazing team manager?'

Laura's face softened. 'Oh, you don't know how much it means that you guys took the trouble to nominate me and that means the world to me. Whatever the result, nothing will ever take that away - that's something I'll always cherish.' She peered over briefly toward her young apprentice, so young and enthusiastic, with her whole future still mapped out ahead of her. 'I would love to see Charlotte win this more than anything. I know she didn't have one of the best starts in life with her dad running off when she was a baby, but her mum saw to it that she would have the best education possible.'

'It couldn't have been easy,' agreed Karen. 'Especially with four older brothers mixed into the equation.'

Laura nodded. 'I know I've got to be seen as being unbiased when I'm interviewing for deputy, but I would really love her to be successful, because if anyone deserves a lucky break, it has to be Charlotte.' She glanced briefly towards her, seeing the animated expression on her youthful face, expressing clearly how much fun she was having with her friends. 'But at the same time, I know I also have to play it by the book and give every candidate a fair chance.'

Their attention was drawn again towards the stage where Donald continued his speech.

'I'm sure many of you are wondering why I've invited Edwina on the stage, and I'm sure *she's* thinking exactly the same thing!' There followed peals of laughter as the Customer Service manager stood there smiling, but appearing a little bemused.

The CEO continued. 'Although it's always delightful to have your company, Edwina, I *do* have an ulterior motive. A little bird tells me that after thirty years, you'll be *leaving* the company to take a well-deserved break!'

Although this was no longer a secret, everybody in the room groaned in disappointment.

Donald gave one of his winning smiles that melted all the hearts of ladies of a certain age in the room. 'Well, we *couldn't* let this occasion go without showing a little appreciation for all the hard work you've done in helping Global Life become the phenomenal success that it is today!'

With that, Bernadette came on the stage, bringing a huge mixed bouquet of flowers in various shades of yellows, the colour that Edwina had always favoured. From the look of complete surprise that showed on her face was genuinely not expecting this to happen.

Laura's could see her manager was clearly moved and for a moment was at a loss at what to say. She quickly composed herself before going back to the beginning of her journey at Global Life when she came as an apprentice after completing her university degree. Edwina went on to say that at the time as far as she was concerned, she came to the company believing this would be just a temporary stopgap before she found another job more fitting with what she had learned through her studies.

With a wry smile, added that little did she know at the time that the *temporary* period would end up being thirty years as she made her way from apprentice, deputy, team manager, business improvement officer, before finally moving up to her final role as customer service manager for the entire Minsden office.

Looking for a moment down at the beautiful bouquet in her hand, her attention focused back to the audience as she added with sincerity that one of the many amazing things she loved about Global Life was the fact that just about *anybody* regardless of their background had the opportunity to flourish and climb as high as they wanted to up the career ladder. Announcing that although her time with the company would be coming to an end the following week, promised that the new Customer Service manager would be finally announced.

She paused for a moment in contemplation, looking emotional as she revealed as much as she was looking forward to her move to Dorset and spending some quality time with her family, in particular with the grandchildren, would miss being part of Global Life family, but would be leaving with very fond memories of all the many friendships she had formed during her time there. She removed a tissue from her handbag to dab a tear away from her eye as she said she wanted to thank each and every one of them for all their hard work and for making Global Life into the huge success story it had become.

Clearly moved and on the brink of tears, Bernadette joined her boss on the stage before hugging the well-loved customer service manager and placing a kiss on her cheek. Everybody cheered loudly in appreciation, followed by a huge round applause and a standing ovation.

'I'm really going to miss Edwina,' Laura said with sadness as a tear slowly slipped down her cheek. 'When I came to the company she just gave me so much support. I don't know what I would have done without her.' She looked at Karen meaningfully. 'The same goes for you too. I've got you alone to thank for getting me into Global Life. Heaven knows where I would have been if I hadn't met you at the bar of the *Maple Leaf*

Hotel!'

Karen's eyes filled with tears. 'Oh, *please* don't start me off! You know how emotional I get after a few drinks - I start blubbing at the drop of a hat! Well, I believe in fate and meeting you that night at the bar was so meant to be! If I hadn't stormed out the house after that row with Graham, then our paths might never have crossed.' She peered over towards Edwina as she wiped a tear away from the corner of her eye. 'I'm sure if she didn't have that minor heart attack, she wouldn't have made the decision to leave the company.'

'I really don't blame her,' said Laura with meaning. 'When something of that nature happens, it's a wake-up call and makes us realise where our priorities lie.'

A troubled frown creased Karen's forehead as a thought occurred to her. 'Do you think that now you've got in touch with your mum and sister, that you might consider moving back to Dorset?'

This was a thought that had crossed Laura's mind on more than one occasion since the big reunion had taken place. She knew without a doubt that Mum was hoping after her weekend visit she might consider going back home for good; but she wasn't so sure she could take that next step, not when there had been so many bad memories, too many ghosts to lay to rest. The only way she would find the answers would be by returning home, back to where she had spent the best part of her life.

Seeing the look of concern written on Karen's face as she waited for an answer to her question, gave a shrug. '*Oh*, I just don't know. To tell the truth over these past three years I've come to look on Minsden as my home town - I feel settled here with great friends and a job I enjoy. Why would I want to move?'

Karen smiled, feeling deeply moved at her loyalty, but wondered if her friend was saying this as much to convince herself. Yes, it was true she seemed more settled than she had been for some time, and was also true her career at Global Life had gone from strength to strength. But as for friends, as far as Karen was aware, she was her only true friend in Minsden.

Although considered a friendly person and was clearly well liked enough to have been nominated for this award, Laura did tend to detach herself from becoming too close to people, preferring to keep them at arm's length. Although Karen herself had become great friends with her, knew there was much she was holding back about her life before moving to the town. At least the reasons that made her leave her home and come all this way. Without a doubt, Edwina knew everything about the situation, but being the professional she was, never divulged details with anybody. She guessed that her boss would be taking that closely-guarded secret with her when she left the company.

They sat back on their seats as Edwina left the stage with the applause finally coming to an end as the main event began.

The first award to be presented was for Best Newcomer which went to the an up and coming called Tony Jefferson who worked in the Claims team.

'Well deserved,' agreed Laura giving a nod of approval, as she applauded with the audience. Tony joined the company less than a year ago as a customer service representative and had proven himself to be indispensable by going the extra mile to ensure his team kept well within the accepted service levels through challenging times.

Photos were taken as he stepped onto the stage, smiling proudly with Donald shaking his hand firmly before presented with the prestigious Global Life trophy and Amazon voucher.

'No doubt he'll spend that on something football-related,' Karen remarked with a grin. Tony was a keen Manchester United supporter and was a key player in the Global Life football team and proved to be an outstanding goal-shooter.

Due to the tight schedule of the evening, meant there was no time allowed to make speeches, much to the relief of most of the nominees.

After the applause died down, the next category was

for *Most Helpful* and was won by Liz Pratchett in Drawdown. The look of disappointment was unmistakable on the face of Lawrence in the Investments team who was amongst the finalists. Laura shared his pain as everybody in the team was sure he would win as was always doing overtime to make sure something urgent was completed and always helping out other areas of the business when staffing levels were down.

'Poor Lawrence,' Karen sympathised, watching the young man forcing a smile as he joined in with the clapping. 'He's taking it so well all things considered, but I hope it doesn't put him off from continuing his hard work.'

Laura agreed. 'Me too, but sadly there can only be one winner in each category. Next week I'll have a friendly chat with him and emphasise he did us proud by getting as far as being a finalist - I'll make sure he gets a £20.00 Amazon voucher. It's the least I can do.'

Next came the award for *Unsung Hero*. There hadn't been any nominations chosen for Investments and had been won by Martin Bradley in the Bonds team. Nobody doubted that the young man deserved to win and the reason why he'd won was well documented after successfully foiling a scam.

Thanks to Martin's quick thinking, immediately reported it to the Financial Crime team who after some further investigation realised the policy holder's details had fallen into the hands of criminals and managed to avert a sustainably large sum of money from going to them. The policy holder was extremely grateful, feeling reassured that with Global Life his money was in very safe hands. In recognition of this had placed a large sum of money with the cancer charity that the company diligently supported.

Next on the agenda came the trophy for *Most Innovating* and that went to Selina Howard in New Business who came up with a particularly good idea for saving on unnecessary printing by immediately scanning information, so this could be immediately encrypted and emailed instead of posted. She also had come up with a number of other good ideas that had saved the company a substantial sum of money.

As her attention focused on the stage, Laura blinked as her vision became slightly blurred; hoping this was more down to tiredness than the migraine as wanted to feel well for her trip home the following morning.

But as the award came for *Personality of The Year*, won by the likeable and happy-natured Oliver Trimble in Sales, she could feel that tell-tale throbbing at the side of her temple and was getting more intense by the minute, especially with the huge round of applause that followed.

With everybody getting clearly into the spirit of the evening, the Investments team were eagerly awaiting to see who would win the final two categories of *Most Loved Colleague* and *Most Loved Manager*.

'Hope you're well prepared to go on that stage and receive your award from the delectable Donald,' remarked Karen with a grin.

'I wouldn't be so sure of that,' said Laura dismissively. 'Not with who I'm up against.'

'*Hey*, are you sure you're feeling ok?' asked her friend noticing her face looking distinctly pale.

Despite the pain becoming increasingly unbearable, she forced herself to smile. 'I'm fine. Nothing what a good night's sleep won't fix. 'Never mind me - it's time for *Most Loved Colleague!*' If there was anybody that deserved this was their very own Charlotte, she thought. Her vision still out of focus, glanced over to the young girl, nervously biting her bottom lip as she contemplated the disappointment after Lawrence not winning.

The video screen displayed the images of the four finalists, her colleagues shrieking with delight as Charlotte's name was called out. She yelped with joy, hugging those closest to her as she eagerly went onto the stage to collect her award and voucher, with all in the Investments team taking photos with their smartphones.

Laura watched her with pride, feeling so proud that her

young apprentice was flourishing in her career and felt certain if she chose, could go way to the top just as Edwina had. She knew it was extremely unlikely that she herself would win the final award of the evening, but to see Charlotte win so deservedly had made this the highlight of the evening as far as she was concerned. Karen took a picture with her phone which was swiftly posted onto her Facebook page.

Finally, they come to the last category for the evening, for *Most Loved Manager*. The whole team became silent, their chatter ending abruptly as they waited in eager anticipation for the winner to be announced. Although Laura felt there was no chance of her winning, was beginning to feel tense which only added to the intensity of the sharp, stabbing pain in her head that was becoming increasingly unbearable.

Giving little regard as to whether or not if the time had come where she could take another couple of tablets, rummaged frantically through her handbag. She silently cursed the dim lighting which made it almost impossible to see anything clearly. Finally, her persistence having paid off when she found the box tucked away towards the bottom which held the two remaining pills. Quickly, swallowing these with some water, snatched the tail end of the finalists flashing onto the video screen. She felt a slight twinge of embarrassment seeing her photo smiling, sandwiched between those of Amanda

Newman in Equity Release, Bob Chapman in Drawdown and Lilian Peters, Manager of the Bond team.

Shrieks of delight erupted from all of her team and from the others at the surrounding tables as her name was called out, announcing her as *Best Loved Manager*. Laura peered at the screen in disbelief then towards the others who peered at her with undisguised elation as they clapped their hands loudly.

'I knew it! *I just knew it*! cried Karen as she dabbed away the tears of joy that ran down her cheeks. She paused for a moment to study Laura and took her very pale face to be surprise at the announcement. 'Hey, I *think* that's your cue to go on stage - no time for getting all stage-struck now!'

As she got up from her chair, feeling nauseous from the violently painful head, by far the worst one she had experienced in her entire life, felt Karen gently squeeze her hand as she whispered in her ear. 'Your mum's going to be *so* proud of you!'

Knowing there was no way she could allow her dearest friend to see her suffering, forced herself to smile, gently squeezing her hand in return.

With her vision now badly distorted, somehow made her way up to the stage, with Donald displaying his brightest smile as he eagerly placed a kiss on her cheek, before presenting her with the award. 'Congratulations, my dear!' he beamed, 'And so very well deserved. Well, from this standing ovation, it looks like you'll definitely have to be starting up your own fan club!' With that everybody cheered louder, the sounds only succeeding in exasperating the already unbearable headache.

She took hold of the trophy Donald handed to her, along with the Amazon voucher, as he kissed her tenderly on the cheek. Despite the overwhelming pain and her distorted vision, she grasped the award, looking at it proudly. How proud her mum would be she thought, peering briefly to Karen who was excitedly capturing the moment on camera. Then her thoughts turned towards her darling Oscar who would be so delighted, if only, if only...'

Her eyes opened widely, giving her the appearance of astonishment, feeling as if her head was exploding with an eruption of a molten red-hot fury of pain, crying out loudly, before succumbing to a white-hot brightness.

With what appeared to be mere seconds, she drifted through the bright light, the pain being superseded by a feeling of calmness, an inner peace that had been missing from her life for a very long time; knowing without an edge of doubt that the relentless agony of all her heartbreak and headaches had finally come to and end.

A feeling of immense joy immediately enraptured her when through the white light appeared Oscar, walking towards her with that roguish smile she had come to love; his dark wavy hair looking slightly ruffled, those small imperfections only adding to his charm. In what she could only describe as an intense bolt of lightning coursed through her, a moment of realisation seemed to rip through to the core of her soul, as she gazed at the pale blue shirt, so familiar, along with those worn denim jeans.

He watched her intently, the love unmistakably clear, sparkling in his warm brown eyes as she peered at him with astonishment, no longer withholding from herself all the happy memories they had once shared.

'You look so incredibly beautiful, my love,' he remarked softly, drinking in the appearance of the emerald dress that complemented the colour of her eyes so perfectly. 'I'm just so very proud of you darling, and I know whatever memories your friends and family may have of this evening, they'll be so happy that you won that award and had your perfect moment.'

In the background, she heard their special song playing, *Beautiful Tonight* by Eric Clapton.

From his pocket, he retrieved the emerald and diamond engagement ring that matched perfectly to her earrings and necklace, placing this on the wedding finger where it belonged.

Gently, he enfolded his arms around her as she nestled her head on his shoulder. Slowly together, they danced in rhythm to the magical melody that they had always considered as *their song*. Everything that she had previously denied herself for so long, came flooding back, finally washing away forever all the feelings of sadness to make way for the love, happiness and joy to return in abundance.

'I've missed you *so much,*' she said softly.

'Missed you too darling,' he whispered in her ear, before gently placing a kiss on her lips.

Oscar paused for a moment, looking intensely into her eyes. 'But you're home now - your time has come to be where you belong.' He studied her face as she stroked her hair. 'Are you ready for that?'

She nodded in confirmation. 'Yes, *I am*. I need to see Jess.'

He smiled, happy with her answer. 'That's great. Shall we go? Remember I said we had a party to go to after the Global life awards? Well, let's get going!'

Together they laughed, happy and carefree as they continued to dance in each other's arms, making their way through the intense bright light, before disappearing without a trace.

Both seemed happy and oblivious of the scene they had

left behind; of the beautiful woman in the emerald green dress, lying on the stage, her face so pale with her eyes staring lifelessly towards the ceiling. The paramedics had been seeing to her for some time, but despite their best efforts one shook his head apologetically as Karen screamed hysterically, screaming '*No! No! No!*"

Edwina, also on the stage sobbed uncontrollably as Donald took from her the trophy and voucher that she had picked up from the floor as their much-loved colleague collapsed in front of everybody. Many stood around in stunned silence, with others in realisation, beginning to weep uncontrollably.

CHAPTER SEVENTEEN

Her face solemn, Karen stood in the scenic grounds of Global Life along with the rest of Laura's family, friends and work colleagues. Edwina had now been retired for just over two months and was already settled into her cottage in Dorset, not too far away from Laura's mum, Angela, and sister Louise who had also come down for this very special occasion. Now well acquainted, the former customer service manager had insisted on driving them to Minsden.

Had it not been for the bittersweet reasons that brought everybody together today, most would have considered this the perfect weather for late September, with its clear blue sky and not much in the way of clouds to be seen. That distinct bite of an autumn chill in the air now very much in evidence, with some of the trees beginning to shed their leaves, falling gently onto the grass below, creating a kaleidoscopic carpet, in shades of bronze laced with reds and yellows.

Despite all the immense emotional trauma she had been

through, on the outside, Angela appeared calm and composed, and that was mainly down to her partner Bob at her side, holding her hand in support. Unsurprisingly, she had lost some weight making her appear gaunt and the dark circles shadowing her eyes told a story of many nights of broken sleep. All very understandable when considering the endless hearbreak she'd experienced one way or another over the past few years, Karen mused.

The memories were still painfully raw of the funeral, and the sound of Laura's mum's loud sobs echoing throughout the church would stay with her forever. Just in the way the memories would last a lifetime of that fateful night at the awards ceremony, seeing her dearest friend literally dropping down dead on that stage; that had shattered her heart into a million pieces, her only respite had been a sedative prescribed to temporarily take the edges from what she'd witnessed.

Louise now stood alongside her husband Michael both looking grim with Toby mirroring the same expressions of all the strange people he studied. Never having met them before, was unable to comprehend what the occasion was all about, only knowing that his Aunty Laura had gone to heaven to be with her loved ones who would now take care of her.

During the past two months, Karen had learned so much about her friend, realising that until now had never truly

DREAM ESCAPE TO ROSE COTTAGE

known her; as a result, her own life would never be the same again. She thought back to the beginning, just after the shock at seeing her dearest friend die on the stage in front of all her friends and colleagues at the Global Life awards ceremony.

A post mortem had been carried out some days after Laura's death, concluding that she had died from a brain aneurysm. All along she had been living on a massive time-bomb, believing that the headaches were the hereditary migraines suffered by Angela and Louise and had no cause to question these as both sometimes displayed very similar symptoms.

Angela revealed for some time, Laura suffered from very high blood pressure after going through a stressful time and was very possible that the aneurysm which she might have been born with was exacerbated by this. It came to light after moving to Minsden, for some reason had stopped taking her blood pressure medication. If only she'd nagged her more to go to the doctor, Karen thought sadly, then just maybe there was something that could have been done to prevent that fatal outcome.

Within a couple of days numbed by shock and grief, Angela and Louise had driven to Minsden to formally identify Laura's body. Witnessing their loss at firsthand, cut through Karen's heart like a knife, as no parent should ever have to

379

witness the death of their own child. Apart from the shock of her sudden death, there were even more shocking revelations coming to light. Over the days that followed, discovered much to her surprise that Laura had left her Dorset village after being unable to come to terms with losing her husband and daughter in a tragic accident. In her previous life in Dorset, Laura had been a solicitor employed by a small law firm which would often mean working long, irregular hours.

On the fateful day that was to change Laura's life forever, came when much to her husband's objections had felt the need to work on her 40th birthday, due to a particularly complex divorce case which needed to be concluded. Anxious for her daughter to take a much-needed break so she could celebrate her birthday with a weekend away, Angela had offered to look after her granddaughter while the couple spent some quality time together. As much as she loved the idea, Laura felt she needed to close her current case that had been dragging on for a considerable length of time. After Laura confided to Angela later about her husband's bitter disappointment with her decision, made a compromise by suggesting to go out for a meal as a family, inviting her best friend and her husband, and to rearrange the break for the following weekend.

Karen would never forget the look of devastation etched on Angela's face as she revealed what was to follow next; an event so horrendous that was to change the course of Laura's life forever. On the day of her birthday, she had been running behind with work but had managed to conclude the divorce case in a manner that would be satisfactory to all parties concerned She called her husband on his mobile to let him know although she was running late, would meet him in town after driving the car home and taking a taxi to the town centre and as previously arranged, to meet everyone at the hair salon which her friend and her husband co-owned.

When Laura travelled in the back of the taxi, noticed fire engines, police cars and ambulances flashing their blue lights swiftly passing by in the direction she was heading, but thought little more of it as was accustomed to see the emergency services rushing through town. She tried to call her husband to let him know she was on her way, but received no response, assuming there was a problem with the network. But when she was to arrive, found that the road had been cordoned off due to an '*incident*' as the policeman put it. It was at that point that Laura realised something terrible had taken place and jumped out of the taxi, much to the objections of the emergency services, making her way to the scene. What she saw next would change the course of her life forever. A lorry had ploughed into the window of her friend's hair salon, killing instantly her husband, daughter, along with her best friend and husband, and the driver of the vehicle.

Karen's thoughts leapt forward to the days following Laura's death. She'd received a call from Louise who found Karen's number on her mobile. Knowing how fond her sister had been of her and in many respects had been closer to her than her own family in recent years, asking if she minded coming along to the flat as they came to see to things.

Glad to carry out this one last act of love for Laura, hugged them both with tears spilling down her face as she met them outside of the flat. Angela, wearing black, making her pale skin even paler, gazed at her through eyes red and swollen from many days of weeping, still understandably in shock. Louise, her complexion very pale and waxen gave a weak smile of appreciation for Karen taking the time to help. 'We left Toby with Mike,' she explained. 'He wouldn't understand what this was all about.'

There were more shocks in store when they entered the flat, with both Angela and Louise staring in undisguised shock towards the painting of Rose Cottage hanging across the living room wall.

Karen quickly explained Laura's dream of the man, Oscar Devereux she fell in love with and met in numerous dreams, in a village where she become acquainted with his daughter Jessica and the painting on the wall was of their home where they would meet often.

Her face a deathly white, Angela seated herself on the leather sofa, and for a moment Karen was worried the woman was about to faint. Louise also clearly in shock sat herself next to her mother, gently holding her hand whilst Karen went to the kitchen to make some black coffee, the milk in the fridge she had already disposed of as well passed its use by date.

Joining them back in the living room, Karen studied Angela as she scooped two heaped two teaspoons of sugar into her mug. To compose herself took a sip of her coffee, hot and scalding on her tongue. 'You wouldn't be aware of this, but that cottage you see on the painting, Rose Cottage, happens to be where Laura lived with her husband Oscar and their daughter, my beautiful granddaughter, Jessica.

Numbed with shock at hearing those now familiar names mentioned by Laura's family who she barely knew, stood up from the armchair and beckoned the two women to the bedroom. 'I feel from what you've told me, you'll find something that might possibly give some answers to the many questions I had.

As they entered the bedroom, their attention was immediately fixed to the portrait of Oscar in his blue shirt smiling warmly with his love for Laura burning brightly from his eyes. Next to this hung her later masterpiece of Jessica, with her hand on Toby's shoulders and Duke close by.

As Angela wept, barely unable to prise her eyes from the images of her loved ones so cruelly taken, Louise confirmed, 'Yes, that's Oscar, Laura's late husband.' She studied the painting of the children, her eyes filling with tears. 'I can clearly see that's Jessica with Toby and *Duke*, her Westie...only Jess seems a few years older, how she would've looked if she hadn't...'

If she hadn't died, pondered Karen with sadness.

Composing herself Angela revealed how Duke had died suddenly from heart failure a year after the tragedy. Looking upon him as the final link to the ones she'd lost had played a major part in setting back Laura's recovery.

They returned to the living room in silence, each lost in their own thoughts. No doubt Becky was the best friend who also perished in the devastation. How terrible to have lost your husband and child, not to mention your best friend and her husband.

Louise had brought along her iPad, showing her photos of her sister's wedding day, with Laura looking radiant and beautiful in the white wedding dress with a crown of flowers on her hair which was long and hanging down to her waist. Angela explained after everything that happened, she decided to have her hair chopped off into a shorter style as a way of beginning a new chapter of her life, but her mother admitted she did prefer her hair longer.

Karen mentioned about the spare room that Laura kept very private and suspected it may well hold further answers to many questions she had. 'I remember the door was locked when we came the other week,' Angela admitted. 'When she left to come here, she did bring along all her photos along with her.'

During Laura's time in Mindsen, there was never a single photo or any personal memento of hers to be seen; none of the usual knick-knacks that made a house or as in this case, a flat into a home. This time the spare room now unlocked, and after some searching, their patience finally paid off when they located the many photo albums hidden in the bottom drawer of her dressing table. Further photos were discovered of Laura and Oscar's wedding day, others of Jessica as a baby and more into her later years. Others went back even further in time to Laura' own childhood and her teens, back to happier days with her best friend Becky, beautiful and vivacious with her long fair hair.

Despite her grief Angela gave a rueful smile. 'Becky was what you'd call a lovable minx. A bit of a rebel - in Laura's own words, *a real party animal*, you know what I mean...the life and soul of any party. Really, quite the opposite of my Laura who was always the quiet and studious one, but somehow their friendship worked well and seemed to complement one another.'

Intrigued, Louise came across a scrapbook at the bottom of the drawer. 'I never knew about this one,' she admitted, studying the contents with a frown. Inside, were newspaper clippings of the accident, with photos showing a scene of a large delivery lorry that ploughed through the window of the hair salon, ironically at 5pm on the dot. With a large part of the building demolished by the vehicle, fatalities might have been even higher had it not been closed up for the day with the last client having left 30 minutes earlier. Marsha their other stylist had left earlier due to a sickness bug, her life thankfully spared. Even more miraculous that no pedestrians had been killed with just a few having sustained non-life-threatening injuries. One newspaper article named the driver as Jeremy Turner who'd suffered a fatal heart attack at the wheel. Apparently, there hadn't been any previous history of heart problems and nobody could have foreseen this happening.

Putting on her reading glasses, Karen studied the photo of the plump, middle-aged man of fifty-four, his kind looking face smiling into the camera, oblivious of the fate that would one day await him. 'Laura often spoke about meeting a Jez Turner in her dreams in the village, so I guess this has got to be the man she was mentioning.'

Neither Louise nor her mum held any malice for the lorry driver, understanding this was just one tragic accident where everybody concerned just happened to be in the wrong place at the wrong time.

Within the scrapbook were other newspaper clippings about the Dorset village of Broadcote where Laura lived with her family. These were packed with old photos of bygone days and its residents. Karen read with interest an article showing photos of the local primary school during the early 1960's paying tribute to their much-loved school assistant Evelyn Lock who passed away after a fatal heart attack. With her plumb round face and her grey tied back in a bun, reminded Karen of her own Granny Mildred when she was alive.

Karen learned with great sadness how Laura had needlessly blamed herself for the deaths of all those she loved. Her argument had always been, if she'd listened to Oscar and not being so wrapped up with her work, would instead have been enjoying a weekend break with her family. Most likely her friends would never have been killed, having gone home for the day, instead of waiting close to that shop window for her to arrive late home from work for her birthday meal. As a result of her loss and the guilt she needlessly felt, Laura suffered a complete nervous breakdown where she needed counselling to help her come to terms with what happened and to help make her realise that none of this was her fault. All this explained to Karen why her friend was never keen on celebrating her birthdays.

Later she was to recall Laura briefly mentioning Maggie the solemn barmaid at the village pub in the dream. Maybe she was being over-imaginative, but wondered if it could possibly be Dan's deceased girlfriend Margaret who was sometimes known as Maggie. Her job had been as a waitress at one of the restaurants in town and sometimes would help out behind the bar when short-staffed.

Angela revealed sadly, despite everybody's best efforts, although her mental health improved, Laura was never really able to come to terms with what happened. One day out of the blue she had simply packed her bags at Rose Cottage where she'd spent many happy years with her family, and drove off, her journey finally leading her to Minsden where she'd stayed ever since.

Tucked away where the photos had been hidden, laid a small velvet box in silver. Intrigued, Angela opened this to find a sparkling emerald and diamond engagement ring that matched perfectly as a set to the earrings and necklace that Laura wore to the Global Life Awards ceremony. As she dabbed away at the fresh tears slipping down her face, revealed the jewellery was a gift from Oscar when he proposed to her on holiday in France and wore these on her wedding day. As Karen studied one of the wedding photos in detail, could see the green gems radiantly complementing Laura's beautiful white wedding dress.

Karen recalled that first bittersweet day when they first become acquainted as she sat at the bar of the hotel lounge, nursing a drink, contemplating her own messed up relationship. In true Laura fashion of always putting others needs before her own, could see she was deeply troubled, revealing much to her astonishment how practically on the spur of the moment she'd decided to leave her old life behind and start afresh, choosing Minsden at random after seeing the picturesque market town on some internet site.

A completely crazy but at the same time, very brave step to take she mused as her eyes filled with fresh tears. And thank goodness she'd taken that plunge and had thrown out her now ex, Graham and came to meet the woman who was to become the best friend she'd ever had. Knowing what she knew now, had little doubt that helping her to get a job at Global Life had probably saved her sanity, not to mention her life.

Her mind came back to the present to the days after Laura's death. Edwina finally admitted the young woman had confided in her of the reasons why she'd left the village in Dorset, but had been sworn to secrecy with the exception of the executive board. By an amazing coincidence Edwina already knew of the tragedy though her daughter and son-in-law who also lived in the same county where there had been much local media coverage. Karen could now remember there had also been some mention of this on the national news at the time, but never connected this to her friend who always used her maiden name instead of Devereux. This explained why there had been something familiar about the painting of Oscar, and recalled her shock at the painting of Jessica with the green eyes so similar to those of Laura.

She thought back to her conversations at the flat with Laura's family about the dream world that she entered almost on a daily basis, meeting her loved ones even though she was unable to admit this to herself. Was it all part of her breakdown that she would manifest those thoughts into a dream world, perhaps even the brain aneurysm playing a major part?

The three women had discussed this at length and agreed that it could be argued until the cows came home, but they would never truly find any answers. But they all were of the theory that perhaps with Laura's condition, Oscar and Jessica knew it would be her time soon and were waiting for her to reunite with them. Karen loved the idea that she had finally found peace and had re-joined the family she loved and missed so much until her dying day.

Back to the here and now, their attention focused on Edwina, along with the rest of the other members of staff that had all gathered together for this special day, to remember Laura in the tranquil wooded grounds of Global Life. Apart from Karen, along with most members of the Investments Solutions team and some of the directors, many of Laura's Dorset acquaintances were unable to make it on the long journey to her funeral.

In her honour, a park bench had been placed in the grounds, overlooking the duck pond which Laura would often gaze towards during her lunch breaks on a summer's day, occasionally offering some bread to her feathered friends. With a brass plaque where her name had been engraved, placed on the middle of the back-rest, ensured she would be remembered for years to come.

To her audience, Edwina shared some of her fond memories of the young woman, how she came to Minsden in unexpected circumstances and beginning her career journey at Global Life, soon making her way very quickly from customer service representative, to team manager. With a smile, she remarked how Laura had quickly recognised talent within her staff, encouraging them to be the best versions of themselves. Charlotte listened with sadness as she wiped the tears running down her cheek. One of Laura's last wishes had been granted and she had been promoted to deputy of the Investment Pensions team. Although Karen was now officially in her role as team manager, the decision had been made for her to revert back to her original team for the time being as knew this what Laura would have wished.

With a discreet nod from Edwina, Charlotte untethered the green balloons that had been tied to the large oak tree, overlooking the pond, handing these out to everybody present. Each and every one in the colour that matched the green colour of Laura's eyes and the beautiful dress she wore that fateful evening.

As they stood in a minute's silence to remember the young woman who brought so much hope and happiness into their lives, everybody released their helium balloons, each one floating away freely, high into the sky. Many releasing their pent-up emotions, sobbed as they remembered the friend who had lost so much in her relatively short life in this world, with her own ending abruptly.

Louise wiped the tears from her eyes as she looked down, placing her hand gently over the gentle swelling of her stomach. On the day that Laura was due to visit her family was about to announce her pregnancy to her sister. She recently discovered that in four months' time she would be giving birth to a baby girl who she decided would be named Laura Jessica, in honour of the two very special people who would always live on in their hearts.

Karen gazed up to the sky, almost oblivious of the tears running down her own face, feeling that nothing would ever take the ache away from her heart of missing her friend so much. As a large white cloud drifted along in the otherwise clear blue sky, momentarily blocking the rays of the sun, her attention focused on three of the balloons that floated and merged together as their strings became entangled. An opening in the cloud allowed the sun to finally shine through, before they finally floated away without a trace. The sight gave her a glimmer of hope and some comfort, seeing this as a sure sign that her beloved friend was finally at peace with the two people most special in her life.

EPILOGUE

*T*he loving husband had led his wife to the village green, to the party that that was held in her honour. The turnout had been amazing, with so many people gathered in eager anticipation for her return, to welcome her back; so many wonderful people including her dearest friend Becky, Chris, Jez Turner, and of course, not forgetting the dependable Mrs Lock. For a moment Maggie gave her a solemn look, before she gave an impish wink and her face breaking out into the warmest of smiles.*

But the one person who grabbed her attention immediately was her darling daughter. They hugged and kissed with tears of joy as everybody looked on with unmasked happiness as they witnessed the tender reunion.

Throughout the party there had been dancing and games enjoyed by both adults and children alike until the tangerine sun had finally slipped over the horizon.

Jez came over offering her a bottle of his home-made elderberry wine, along with a basket of some of his home produce of freshly grown carrots, lettuce and onions. For a moment he looked at her with a tinge of sadness, his expression making it clear he was deeply sorry for what had happened. Her warm smile as she accepted his offer, reassured the kindly man that she held no harsh feelings for what had simply been a tragic accident. Feeling immensely relieved, he returned her smile, feeling happy knowing that one day when it was her time, his darling Bella would arrive at the village to join him.

Once all the festivities had come to their end, the happy family returned home to Rose Cottage. Their little girl sitting happily on the living room floor with Duke by her side, sketching her parents seated on the sofa gazing into each other's eyes as Daddy stroked Mummy's hair which was now lovely, long and shining again. As the clock on the wall suddenly sprang into life, with the hand just passing 5 o'clock, she studied her sketch, feeling she had captured well their likeness as they looked at each other holding hands, so happy and so clearly very much in love.

ABOUT THE AUTHOR

Michelle J Nagy

 Michelle's one great passion in life is to write interesting stories, and to bring her characters to life. With the promise of an element of suspense, along with a surprising twist, her own take on life is that a slice of inspiration can be gleaned from even from the most mundane of situations; a good imagination usually helps to see to the rest!

In her spare time, Michelle loves to take relaxing walks around the beautiful quiet Hertfordshire village where she currently lives and having a chat with the friendly locals along the way!

Her debut novel is What's Best For Helena

At present, she is working on her next novel which is expected to be released soon

BOOKS BY THIS AUTHOR

What's Best For Helena

When tragedy strikes after her elder sister is killed in a car crash, Helena Broadhurst leads a lonely and sheltered life in the quiet Hertfordshire village of Little Green.

With a promising career as an illustrator, her health suddenly takes a turn for the worse. Suffering from seizures, and losing her artistic flair, begins to experience memory lapses. With overly protective parents, her father a retired research physicist and mother, a former special effects artist and close family friend Peterson, known affectionately as Uncle Ian, a sudden twist of fate brings her together with Kelly and Lee.

As Kelly and Lee's own relationship deepens, are curious to learn more of the elusive companion Hugo, Helena often mentions, suspecting he exists only in her imagination.

On a quest to trace Helena's lifelong friend, Katherine Jolley, a Pandora's box of revelations opens that completely turns around everything they thought knew about Helena…

Printed in Great Britain
by Amazon

62899758R00231